Eyes to the East

Sam Lewis

TSL Publications

First published in Great Britain in 2022
By TSL Publications, Rickmansworth

Copyright © 2022 Sam Lewis

ISBN / 978-1-914245-62-6

Dedication

To my Grandparents and the Malvern Hills,
where the inspiration came to begin writing

Li Xiao Mei, a businesswoman in Hangzhou, China, was sitting in her office on the 30th floor of a brand new skyscraper she had paid to be built. Sipping on green tea from her tea plantation situated in the rolling leafy green hills near West Lake, she watched as the rain outside crashed angrily on the floor to ceiling window which overlooked the Qiantang river. It was a biting February day and she had just returned from her familial Lunar New Year celebrations. The clouds outside were dark and the shower of water so heavy that the view out of the window was blurred.

Inside the office, the walls were adorned with ancient Ming Dynasty artwork, characterised by the rich dark brown seal colour and calligraphy which combined to give the painting an ethereal quality. The artistry seemed completely out of place among the glass and firm edges of this modernist structure, built as a monument to an industrialist's life work. Porcelain vases atop hardwood furniture were adorned with fresh flowers each day, in particular roses and lilies, even when Li Xiao Mei was not in the office. On one wall was situated a map of China – Taiwan and 90 per cent of the South China sea proudly symbolised as Chinese property, the 9-dash line swooping to within an inch of the coastlines of Vietnam, the Philippines and Malaysia.

She sat behind a large desk looking out towards the rain, motionless, barely blinking, rather like a doll stuck on a child's shelf, porcelain and pale. She wore a smart suit which comfortably followed the curves of her body – the communist party badge, bright red with a hammer and sickle, proudly displayed on her lapel. At 44 years old, she looked young for her age – in fact, she would have been a rather attractive lady were it not for a large brown mole at the top of her nose to the inside of her right eye. Four prickly hairs protruded out of its fuzzy texture, black and sharp, requiring constant maintenance. The image of herself she kept on her desk notably lacked the blot, for like all her portraits, any wrinkle, crease or crevice had been airbrushed. At the same time, despite the ease of the procedure, requiring a professional to wield a little knife with careful precision, she never dared to have it removed because it was at once a flaw but also a reminder of her childhood, when she had been bullied for it.

Her earliest memory was of growing up in the bitter cold of Liaoning Province, a backwater of northern China, where the temperature reached highs of -10C during the winter days and dipped well below -30C at night. Her parents, who'd married at the young age of 16, had been migrant workers in Beijing, he a manual labourer and she a cleaner at a local school, which left her to grow up in the care of her grandparents on the property her paternal grandfather's family had owned for many generations. During the bitterly cold winter nights, enough to make little toes burn with frostbite, they would light a fire underneath their bed made of brick and sleep with their granddaughter in between them, cuddling for extra warmth.

If Li Xiao Mei had been born 20 years earlier, she might have remained a peasant in the cold fields of the north, or become a migrant labourer like her mother and father, slaving away in some backbreaking, menial, repetitive job in one of the many northern cities. However, she was lucky. She had been born just three years after Nixon's first visit to China which set in motion the inevitable change that followed. Under Deng Xiaoping's policy of reform and opening up, China was reborn economically and could come to terms with its more recent past. A 'communist country' but with all the benefits of capitalism – whether Mao would turn in his grave was taken care of by calling the miracle growth a result not of capitalism, but of *Socialism with Chinese characteristics*. Millions like Li Xiao Mei suddenly had the chance to get filthy rich and, so long as she was a member of the Communist Party who didn't express political opinions, she didn't have to worry about sliding back into poverty.

She remembered 1989 quite vividly despite being only 14 years old at the time, it being a year of many world events. She remembered watching the news stories in May with quiet concern – her parents were in Beijing at the time. Students protested in the centre of the city, gradually joined by more and more ordinary citizens from all walks of life until the numbers swelled to over a million people in that fateful square which had seen so much Chinese history played out in it.

Even at 14 years old, she could tell this was a big event, filled with wonderment and a general feeling of abrupt change occurring in the spirit of revolution. Then on 4th June, everything went silent. There was nothing on the television news about the protests, as if they had suddenly ceased to exist. She didn't think much of it at the time, for whatever happened must have been for the best. She still had food to eat and study to keep herself busy, what did it matter to her if things were happening elsewhere in the country, they were out of her control anyway.

Self-taught English and the ability to study at university in Shanghai brought with it a great array of opportunities, with which Li Xiao Mei excelled. By the age of 25 she worked as an accountant in Shanghai, a menial job but one that established in her a firm business awareness of bookkeeping. By 30, she'd moved to Hangzhou to work alongside a young investor named Jack Ma, an eccentric individual, but a joy to have as a mentor. By 35 she had left Alibaba to create her own venture in business – a clothing manufacturer which, she hypothesised, was the first product people bought when they had taken care of the essentials of food and shelter – she realised the potential for a market about to explode with demand. As a result of her contacts with the largest e-commerce giant in China, she had a wonderful supply network.

By 40 she diversified her portfolio of assets with investments abroad and at home, from steel to schooling. At 42 she decided her legacy required a huge building in the city that made her rich, Hangzhou. This was where the idea came for a 30-storey colossus housing the HQ of all her businesses. Here it stood as a testament to a penetrating willpower and unconquerable ruthlessness.

However, despite her many hundreds of millions of dollars, something still seemed elusive. She had a 23-year-old daughter studying in New York, and a 20-year-old son leading a bachelor lifestyle in Shanghai. The fact that her daughter was not yet married deeply troubled her, and she feared that should she reach the age of 28 without marrying, then she would never find the one. Time was of the essence. Five years had swung by since her joyful innocence of 18, who was to say she would not reach the dreaded number 28 in the next blink of an eye?

There was a knock on the heavy wooden door, dark and creaking, more at home in a castle than an office, and her secretary walked in. Its giant clunking doors required her to push with both hands, throwing as much of her skinny weight into moving it as possible.

'What is it, Fu Gui?' Li Xiao Mei snapped in her strong northern

Chinese accent, which made conversation with her in her native language clear and concise.

Fu Gui was a tall, northern Chinese lady who had been Li Xiao Mei's personal secretary for two years. She was young, only 28 years of age, but had been the only secretary to last longer than six months. She had long dark hair, neatly tucked behind her ears, and a pair of fashionable glasses sitting on her high, flat nose. After the energy she expended on opening the door, she panted a little, her heavy breaths making her look as if she was bowing her head slightly, in deference to her boss.

'The new English teacher Charlie has arrived,' came the reply.

'OK let him in,' Li Xiao Mei responded with a great sweep of her hand. 'How many other meetings do I have today?'

'Five. You have a call in half an hour with your husband.'

'OK, OK, bring in my lunch once I'm done with the foreigner,' she said.

Fu Gui gestured behind her with quick, short motions as if calling over a dog. A tall, lanky, round-cheeked white man meandered in. Dressed in jeans and a shirt, sporting a black winter jacket with a white collar, he stumbled across to Li Xiao Mei. His long steps seemed to stride slightly further forward than they were meant to, making his head bop up and down as he moved. He held out a sweaty palm which clasped Li Xiao Mei's without her having to move towards him. He looked tired and a little confused, he'd just spent 25 hours travelling from the UK to get to this meeting.

'Welcome to China, Charlie,' she said, speaking English with an oddly clipped British accent, her poise assuming that of a member of the upper class.

'Thank you, Mrs Li,' he smiled back, eager to make a good first impression.

'Please call me Lesley.'

How old is this woman? Charlie thought. They all look either 25 or in their late 60s. He hypothesised that there must be one day where the transformation took place. Where the wrinkles would finally appear, and all the hard work of maintaining a pale white face with dodgy cosmetics did more to worsen their skin condition than it did to improve.

Once they were sat down on the comfortable chesterfield brown chairs, she poured them both tea.

'How was your flight?'

'Slow. I had a long layover in Chong-king.'

'Chongqing.'

'I'm sorry?'

'Chongqing, you use a "ch" when you pronounce q's in Chinese.'

'Oh, sorry.'

'It's OK. Every foreigner struggles with speaking Chinese properly ... Anyway, tell me a bit more about yourself. Where did you grow up? What did you study at university?'

'Errr, I grew up just outside of London, near a place called Guildford.'

'Guildford? No, I haven't heard of it.'

'After that I studied Law at Edinburgh University.'

'Edinburgh, that's the north of England, right?'

'Well no, not really, it's in Scotland.'

'But Scotland is part of England, isn't it?'

'Not quite.'

'So why did you go to another country to study?'

'I didn't.'

'But you just said Scotland wasn't a part of England.'

'Well, no it's ...'

He grabbed his cup ungracefully from the table and slurped the tea. The lukewarm water made him feel more alert.

'Yes, I guess you're right, I went to another country.'

'Aha, can't fool me,' she jovially smacked the table before continuing. 'You're obviously someone who likes a bit of adventure, first Scotland, now China. I think you've made a good choice coming here, there's a lot of work for someone like you.'

'Someone like me?'

'Yes, someone like you.' She poured Charlie some tea as he shuffled awkwardly in his seat. 'You see, there's a pride in being able to hire English speaking foreigners to businesses in China. You're a rare commodity. That's why I pay you so well. More than four Chinese teachers combined.'

'Er ... that's nice.'

'Do you like China, Charlie?'

'Yes, I suppose I do.'

'What do you like most? Why did you come here?'

She tilted her head, smiling slightly as she waited for a compliment.

'I haven't seen much so far but the people seem friendly, even if they randomly take videos of me. I almost felt like a celebrity.'

'I told you, you're a rarity here. Have you been to West Lake?'

'No, I've only been here a few hours.'

'Then go, I think you'll find West Lake far more beautiful than anywhere else in China, that's why I chose to set up business here. Look at this painting,' she said pointing towards the Tang dynasty canvas on the wall, 'this is what West Lake looks like when the clouds are low and it's early in the morning on a fresh day. This is the last part of China where you can still experience what it was like in ancient times.'

'Not even in the countryside?'

'No, the farmers build new houses, concrete monstrosities but a sign of progress nonetheless.'

'What did they live in before?'

'Mud, wood, bamboo. A mix of three depending on where you were in the country.'

Charlie took another sip of the tea.

'You see, this is why I came to China,' he started, his eyes lighting up with interest, 'why I find it so truly fascinating. To think that 40 years ago China was mostly in poverty, and now poverty is nearly eradicated.'

'Anything is possible when you put your mind to it.'

'Something of that attitude is what I think the West is missing,' he said glumly.

'The West has much to teach China,' Lesley continued grandly, 'but soon China will overtake the West and the West must learn from us.'

Charlie gulped.

'So how long have you wanted to be a teacher in a kindergarten?' Li Xiao Mei asked.

'Ha,' he awkwardly replied. 'I didn't think I would be doing this if I'm honest. I just finished studying and wanted to find a way to come to China for a gap year or something. I don't know why China, it just seemed like such a mystical place. Like a land far away that few had been to before.'

'Like Scotland?'

'Er yes … like Scotland.'

'I'm happy you say that Charlie, I think you'll find China is no more different to London than Scotland is. You don't need to worry about mysteriousness. A lot of your local colleagues will be dim-witted and slow in comparison to you and me but you'll get used to that. They're easily replaceable so if anyone, and I mean anyone, says anything to you that you don't like, just tell me. And on that note, if there's anything I can ever do for you, please let me know.'

'Thank you,' Charlie replied dumbly.

A bird flew past the window which caught Charlie's eye and he turned his head towards it.

'Beautiful view,' he finally said.

'Yes,' she said dismissively before asking, 'Do you know how we work at this kindergarten?'

'Not at all.'

'OK, well the other teachers will fill you in but I can give you an overview. You'll have two classes you're assigned to, in the morning you'll teach one class English whilst your afternoon class is taught by their Chinese teacher. In the afternoon you swap to teach the second class English whilst your morning class learns from the Chinese teacher.'

'Sounds simple enough.'

'Good, I'm glad to hear that.'

She poured them both some more tea before delicately placing the pot down. The water in the small cups swirled gently before coming to rest.

'Hmm, you know Charlie, if you keep at it with me you can make a lot of money this way. It's why I invested in these schools. I charge about, errrr what's the exchange rate … 9 err 10,000 pounds per year for each student. Three students' fees per class pay for their class teacher's salary. You foreigners earn 20,000RMB per month whilst the Chinese teachers, of which every class has two, earn 5,000RMB each. Almost all the rest goes to me, I make good profit per year. This kindergarten you are about to start in is only two years old and already 300 students. I have three kindergartens at the moment with a plan to open another in Shanghai soon. It's wonderful, isn't it!' she said, beaming with pride.

Charlie sat in silence. Should he laugh or stay silent? He thought. Why was she telling him this?

Not quite sure how to react as she continued to disclose precisely how much money she made and what her costs were, he fiddled with his tea cup, trying to make the liquid last so he wouldn't have to awkwardly stop her mid-flow of conversation.

Looking at her talk as she sat opposite him on the sofa with the backdrop of this odd office, it felt quite surreal, as if the feng shui of the surroundings was meant to draw all attention to the seat Lesley occupied. Charlie smiled at the thought that this was a subtle yet deliberate action which amplified Lesley's importance in her own mind, and that of her guest. A more interested party might have been better engaged with Lesley's financial musings, but it was too much for Charlie to feign intrigue – not that Lesley cared to pick up the signs that she was boring her new employee. It was as if she was expecting him to obsequiously agree with everything she said, and praise her business acumen. When this wasn't forthcoming, she decided to change subject.

'How old are you Charlie?'

'I just turned 22,' he said, startled again at her directness.

She expertly picked up her cup of tea in thought, sticking her little finger out as she raised it to her lips, without a vibration on the surface of the dark, sweet liquid. Tea to her was ritualistic, it contributed to the process of thought and improved the functioning of the gut. On average, she must have drunk at least 20 cups per day of the same tea leaves, refilling the tea pot with water kept at a boiling temperature nearby.

'Hmm, my daughter is only one year older than you. Maybe you would like her ...'

She took out her phone, large and shiny, and proceeded to scroll through photos, showing Charlie every so often a generic smiling Chinese girl wearing a graduation gown. After swiping through a few more pictures, she showed one of her daughter at a beach with Li Xiao Mei also in a bikini. Charlie blinked in disbelief and looked away briefly in embarrassment before taking a longer eyeful of the brightly coloured bikinies.

'You would like her I think, only 23. At the moment in New York completing a Masters.'

'Yes, I do have a thing for older women,' he said jokingly, hoping she would change the subject. This was lost on Li Xiao Mei who thought he had instead complimented herself. She giggled in appreciation before correcting her girl like outburst into the forced deep voice of a woman operating near the top of a country dictated by men in dark suits.

Her now booming laughter was interrupted by the phone ringing. She stood up and strode across, picking it up with an exaggerated grace. It was a vintage rotary dial phone, reminiscent of the 1960s.

'Hang on a moment, dear,' she said in Mandarin before switching back to English and placing the phone to her chest. 'It was nice to meet you Charlie, Fu Gui will show you out. I think you will go to the school now … Oh and welcome to China.'

As he got up to leave, he took some dates from the enormous bowl of fruit on the coffee table, and popped them in his mouth. With a huffing effort, he pulled the door open and was about to let it naturally shut behind him when Fu Gui rushed over and gently completed the move so as not to create a loud clank as wood hit wood.

'What you think?' Fu Gui asked in broken English.

'She seems nice.'

'Yes, she can be. She can also be not nice.'

They started to walk through the waiting room.

'She has some odd opinions,' Charlie finally said.

'She is nice to those she likes. Not to those she do not.'

'Does she like you?'

'I think so,' she smirked. 'I can tell never.'

'Do you like her?'

'Yes! She give me job, how can not like?'

She led him to the lift where they were joined by a short but shifty looking man in a suit and tie. He had dark eyes and stank of cigarette smoke.

'This be driver Lesley. He take you school. You know, if you feel lonely, I have friends, we can go to play.'

'Play?'

'Oh yes,' she laughed. 'I forget. Play mean something else in English. We can go and "hang out".'

'Oh yeah sure.'

'If not, I don't mind. Let me know. Maybe China scary but we are friendly. I give you my WeChat.'

After she'd typed her number in his phone, she gave him a smile and turned to her desk.

'Welcome to China!'

As the car sped along, Charlie wondered what he had got himself into, as if a woman having second thoughts about a baby when her due date was the next week. This was a mystical land that he'd read about since a young age, but he was overwhelmed by the energy he felt emanating from everyone he talked to. Little children on the plane across had come up to him to talk in their limited English. Old women had been very kind, offering sweets and snacks, whilst their husbands looked on with toothless smiles, their eyes disappearing behind what looked like closed eyelids.

'How long will the drive be?' Charlie asked in English.

'Sorry?' the driver replied.

'How long?'

'Sorry, no, sorry.'

Well that's two words more than I can speak of Chinese, he thought. He reverted to looking out of the window at the passing buildings, almost all of them at least ten storeys tall.

The weather had calmed now, but the pollution made the sky a fuzzy grey and a haze covered some of the more distant buildings like a dirty fog, adding to the mysticism Charlie felt. It was unlike any of the pictures he had seen in books of ancient long flowing robes, and ponytailed men walking around, passing shops with wrinkled elders on wooden beds smoking long opium pipes.

The roads weren't particularly busy this Friday afternoon but the other cars were weaving in and out of traffic like maniacs. Charlie assured himself he'd be safe and tugged on his seatbelt, wondering if the inside of the head of the seat in front of him was made of brick or soft fluffy cotton. He resigned himself to following the journey with the maps on his phone.

2

'Baby shark do do do do do do, baby shark do do do do do do, baby shark …'

'Run awayyyy!!!' the children screamed as they sprinted in all directions across the classroom, knocking over chairs and toy blocks. They loved this particular song, it was by far the best of all the nursery-aged rhythms out there, the competition being fiercely saturated by many equally obnoxious, repetitive tunes. Conversely, for the teachers it was a tedious and messy affair, which always ended with one kid knocking another over, leading to fits of tears and the fear that one of the parents might throw a tantrum in case their precious baby had so much as a small bruise on their body.

'OK, OK, go back to the front of the classroom!' their Chinese teacher shouted in their native language.

When the children were seated again in two rows of small wooden chairs, barely big enough for anyone above the age of six, their English teacher picked up a large picture book. Each child panted in exhaustion, with beads of sweat streaming down their foreheads to the wide smiles on their faces in excited anticipation of the story to come. The book was too big to comfortably hold, and their teacher had to read it whilst cautiously perched on a child-sized chair. His legs began to cramp as he awkwardly turned the pages of the large swaying book.

'Teacher Kevin! Mouse!'

'Teacher Kevin! Dog!'

'Teacher Kevin! … err I don't know,' the children would say after each flip of the page. It was a book about animals visiting different parts of the world, flying on the top of a large white aeroplane.

As Kevin reached the end of the book, he looked at his watch and saw there were still five minutes left before he could let the children play outside. This was something they were always willing to do, like dogs agitating to go for a walk. It was also something Kevin was always willing to do as well, because it meant he could be left alone with his thoughts whilst the children scuttled around aimlessly. With a huge sigh, he chucked the book to his left and reached behind him for another smaller book. As he fiddled through the small collection by the teacher's desk, the children screamed titles they wanted to be read.

'Teacher Kevin, that one!'

'Teacher Kevin, *zhe ge.*'

'Teacher Kevin, *na ge.*'

Their chubby little faces creased as they tried with all their might to create the loudest noise. Kevin, a little tired from lack of sleep and furious at their volume, turned around and shouted. 'OK, quiet!'

The children immediately thrust their hands onto their knees and stiffened their backs and legs at perfect right angles like obedient little robots. Kevin smirked. They looked both scary as carbon copies of each other moving in sync, but at the same time reminded him of the old Chinese men he'd seen sitting outside restaurants burping, spitting and drinking Tsingtao with their hands straightened in a similar way directly onto their knees. In their case, it was done to keep large, swollen bellies snugly placed within their legs. In the case of the children, they simply imitated what they saw their parents and grandparents doing.

'OK, well done … this story is *The Lorax*, by Dr Seuss.'

After he'd finished reading the book, he looked towards the clock suspended on the wall and breathed a sigh of relief. Only half an hour more, he thought, and then he could be rid of them. Unfortunately, however, it was drizzling outside, in bold defiance of anyone's wish to enjoy the few remaining hours of outdoor light.

Thank God it's Friday, he thought, he couldn't take much more of this. Maybe he needed to find a new school or go back to teaching older kids. He took out his phone and looked at his plans for the evening. Where should he go tonight, he wondered. He had, like most weeks, a standard formula. Chinese club – dark, sweaty, smoke-filled place with music that was far too loud yes, but, there would be plenty of locals to warm him up for the evening.

It had been his prescription for a good night out for many years and he always enjoyed its prospect more than anything else.

Kevin looked towards the darkening clouds outside. One class had braved the playground in brightly coloured raincoats whilst their bored parents waited under shelter nearby.

As he shuffled to the softly padded floor surrounding the wooden blocks the classroom had, he wondered if he'd forgotten something. What was it? Oh yes, new flatmate, goddammit, what if we don't get along? What if he doesn't drink? What if he doesn't like girls?

He lay down on the blue mat and spread himself out. He knew the teachers didn't like it when he did this, but he did it anyway.

He sighed as he thought about how he should act around his new flatmate. If only he'd come on a different day. Actually no, if anything, the best time to meet someone would be on a night out. It would be odd getting into a taxi with him, they were strangers after all but then again, as an expat, they would have some form of bond.

A kid came up to him and squatted nearby to pick up a wooden brick. Kevin snatched it and threw it across the mat.

'Ayaaaaa,' the kid screamed.

Kevin chuckled before seeing the dirty look the class teacher gave him which made him abruptly stop.

As the half hour came to a close and 17:00 approached, he slowly stood up and grabbed the games he had played with the children – today a version of hopscotch that involved none of the lines of demarcation being honoured – and strode out saying a quick goodbye to his Chinese colleagues.

'Bye.'

'Bye bye Kevin,' one of them smiled.

He shuddered as he exited the class. He had an odd belief that he had been punished ever since he'd arrived at the school by being placed in a classroom with what he considered to be the least attractive women in the kindergarten. No matter how nice they were, he was short and curt with them.

When he got back to the foreign teachers' office, everyone was already there and circled around something.

'Alright bumders!' Kevin shouted with an exaggerated West Country accent as he cockily strolled into the room, dumping an armful of games by the door without bothering to store them tidily.

'Oh Kevin,' one of the girls said, 'this is your new flatmate, Charlie.'

Kevin looked Charlie up and down. Well there he is, he thought. Nothing threatening in those gangly legs at all.

Most of his thoughts when confronted by someone new referred to their looks, whether they were boy or girl didn't matter. Kevin had a strange outlook that the sum of one's life was expressed in their posture, facial expressions and poise. To him, those who were good looking were evidently better to deal with than those who were ugly, who must've been that way through some fault of their past. It didn't endear him to his colleagues who viewed his tendentious beliefs with quiet bemusement, for they weren't sure what was a genuinely held conviction and what wasn't. Sometimes he would take positions in their conversations which were antipathetical to a university educated individual, but then the next day take a contradictory position. No one could ever truly place his philosophy.

'Alright mate,' he said as he walked across and shook Charlie's hand. 'How long you been here? Old lady Lesley given you a breakdown of how she runs the school and exploits the kids?'

'Yeah,' Charlie awkwardly laughed. 'I was a little confused when she started going on about how much money she made off the parents here.'

'Yeah well, it's the same all over this fucking country.' Kevin continued, 'I've been here seven years now. Six different cities and schools and they're all the fucking same. I tell you, when I was in Guangzhou, the boss told me she'd pay for me to come in on a weekend, and then told me not to tell the other Chinese teachers I was getting paid, because she had no intention of paying them.'

'Yeah same with me and Vivian,' a large, round figure by the name of Elijah interjected in a strong American accent. 'She's a teacher at an international school and it's the same there. All kids are to them are dollar signs.'

Elijah, who had large round red cheeks and a constant quizzical look in his bright blue eyes, gruffly picked up some leftover dumplings he'd bought at lunch and plopped them in his mouth without bothering to use chopsticks. The congealed grease from the sauce they had been in trickled onto his clean-shaven chin as he wiped his hands on his shorts. The other teachers conceived that perhaps it was an American thing, but Elijah always wore shorts which exposed his hairy unkempt legs, even when the temperature was below zero. The fact he also often only wore t-shirts which exposed an array of tattoos didn't lessen their belief that mid-West Americans were made of stern stuff.

The group asked Charlie about his background and what he'd been up to before coming to China. It was a story they'd all heard somewhere before, as if there was a strain of commonality between all expat teachers and the groups they circled in within China. He'd had some very good promise at school. He then went to a university of some reputable name to study a good degree only to find that the saturated job market wouldn't take another lawyer, or physio, or English major, or whatever else. Out of desperation he applied for a 'gap year' in China to teach English and travel.

'Haha, only a gap year,' Kevin laughed, 'you're innocent man.'

'What? Is that not normal?' Charlie replied, glancing from individual to individual.

'Yeah it is,' one of the girls who'd introduced herself as Daphne said, glaring at Kevin. 'But we all thought the same and ended up staying a little longer, but that's because I enjoy it, not because I am trying to avoid going home. I've been at this school since the beginning and just married. I think apart from Amelia and Perry,' she said pointing to a short brown-haired girl and a tall spectacled cropped-haired blond who had his arm round her waist, 'who started six months ago, we've all been in China for at least two years.'

'Oh wow, that's nice,' Charlie said, before adding, 'You must love your jobs.' The others shuffled in their places as they laughed nervously.

'I do,' Daphne said proudly, 'it's about how much effort you put in. If you plan your lessons well, you'll enjoy the outcome. If you expect like some,' she exclaimed rolling her eyes in Kevin's direction, 'that it's all a piece of cake and you can turn up with little or no preparation, no one's going to end up happy.'

'What can I say?' Kevin pondered aloud as he turned off his computer. 'I'm just bloody magnificent.'

The rain outside pattered on the windows as Charlie swivelled slightly in his chair. The desk in front of him was empty bar a computer and keyboard though there was a circle engrained into the desk as if a plant pot had been there before.

'So who's everyone else?' he finally continued.

One by one he was introduced to each of his new colleagues. In addition to Kevin, Daphne, Elijah, Amelia and Perry there were two others sat on a desk, who had spent the whole conversation in silence. One had a great frizz of blonde hair and wore tight clothes which accentuated her large bust. She had bright green eyes and a nose which was too small for her face. This was Ellie. Sat next to her was a small man who had a wispy beard which gave him a French demeanour. His short and stylishly waxed ginger hair added to the suggestion that he was in his mid 20s but the crow's feet around his eyes gave away that he had actually just turned 30. There was a twinkle in his eye, and he held Charlie's gaze for a few seconds longer than felt normal. His name was Bryn. These were the only other two foreign teachers who had been at the school with Daphne since its opening. Apart from Daphne, Kevin and Elijah, they were all Welsh.

Amelia and Perry were the first to leave, kissing at the door before holding hands as they walked out.

'They won the MOAC award at their school,' Elijah whispered.

'MOAC?' Charlie asked quizzically.

'Most Overly Affectionate Couple award.'

'Oh, I see.'

When they reached the lift, Amelia and Perry shared a passionate kiss which made a few kids shout 'ewwwww'. Ellie and Bryn exited soon after, followed closely by the ever-cautious Daphne, who put on her bicycle helmet and arm pads should the worst happen when she was cycling; this on top of the plastic coverings she placed on her shoes which looked like a cheap tacky see-through boot, designed to keep the rainwater off her shiny white trainers. As Elijah picked up his motorcycle helmet to head out, he double took.

'You boys fancy some drinks and a game of poker tomorrow night? Vivian's in Shanghai for some conference.'

'Sure. Sounds good,' Kevin responded for the both of them.

'Ace,' Elijah replied before waddling out, his large thighs clapping as he whistled his way into the lift.

Kevin looked Charlie up and down again, unsettling him with his penetrating blue eyes.

'Well champ, got your bags? Right, let's go,' Kevin finally said.

The walk back to the apartment was a pleasant one. As they walked through an avenue of recently planted trees next to the main road, the sky looked grey and threatening. They passed stray dogs and small children on leads being walked by their grandparents, sometimes bustling with energy which forced their grandparents to yank them back.

Kevin explained it was the business district of Hangzhou, built within the last ten years, but, despite this, looked as if it had been there for at least 50, its peeling buildings, unlike their occupants, maturing faster than their age. Whether it was the shoddiness of the quality of building or the effects of the bitter cold in winter followed by the dense humid heat of summer, either way it gave the area a certain depressing character. Charlie's first impression of China from the plane as they were landing was of a land littered with a mix of communist buildings that looked the same, and villages that looked like they belonged in the middle ages, almost like mud huts from above. He later discovered on the ground this wasn't the case at all, because the neighbourhoods they passed had a distinct make up to them, welcoming and homely. Each neighbourhood had 20 buildings of 10 storeys each towering into the sky, but they were not slum like, they were well looked after and clean.

'So you were at Edinburgh?'

'Yeah.'

'Once had sex with a girl from there.'

'Fascinating.'

'Aye, I've got family up in Aberdeen, not too far.'

'And where did you study?'

'Manchester.'

'What did you study there?'

'Geography, but I didn't enjoy it much. I mean a waste of three years if you ask me, especially since I've come out here since.'

'Did you not plan to stay long?'

'No, definitely not, I only came for a laugh and to get away from my ex. Like Daphne said, we all planned to have a gap year, but you end up just sort of staying.'

'What made you want to stay?'

'The girls.'

'Fascinating.'

'And the lifestyle. It's just so easy man, honestly, we're getting paid the equivalent of £25,000 a year just to wipe snot off a small kid's face, and we basically can't get fired. Well, I've been in the past but that was for a different reason.'

'No way,' Charlie smirked. 'What did you do?'

'I'll let you know after we've had something to drink,' Kevin said, tapping his nose twice.

As they walked, they shared jokes and stories from university and childhood. Most of it was about drinking and girls, but Charlie began to suspect this would be the usual when it came to Kevin. He seemed to have an obsession with women, as if little else in life mattered. As it turned out, he took pride in having slept with over 500 women and made an effort to stress that in China alone, he usually slept with at least one girl a week.

'That doesn't sound very healthy.'

'What are you, gay?'

'No.'

'What's wrong with it? I'd do it back in the UK, only fewer girls are willing to sleep with me.'

Charlie shuddered. Well, everyone has their reason to keep living, he thought.

When they arrived back at their neighbourhood, the security guard at their gate briefly stopped Charlie and said something in Chinese whilst Kevin skirted through the barriers. When Charlie didn't respond, he opened his bag and searched through his possessions. After Charlie had translated into his phone that he was new to the area and about to move into the neighbourhood, the security guard made a sort of belching noise, and opened the gate, staring at him with squinting eyes that suggested he didn't believe this story. Charlie, too tired to try to explain again, simply rolled his baggage through the gate and joined Kevin who'd waited impatiently on the other side throughout the whole exchange.

'That was strange,' he said to Kevin.

'Yeah … they do whatever they want to be honest. A bit like a bouncer at a club, they like to use what little power they have.'

The neighbourhood was large and filled with healthy green trees which had patches of sprouting grass at their base, the type Charlie thought could only be found in the jungle. It was an entirely artificial complex built less than 15 years before, but it seemed to have a grace and peaceful serenity at the same time, as if trying to recreate ancient China, with its idyllic gardens and sculptured landscapes. The apartment blocks had ivy growing on their sides, and the sound of children's laughter could be heard with each breath of wind, even in the cold.

Charlie wondered if the apartment would be similarly grand.

Because of how Kevin had acted so far, it felt strange to Charlie that the first thing he noticed when they finally entered the apartment after a slow lift ride, was a bookshelf full of books on history and engineering. They covered a large portion of one wall, and all their spines were creased, suggesting they had been read from front to back.

'These yours?' Charlie asked, a bit bemused.

'Yeah, have a look if you like.'

In the corner was a guitar case open with the guitar nearby, and a music stand that had the score open to a page with lots of squiggles and notes on it.

The 8th floor flat was not as bad as Charlie had worried it might be. Behind a heavy and, for some reason, sticky door there was a kitchen which had a distinct burning smell inside. Charlie assumed this had something to do with the reason there was a large sign on the door saying 'KEEP CLOSED'. The main living room seemed to be recently refurbished but there was a crack in the ceiling from which flakes of paint descended every once in a while. A large sofa opposite a big TV led out onto a balcony which overlooked the community lake below – an artificial contraption put in when the neighbourhood was built but expertly designed to seamlessly fit in like it was natural and the neighbourhood had in fact been built around this beauty spot.

There were three large bedrooms in the flat, one ensuite and the other two sharing a bathroom. The layout was such that one of the bedroom's occupants would have to dash across the living room in order to get to the shower each morning.

'That's my room,' Kevin declared.

'No kidding,' Charlie muttered under his breath.

As a result, however, Charlie was given the room with the ensuite. He smiled with glee when he opened the door, relieved to see a large double bed and clean space, with recently painted walls of white, and large sliding doors that opened out onto his own balcony.

The third occupant of the flat, Kevin had been telling Charlie, was an American who worked at a nearby high school.

'That's Gabriel's room,' he said, pointing towards a door with a large rainbow flag draped on it, 'but he doesn't like people going in there so try not to unless he says you can.'

'Where is he right now?'

'He works for extra money outside of school on a Friday evening, but he'll join us later on. Now, how about some lubrication?'

3

The sound of a piano could be heard through the ceiling as Charlie opened his weary eyes. His head pounded with a ferocity he hadn't felt since the first time he'd drunk absinthe. His mouth was so dry he couldn't speak. There was a ferocious pounding in his ears, and he stank of cheap cigarette smoke, like the charred ash of burnt wood-shavings; he could feel his heartbeat all over his weak body, from his toes to his fingertips. As he lay in a state of self-pity, cuddling his pillow with all his might, he tried to recall where he'd been the night before, and what he had been up to. All he could remember was swaying from side to side as he entered the club ... but after that, nothing – it was as if a poor quality pirate copy of a movie had been taped over at the point it was about to get interesting.

His room was large and barren. The sliding doors to his right were slightly ajar and the chill from outside had engulfed his room, causing him to cocoon himself even more in his duvet, tucking in as many limbs as he could. There were two cupboards to his left, still empty as he hadn't bothered to unpack before the excitement of the night before, when Kevin had plied him full of spirits which Charlie, to avoid seeming like a sour dud, had hesitatingly drunk. There was a terrible smell emanating from the bathroom.

The piano seemed to get louder and there was a high-pitched shriek-ing, a bit like a child's but deep enough to be an adult's, coming from Kevin's room. Then, a thudding noise grew louder and louder next door as the piano reached its crescendo, building into an exploding cacophony of noise causing Charlie to place his shaking hands over his ears.

'Ughhhh,' he groaned as he burped, the taste of vomit filling his mouth.

Charlie froze with his eyes open, staring at the corner of the room, not quite knowing if he was still dreaming or if he had yet woken. Then the piano and the thudding stopped.

Charlie swung his long legs out of the bed and slowly pushed himself up, his elbows shaking lightly, as if he were an old man trying to get out of a low chair. His back ached like it had just been carrying a sack of sharp, jagged steel bricks – his mattress felt like planks of wood had been substituted for feathers. He groaned again. He wondered what on earth he'd drunk that could cause such a horrible sensation in his head.

He was naked, so he looked to the floor and, from the bed, threw his hand towards his trousers which were scrunched up with his pants still inside them. He fumbled about in both of his pockets before pulling out his mobile phone which had a large scratch across the bottom half of the screen. 13:00! Already! He looked at his messages, a few missed calls from Kevin and some WeChat friend requests from people he didn't recognise.

Charlie chucked his phone on his bed and pushed himself up to his feet with a big sigh, barely maintaining his balance as blood rushed to his head, making him sway from side to side. He stumbled to his bathroom, clutching the doorway to give him some form of footing. As he thrust himself ungraciously towards the toilet, he could see where the smell had been emanating from.

Oh Jesus Christ, he thought.

Not only were congealed chunks of last night's dinner protruding from the shower drain, but in the corner stood a red cup, with a ping pong ball sitting on top of the vomit within it.

He opened the taps of the shower before recoiling from the freezing cold water that cascaded from the shower head; he then began to wash the grime off the floor away as best he could.

Unfortunately, he'd forgotten to plug in his electric boiler before he went to sleep that night. He kept feeling the temperature of the water but it wasn't getting any warmer. He took a deep breath before throwing himself underneath and letting out a screech.

During his shower, elements of the night uncontrollably began to come back to him. He recalled they'd started by having some drinks whilst playing Fifa on Kevin's PS4, then they'd hopped into a taxi to a huge place in the centre of town, more like a diner than a bar. But there was music, he thought. How could it have been a diner? Oh, no, that's right, there was a stage which had a live but terrible band playing.

Then, what happened? He strained to remember as the cold water numbed his shoulders. Kevin had introduced him to a lot of other expats, mostly large, dim and drunken American Football players. From there, the night seemed harder to remember. Kevin and Gabriel had pushed him into a taxi and Gabriel spoke some Chinese and … Gabriel! That was right, Gabriel. He was nice; far nicer than Kevin.

After he'd showered for the two minutes he could bear shivering, he hopped out before running to close the doors to his balcony and turning on the A/C to its heater setting. Following this, he unpacked his bags, changed into some lounging tracksuits and finally opened his door to go into the living room, as refreshed as possible with a pounding headache. There was a pair of white shoes strewn across the floor in front of Kevin's room and a pair of small high heels neatly placed next to the door. Gabriel was in the living room and looked like he'd been up for a while.

He sat on the sofa with his laptop on the coffee table and papers spread out in a neat semi-circle around his workspace. He was in shorts and a maroon hoodie, and wore a pair of Harry Potter-esque circular glasses. His hands were clamped around a cup of coffee soaking up the heat it emitted, whilst the steam warmed his bristly chin. He stared intensely at his laptop with the singularity of vision and purpose of someone absorbed in work. The large A/C in the corner of the room was on its highest setting, and yet the room still felt a little frosty to Charlie.

'Good morning,' Charlie managed to croak.

'Oh hey, good morning!' Gabriel replied, a little startled having been so engrossed in his work.

'You don't happen to have any water, do you?' Charlie asked meekly.

'In the fridge, take as much as you want.'

Gabriel's accent was Californian but there was a soft touch to it and a slight twang which suggested he was actually from somewhere in the south of the US but he was trying to hide it. He looked about the same age as Kevin, but had taken much better care of himself; the daily application of moisturiser showed on his gleaming face. He wasn't a tall and muscular man, but it was obvious he kept fit and possessed minimal fat. His blue eyes sparkled as Charlie returned from the fridge with a large five litre bottle of water and a plastic cup. The kitchen didn't seem to have any permanent features anywhere other than a small fridge and a cooker.

'How did you enjoy your night?' Gabriel asked.

'It was fun!' Charlie replied. 'But my head is absolutely pounding, what did we drink?'

'Baijiu.'

'Baijiu?'

Gabriel stood up before grabbing a bottle from beside the television. It was square shaped, a bit like a bottle of Jack Daniel's whiskey, and covered in Chinese characters; the liquid inside was clear and swished around with the same viscosity as water. The whole get up made it look more like a bottle of cleaning spirit than a bottle of drinkable alcohol, but Charlie still took it and opened the cap intrigued to find out what it actually smelled like. He took one sniff and almost vomited again, coughing and spluttering as he wrinkled his face out of disgust. Suddenly, a whole lot more of the night vividly returned to him.

'Ugh, that's vile.'

'Yah I know,' Gabriel giggled.

'How much of that did I drink?'

'About half,' Gabriel said, 'and that was after we left Wade's with Kevin. You must have had a few beers before I came with this at about midnight.'

'No kidding …'

'You weren't great in the car.'

'What time did we get back?'

'Ooooh, about …' Gabriel put his finger to his chin before tilting his jaw to grind his teeth a little, '6 a.m.'

It was just coming up to 14:00 and Charlie felt more than a little peckish, having emptied the contents of his stomach many times, both in some poor Chinese person's taxi and on his shower floor. He sat on the sofa next to Gabriel and brought his elbows into a self-hug. He shivered a little and put up the hood of his hoodie whilst his stomach rumbled loudly, sounding like a whale's mating call.

'Do you fancy grabbing some lunch?' Charlie asked. 'I'm starving.'

'Sure, give me two seconds.'

After Gabriel closed his laptop, grabbed a jacket and put on some crystal white plimsolls, he led the way out of the flat and into the neighbourhood below. The weather had improved since the day before and now the sun was shining with only a few bright white clouds in the sky. There was still a haze from the ever-present pollution, but the light was warm as it touched Charlie's face. The air wasn't fresh, but it felt good to be outside and his head had finally stopped its incessant banging. As they walked around the path which circled the perimeter of the neighbourhood it became clear just how large the complex was. At three corners there were exits which were the only way in and out – these were guarded by security men who looked a little worse for wear, with large pregnant bellies protruding symmetrically from their coats, like swollen fruits.

They walked past the first exit which, even in winter, was surrounded by flowers and plants and gave the compound an exotic feel. There were palm trees towards the lake at the centre of the compound, but they didn't walk towards them, instead diverting underneath a residential building to another exit. As they walked out of the complex, their faces were picked up by a scanner mounted by the gate. Gabriel waved to the security guard and motioned towards Charlie. He spoke some Chinese and the security guards grinned back, their dark yellow eyes squinting as brown stained toothy smiles appeared on their faces. They quickly put up their hands, as if in sync, and put them down again in a hurried greeting, feigning a little embarrassment.

Outside of the complex they angled left and walked for a few minutes along the main road, trying to avoid stepping on loose tiles on the pavement which hid within them small drops of the previous day's rain. The traffic wasn't too bad at this time on a Saturday afternoon but the pavements were lively with people, even in this supposedly business area of Hangzhou. The shops to their left ranged from clothing stores to restaurants & cafés, each bustling with activity and energy. There was no order to the shops and within a 100 metres, there must have been five hairdressers with bored girls in short skirts mulling around the inside. They smiled and stared as Charlie and Gabriel walked past.

'You know if you want a cheap blowjob,' Gabriel said pointing at the barbershop, 'you just gotta go to one of those that looks right. That particular barbershop isn't, but if you see a place with more girls sitting on their arses than hairdressers behind them, you know you're there. If they're open past 10 p.m. too, that's a giveaway. Ooh but *not* if they give a bad haircut, that's not a giveaway, that's just every damn hairdresser in China.'

'No way,' Charlie replied, a little startled. 'How do you know that? Isn't it illegal? And … well … aren't you gay?'

'Well duh … but here and there, some of the massage parlours you find as well are more than happy if you pay a little extra. Besides, there's 40 million more men than women in this country, I'll be fine.'

They continued walking and Charlie noticed a lot of people turning when they passed and pointing at them, it wasn't just kids but adults too. One of the children in particular pointed before laughing uncontrollably while his mother and sisters, embarrassed, tried to pull his hand down.

'That happens a lot here, doesn't it?' Charlie asked.

'Children laughing? Oh no, not really.'

'No I meant the staring, as if we're aliens. At the airport in Chong-kwing alone random people were filming me and sniggering at the same time.'

'Yeah, that happens but you get used to it … Also it's Chongqing.'

'That's what I said!'

'No you didn't, it's "ch"ing, not "kwing".'

Once they'd reached a small shop which had Arabic writing on the sign outside, they dived in and grabbed a chair – the inside seemed dark in comparison to the street outside, whilst the air was rich with the smell of garlic and spices. The restaurant was the least busy of those they'd passed and there were pictures of food on the walls. Most of them looked the same to Charlie, simply variations of the same dish placed on rice or noodles. At the back there was a counter with a fridge containing soft drinks alongside a large sign in English saying 'NO ALCOHOL'. Through the curtain at the back was the kitchen filled with four sweaty men each wearing a topi. The tables in the eatery were small and the seats mismatched plastic stools which looked like they'd been taken out of a skip.

After looking at the pictures, Charlie went for some soup noodles with beef whilst Gabriel went for a bun filled with shredded beef & chillies alongside a plate of rice & cumin beef. Once they'd sat down on two of the stools by the front door, Gabriel replied to some texts on his phone whilst Charlie cast his eyes around the premises. The other diners all looked at them with odd expressions on their faces, bemused but emotionless. There was something funny looking about them, Charlie thought. They were much more tanned than most people they had seen on the street so far, and their eyes were larger and more wide set. Their noses were, in general, a bit bigger and two of the older gentlemen in the corner had long wispy beards which moved with every twitch of the face, like long grass swaying in the wind. They too wore topis, and also wore thawbs, long tunics in the style of Middle Eastern men that sat below the shins, only allowing a small glimpse of the socks and sandals they were wearing beneath.

Just then, their food was brought out by someone Charlie thought was a Turkish-looking lady in a hajib. Her face was pale and her eyes very circular; she looked like a picture Charlie had once seen of Uzbek people.

'How are you today?' the lady asked in Chinese.

'What did she say?' Charlie turned to Gabriel.

'She asked how we are.'

'Oh,'

'We're OK,' Gabriel returned.

'What did you say?' Charlie asked.

'I said we're OK ...'

'Oh ... makes sense.'

'How's the little one?' Gabriel continued.

'He's OK, I think he looks more and more like his father every day. Xiao An,' she shouted turning around, 'come here!'

A little boy with a large nose ran forward dressed in a long tunic.

'Hello brother Gabriel,' he said shyly in English with a strong accent.

'What did he say?'

'He was speaking English!'

'Oh ... was he?'

Gabriel ignored Charlie.

'How is school for you?' Gabriel continued in Chinese

'It's fun ... do you want to see my cool figurine?'

'That's enough Xiao An, let's leave our two guests to eat.'

The lady turned around, tugged the child on the shoulder and disappeared behind the kitchen curtain.

'Funny looking, isn't she?' Gabriel said as he caught on to Charlie's eyes still looking towards the lightly swaying curtain.

'Is she Chinese?' Charlie asked.

'Uyghur,' Gabriel replied. 'They're nice enough, but a lot more quiet than any other Chinese people I've met, and they speak in a very odd accent. When I first dropped in, they treated me like a king. It almost looked to me like they were bowing as they dropped off my food and again when I paid. I was a little embarrassed. I've been coming to this restaurant for two years now, almost every day. They're much more pleasant than the owners of the other restaurants around here.'

Gabriel took a bite into his greasy bun and expertly started to fish at his rice with a pair of chopsticks, picking up chunks at a time with the grace of a local. Charlie used his spoon to hoover up the contents of his noodle soup, he'd not yet learnt the art of holding chopsticks and knew he would embarrass himself if he tried to pick them up now.

'You know I once came in here and saw her crying in the corner with a large red mark on her face. Her husband had plainly hit her. I think I must have been the only one to ask if she was OK. All the others in the restaurant carried on eating as if nothing had been happening. People keep to themselves in China.'

Charlie mulled this over as he stared longingly into his soup. 'I've seen something like that before,' he finally said.

'You have?' Gabriel replied. 'But you're from England.'

'Yeah, but in Morocco you know, these Muslim countries where women are often slaving away in the kitchen while their husbands sit and drink tea.'

'I guess.'

'And when I went to Dubai, I had to act like my brother's girlfriend was my older sister.'

'No way! How did that go down?'

'It was a bit weird. We got away with it though.'

He fished in his bowl with his spoon, swirling it around in an attempt to pick up loose strands.

'How long have you been here now?' he asked, slurping up some soup after he'd given up trying at the noodles.

'I've been here about three years but only two in Hangzhou. Before I was in Tianjin at a primary school but the winters were too cold and the scene wasn't fun enough. Thought I'd try here instead and teach older children. Besides it's closer to Shanghai which has a big gayberhood. I like Hangzhou. It's the greenest city I've seen so far in China and it's got great links to the rest of the country. Only four hours by train to Beijing, and an hour's flight to Hong Kong.'

'How is the gay scene?'

'It's so easy here, oh my god, like I could pull anyone. A bit like if you're straight too, I guess. But the thing about Asians is that they're not really allowed to be gay so they are even more secret about it. In our neighbourhood alone I've already met two who haven't even told their parents they're gay, but they were so open about it with me … It's more fun … It feels like it's illegal, but it's not.'

'Hmmm,' Charlie laughed awkwardly, 'sounds just like Kevin.'

'I'll take that as an insult.'

'Oh no, I didn't mean it like that,' Charlie turned red.

'Yeah I know, I'm just teasing,' Gabriel winked.

'And when did you first meet Kevin?' Charlie asked as he probed his soup for the final contents that had sunk to the bottom of the bowl.

'Oh Kevin,' he said in thought, 'he's been my flatmate for a year now.

Our agency put us together. At first, I thought he was such a dick. Very self-centred and, honestly, his ego drives me potty. But he's nice once you get to know him. If anything, I sometimes wonder if he's bi the way he is around me. Very open and expressive. He's got a weird presence.'

'Hmm, yeah I noticed that about him. The way he spoke though, you'd think he'd only come to China for girls.'

'He's not the only one,' Gabriel laughed. 'You know he's been fired before from three of his previous jobs for having sex with some of the parents at the schools he's been at. There's even a rumour he had sex with one of the 16-year-old students at a high school he taught at, but I doubt it, because he definitely would've been deported if that was the case.'

'What!?' Charlie gasped. 'I mean I don't even know where to start with that … How do you know about it?'

'Just rumours man, but he told me about the parents. Didn't go into too much detail.'

'So how many schools has he taught at?'

'Errrr six, I think. But having sex with a parent isn't that hard from what I've heard. Most of the schools that hire foreigners are expensive anyway, and the dad is usually some ugly guy who's rich and their bored-as-fuck wife can't wait to take their children to school and flirt with the foreigners.' Gabriel paused in thought. 'It seems to me Kevin gets into trouble wherever he goes, then once the one-year teaching contract is over, it isn't renewed and he goes onto the next job. You see the demand for white English teachers here is through the roof. As long as you don't have a criminal record, any school will hire you, literally anyone.'

Charlie sat in silence.

'Huh, so I guess the guitar and books were yours then,' Charlie concluded, slurping up the last of the soup.

'Actually, no they're not, those are his,' Gabriel nodded. 'But I think he initially brought them when he first came seven years ago, and he just takes them whenever he moves around.'

'Does he play the guitar a lot?'

'Not much anymore. I think he just set things up like that to make the flat more homely. Apparently he used to be really studious.'

'That can't be true, he's a wreck.'

'I know what you mean, but I don't think he was like that when he first came to China.'

'He only told me he didn't know what to do and wanted to escape a girlfriend.'

'That's my point. I can't even begin to imagine Kevin with a girl-friend. I mean seven years is a long time, he's probably changed a lot during that.'

'Have you?'

'I haven't been here that long.'

'But have you still changed a lot?'

'A little. I've become more lazy definitely, more unwilling to go home to the US. I don't know what it is about China but I'm just so drawn to staying here'.

'Kevin said he likes the easy life.'

'It's definitely part of that, but it's something more too. Here, it sort of gets into your head that you're different, as if that makes you special. When people film you randomly or want to take pictures with you because they've never seen a foreigner before, that makes you feel famous. It changes you.'

'But you say it hasn't changed you.'

'Not as much, I think it's different for me though. I'm gay, I've always been a bit of an outsider that has attention, both good and bad, that comes with being gay. For straight white men it's different. There's nothing particularly special about them back home, at least nothing that would turn heads, but here, everyone is aware of them, not because they're actually special but because they look different to the locals. Add that to the fact that pale white skin, large eyes and big noses are consid-ered more beautiful by Asians, and you're left with egotistical arseholes.'

Charlie took out some cash as they were about to leave but Gabriel laughed and waved his arm in a way to say he'd got it.

'China's ahead of the West in some things,' he explained. 'This is one of them.'

He took out his phone and scanned a QR code beside the till before typing in the cost of the meal.

'Nifty right,' he said before turning back to man behind the counter. 'Busy day?' he asked in Chinese.

'No, slow morning,' the man behind the counter smiled. 'Thank you for your custom.'

'Oh stop, you know I love coming here,' Gabriel smiled back. 'See you tomorrow.'

He led Charlie out and onto the now quiet street. It was nearing 15:00 and the sky was already beginning to darken as they strode back to the gate of their community.

When they returned home, they noticed the girl who had been in Kevin's room was gone and Kevin was now ungracefully splayed out on the couch, scrolling through his phone with an index finger as he held it directly above his head, his eyes slightly crossed staring at something so close to his face. He'd just come out of the shower and had only a towel around his waist, which it seemed was the only thing that was dry as there was a long trail of puddles to the couch, and his still dripping hair had formed a large dark spot on the sofa beneath his head.

On his chest, just above his heart, was a tattoo that looked a bit like a university crest, while there was a quote in slanted writing across his toned midriff. His thigh had a solid black band which circled the whole circumference of his hairy upper leg, the dark ink already fading in a way to suggest it had been done a few years before. He was muscular but the alcohol he had drunk the night before made his body look both puffy and dehydrated. In this moment he looked about double his age.

'Alright bumders,' he said, looking quickly below his phone and back to his screen.

'What happened to you last night?' Charlie asked.

'Oh, same old, same old,' came the reply. 'Do you boys wanna head into town to grab some drinks before we head across to old man Elijah's later?'

'Actually, I was thinking of heading to West Lake to look at some of the touristy things,' Charlie replied. He also didn't fancy the prospect of another drop of alcohol to add to his hangover, even if it had mostly subsided.

'Oh sure, I can show you everything,' Kevin said. 'Give me a sec to change.'

He jumped up with a surprising amount of energy for someone who must have drunk at least as much as Charlie the night before. When he'd reached his bedroom, he left the door wide open before stripping naked and throwing clothes on. Charlie, to avoid having to see him naked, walked to the living room balcony and peered out across the skyline. In the distance, the lights of the buildings slowly flickered on. The sky was cloudless, but there was no prospect of stars tonight. A plane descended in the distance, but no noise could be heard from its landing. A few frogs croaked by the neighbourhood's lake as the water lapped against its edge.

4

Four weeks had passed since that first weekend in February, and the weather had begun to warm up with the promise of a pleasant spring in the air.

Kevin and Charlie paced along a boulevard in the newest area of Hangzhou, Xiaoshan, where the buildings were taller, the roads wider and the cars shinier. This area was dubbed the next Silicon Valley though neither of them could say why. As they pounded the street, each step producing a large clank of heel on ground, the sky drizzled and cars sped by, spraying them from the day's puddles that had formed on the side of the road. Since Charlie's relatively smooth entrance into the Hangzhou expat scene, and with his talent for gambling, a group of them now met once a week to play poker at Elijah's house. The stakes were low but the alcohol flowed and the conversation was varied. Vivian, Elijah's fiancée, had been promoted to become one of her school's management, and now spent most of her time in Shanghai planning for a new addition to the International School she was employed by. Elijah didn't mind as it meant he had the flat to himself most weekends. Also in this case, given Vivian's vastly higher salary and larger accommodation grant, they could afford to live in the penthouse of a high rise in most expensive district of Hangzhou.

When the two boys had escaped the rain into the lobby of the apartment building, they shook themselves like dogs rising out of a lake. They looked at each other in bemusement before laughing, walking to the lift doors, and pressing the button to wait – leaving droplets of water in small puddles on the floor behind them to the visible annoyance of the concierge. They each had a bottle of whiskey in their hands and carried beers in a carrier bag which clanked as they walked.

Charlie had come to enjoy spending time with Kevin. They'd formed a bond in the few weeks they'd come to know each other which transcended all Kevin's previous acquaintances in his many years on the mainland. Given they both lived and worked together, their colleagues had suspected they wouldn't be able to stand each other after a few weeks, but this turned out to be false. In fact, the more time they spent together, the more they enjoyed each other's company, as if a newly married couple enjoying a grace period akin to a romantic honeymoon. Most evenings Kevin was busy, but this didn't matter as Charlie had taken to learning Chinese from Gabriel who had a thorough grasp of its intricacies. On weekends, however, they would be inseparable, drinking, eating and working out together.

Once they'd reached the top floor, they exited the lift into the corridor, only to be hit by the thumping beat of music, its vibrations almost visible in the air. The music, loud enough to feel they were backstage at a concert, filtered out of the wide open double doors ahead that comprised the entrance to Elijah's apartment. Because the building was brand new, the other flat on the top storey hadn't been occupied yet, allowing the men to commandeer the entire floor for the evening. They walked along a tunnel of glass which overlooked an empty roof garden with bar, table and furniture stacked up, under covers to protect them from the rain. The panoramic view was large and captivating, following the Qiantang river as it meandered through the fields in the distance, as far as the eye could see.

'I wonder if Elijah popped the question out there?' Charlie mused.

'Doubt it, I think he did it in a bar. From what Vivian's told me he doesn't have one romantic bone in this body.'

Entering Elijah's flat was a bit like entering the temporary luxury of a suite at a 5* hotel. The flat was fully furnished with white leather that creaked when sat on, and windows made of floor to ceiling glass, giving anyone that stood in front of them, staring at the ant-sized people below, the simultaneous feeling of superiority and vertigo. There were designer paintings on one side and a plasma-screen TV suspended above a not too obviously fake fire on the other. Everything within looked sleek and brand new in a fashionable, minimalist way. The view from the living room was just as expansive as the view from the roof terrace, overlooking almost all other buildings in the surrounding area. Even in the cloudy weather, Kevin and Charlie were in awe at what Elijah woke up to each morning and saw last thing before bed each night.

As they sat down to start their game of poker, they were joined by two of Elijah and Kevin's American Football mates – Gabriel hadn't been able to make the night because he had found a date on Grindr. The American Football players were almost carbon copies of Kevin. All had a similar sense of humour and a vulgar interest in the local women. All had been teachers in China for at least three years, and had spent at least one year in Hangzhou.

'The gurls 'ere are t' best,' bragged one named Albert, in a thick incomprehensible Yorkshire accent. He was ginger with pale skin and a few freckles on his large nose. His bright green eyes made him attractive, but he didn't help himself by slumbering to one side which accentuated his appalling posture and gave him the appearance of lacking in confidence.

'Couldn't agree more,' the slightly shorter, fatter one named Will concurred. Will had brown hair and dull brown eyes, but a forgettable face.

Kevin, whilst staring intensely at his cards, also nodded his head in slow appreciation; he was too busy having a bad night to take part in the direction of the discussion. He was determined to salvage some money before the conversation turned to the inevitable debasement he knew they were capable of without female company.

'What makes you say that?' Charlie inquired innocently.

'Aww mate really?' Will said. 'They're just so fit. They're like a mix of north and south. The tall, strong but squinty-eyed northerners and the small, well-shaped, large-eyed southerners. A lot of them speak English and they're all dead keen,' he continued boorishly. 'I don't think you'd know cos you just got here, but, believe me, you've hit the jackpot.' Will placed his arm over the back of the chair as his hairy belly protruded under his t-shirt. A shiver of disgust darted up Charlie's spine which made him sit up straight.

'How many 'av' you 'ad so far lad?' Albert spluttered whilst taking a swig of his beer.

'I assume you're referring to girls? None so far, but there's a Korean one at Kevin's salsa I'm interested in, might ask her on a date.'

'Wahey Charlie boy!' both Will and Albert replied with a lewd cheer.

Kevin, who had been silent for a while, trying to concentrate on how to win back some money, thought this a bit untoward and that the conversation needed to move along, 'Come on guys, show a bit of respect would you. They're not meat.'

'Says you!' Will screeched in reply.

'It's only because he's losing,' Albert hypothesised.

Kevin had indeed let the losing get to him, but there was also something about the girls at his salsa class which lit a chivalrous beacon within him.

'I'm just saying, treat them right, they're not meat,' he repeated.

'And when did you come to that conclusion?' Will asked.

'Just … you know. There are some girls who are one way and others who are another. The girls at our dance class are partners.'

'Oh, not this again.'

'Not what again?' Charlie asked.

'Kevin's theories on girls,' Albert explained. 'He seems to think there are three of them.'

'It's true,' Kevin stated.

He put down an ace of spades but regretted it immediately.

'Fuck sake!' he shouted. 'Shouldn't have done that!'

'Well go on then,' Charlie gestured. 'I want to hear your theory.'

'I give up, guess it's only a tenner,' he said, throwing his cards down. 'Alright, alright. The thing is this, there are three types of girls which can be put down to "the three p's" …' He put up three fingers, counting each one off, 'partners, passengers, parasites. The partners are the ones everyone should look for in a relationship. They don't want anything from you, instead they only want to make you stronger, more confident. Passengers are there for a good time but you shouldn't make plans for them in the long run, they're dull. But the parasites … they're the ones you should avoid. They leech off of you, remove you of the will to live. The problem is that they're usually the ones who are best in bed. The graph is inversely proportional. Partners are the keepers but useless in bed. Passengers are decent enough but only average in the sack. But the parasites, my god, they're the best.'

'Did you actually just refer to it as inversely proportional,' Elijah burst out laughing. 'What are you, a bloody scientist?'

Kevin smirked a little.

'No that's not what I mean … anyway,' he said turning back to Charlie. 'The girls at the dance class are partners and passengers. I've never met a parasite there. Most of them are the ones I meet in night clubs but for one night there's nothing wrong with a parasite.'

Charlie stared at him bemusedly. 'I mean … I don't really know what to say to that to be honest.'

'Don't say anything,' Kevin replied, 'you're young … Anyway,' he stood up and walked to the fridge, 'I think Charlie has his eyes on the parent in Lily's class. Xiao Bao's mum. Now she is *definitely* a parasite.'

There was laughter around the room.

'Who doesn't!' Elijah interjected.

Charlie's face turned bright red.

'Who's the English teacher in that class now?' Will asked.

'Errr, it's Amelia right now but I think the school's getting some more children starting in a few weeks so we might be shuffled about again. Amelia's better with the younger kids but Lily's class is the oldest in the school,' Elijah explained.

'Huh, anyone fancy their chances?' Will stated generically.

'Yeah, me,' Kevin winked. 'Have you seen how ugly her husband is? She's leeching off him for sure. Probably desperate for someone else's attention.'

'You know, I've never found Chinese girls that attractive on the whole, but for her I'd make an exception,' Elijah said, swigging on his beer before letting out a large belch.

'I mean you do have a girlfriend of ten years,' Will pointed out.

'Yeah, but even so, I just never would. Maybe it's to do with the fact their food stinks and they're a bunch of weirdos. If I had kids I wouldn't want their mother to be Chinese, she'd take them to the grandparents who would plant notions in their head.'

'Ah see wut ya mean pal,' Albert said incomprehensibly.

'How long have you been in China?' Charlie asked Elijah, with a tinge of anger in his voice. He scrunched his hands into fists.

'Er … three years now.'

'Why don't you leave then if you think it's so bad?' Charlie continued.

'Nah mate, I would, but this is where the international school circuit is. All the jobs are here. I'm not saying I hate China. It's a beautiful place, but the Chinese who grew up under the cultural revolution, and a lot of the men, are just weird. Like truly odd. Before you came, one of the grandparents had been taking pictures of Amelia's bum when she was in the playground and he'd just hang around looking at her the whole time.'

'Yeah, not great,' Kevin agreed. 'The school had to have a word with him.'

'But that happens in every country,' Charlie interjected.

'Plus they're a bunch of racists themselves,' Elijah continued, ignoring Charlie's remark. 'You probably haven't felt it yet, but they really treat people differently. Lesley was offered by the agency a chance to hire a black person but declined despite the fact he'd been teaching in China for five years. In her usual "it's just business" way, she said it was because parents didn't want him to teach. I was just like, "hmmm I wonder why".'

'That's not true, I've seen plenty of black people around Hangzhou.'

'Just because you see them doesn't mean they don't suffer discrimination.'

Elijah let out another belch and stuffed a few crisps into his mouth before continuing his drunken tirade, little pieces of half-eaten chunks spewing onto the table in front of him.

'Forgive me,' Charlie scoffed, 'but I don't think you've ever had to put up with discrimination.'

'No, you're right, I haven't but I know it happens. Believe me I used to be like you, thinking, "Oh isn't this a wonderful place, all mysterious and classical with 5,000 years of high cultural history". It's bullshit, there are a tonne of problems that get ignored, I just know I can't do anything about it, so why bother. As long as I have beer and food I'm not concerned anymore. And concerning race, the simple fact is, that if you were Chinese and settled in America or anywhere else in the West, after one generation, you would be considered to be from that country, and your kids, despite being a different ethnicity, would be considered that nationality. Think Idris Elba, his parents were born in Africa but I don't think anyone would argue with the fact he's British. But here it's different. Here, if I came and had a child with Vivian, that kid wouldn't be considered Chinese. If he or she spent their whole life in China, marrying a Chinese girl, speaking better Chinese than English, they would still be referred to as a foreigner. By my values, that's appalling.'

You certainly seem to pick and choose you values, Charlie thought. He shuffled his cards angrily.

The day after was a beautiful morning. The sun shone with brightness and the air was crisp and fresh. The birds by the lake below chirped as the old went out for their morning workout, keen to hold on to whatever zeal of youth they had left.

Kevin was up at about 10 a.m. after a good night's sleep. It had been one of the few moderate nights of the year where he hadn't needed to sleep with the A/C turned on to either hot or cold. He'd lost a fair amount of money in the previous evening's poker game, but he didn't plan to let the bitter aftertaste of gambling affect his day.

The slowly rising sun outside was powerful, penetrating the room with heat and light; its rays catching dust suspended in the air. Despite the coldness of the previous few days, the atmosphere outside was temperate, which Kevin knew from experience meant spring was fast approaching. He decided that when he went out later, he would brave it in only a t-shirt and jeans.

The grassy patches around the lake outside were boisterous and lively, a lot of the neighbourhood used Sunday mornings to socialise and play; every so often Kevin could see one of his students from a distance with their parents who lived in the same complex. The echoes of children's screams of joy could be heard eight floors up, reminding Kevin of the reason he never wanted children. This morning in particular there was a strong smell of lavender in the living room, where Gabriel had left a scented candle lit overnight. His date's takeaway was still on the dining table and his laptop open but locked; a picture of Gabriel completing a pull-up on some nondescript Californian beach as his screensaver.

It must have been a quick burst of passion, Kevin thought.

He grabbed the leftovers, flicked away a fly that had settled on some rice, and nibbled on their cold remains, his blocked nose preventing the reek of fish from becoming too overpowering. The consistency was good and he polished it off within a few minutes using a bright red pair of chopsticks.

His usual Sunday routine was melancholic. He would potter around the house in his silk dressing gown – opened to slightly reveal his torso – then stretch out on the sofa to relax. After turning on his VPN and scrolling through his UK social media, then drinking his third cup of coffee, he would most often be ready for the gym and a tough workout to sweat out the two previous nights of drinking. This morning, however, as he splayed across the furniture, he felt a little peculiar. An emotion of ennui took hold and he could do nothing more than stare at the ceiling.

The ceiling's crack followed a path like a river, curving and meandering, from one side of the flat to the other. As he lay on the sofa, he closed his eyes and imagined that the crack was the Yangtze, and he was traversing the length and breadth of China. It's such a big country, he thought, why would he want to live anywhere else? If he wanted a desert, or mountains, or the tropics, or a ski season, poverty or wealth, he could experience it in China. He didn't need the UK, not when he could stay here.

He imagined he was starting at the source of the Yangtze in Tibet. To his left were large plain, mushy fields with bunting of all colours spread out. The air was cold and the hairy people friendly but aloof, they looked like distant cousins of the Chinese. As he paddled down the slowly forming river, he went through deserts and canyons that had been carved out many millennia before. Further down, he went through dense forests where he saw lurking wolves licking their lips by the edge of the water, following his boat. After a while, he began to see small towns and villages, full of people who looked like they'd been left behind in the middle ages. Some had their feet bound, others had singlet rings around their giraffe-like necks. The further he went along the river, the more people looked like the Chinese he was used to seeing – they were stronger, healthier, and their skin was pale. As he neared the end of his trip, the buildings grew taller and more futuristic. In the distance he could see Shanghai and the skyscrapers adorned with lights and messages written in Chinese. The people carried smartphones and some wore suits. On the whole they were more Western, and most spoke English.

He opened his eyes slowly to see Gabriel enter through the front door, the living room and dining table were now sparkly clean – there was a stench of bleach coming from the bathroom which penetrated even his blocked nose. As Kevin checked his phone to see he'd slept through to 14:00, Gabriel laughed and sat on the sofa next to him. He'd just got back from his run, having first kicked out his date and cleaned up the flat. The sweat clumped together his fuzzy brown hair into spikes. He was in shorts and a vest, revealing his recently shaved chest and back. He looked immaculately groomed, and with a glaze of sweat, like some Californian beach model.

'How was your date?' Kevin asked dumbly.

They talked openly about Gabriel's night, and took this chance to catch up with each other's week. They had these talks most Sundays, it was the most they got to see of each other and they both found the unbarred conversation therapeutic.

'Y'all know it was so weird last week,' Gabriel said in his Texas twang

'What was?'

'As I was coming out of the extra tuition I do on Friday, there was this guy who walked over and started talking to me. It turned out he was Iranian and I was like "Wuuuuut, my ex was Iranian", and he started talking about his family and kid. Turns out he used to work for the Iranian embassy or something but then became a teacher here instead. He speaks even better Chinese than me.'

'Hmmm sounds interesting,' Kevin said non-interestedly.

'Anyway, he invites me for tea at his house so I go along, not much else to do and I didn't fancy going out with you guys on Friday anyway.'

'Yeah, we missed you.'

'So, I get to his house and we have tea, I meet his four-year-old kid and his wife. I thought it was a bit weird because he was very handsome but she was fat and her face was puffy, not very pretty at all; he could've done way better. Anyway, we have tea and I was about to leave when he says, "Why don't you stay? My wife can give you a massage."'

'Wait, what?' Kevin exclaimed with sudden arousal.

'Yeah, I know, I was a bit freaked out, but fuck it, it was their house. Anyway, she gives me a massage with all these oils and suddenly she's pulling my underwear down.'

'Go on.'

'So, I'm like whatever, I didn't have a boner and she told me to lie on my front.'

'Oh,' Kevin said disappointedly.

'After a while she'd finished and the husband comes in, I'm still naked and he gives me a towel. I wiped down the oil, put on my clothes and said goodbye. It was the weirdest thing. I got a WeChat from him yesterday saying he wanted me to come round again next week.'

'Hm, how odd.'

'Yeah, I haven't replied to him yet, I don't really know what to say.'

'I mean a free massage is a free massage,' Kevin pondered. 'I'd be happy to take over the role if you're not interested,' he winked.

'Yeah, I guess,' Gabriel smirked. 'But you'd take a massage from anything with a pulse.'

A plane flew in the distance as Kevin looked outside. A ray of sunlight touched his foot on the floor, illuminating some dead skin on his little toe. There was a child's scream outside and the authoritative voice of its parent trying to assert control.

Kevin looked back inside and stared into the space ahead of him. As if in sync, they both sunk into the sofa. It was a peculiar thing that whenever they slouched in such a way, they became aptly philosophical, and would venture onto topics of great emotion, as if prying a way into each other's soul, still hidden despite their long close proximity.

'Huh,' Gabriel sighed. 'I just don't get it. All I want is a stable boyfriend. Is that too much to ask? I mean, sometimes I wonder, should I even believe in love?'

'I don't ... I believe only in temporary expediency.'

'How romantic.'

'And you do?'

'I'm not sure ... I guess so ... my first boyfriend. I thought I loved him but now I realise that was just because it was the first boy who liked me in that way.'

'Exactly. And girls are worse, they are master manipulators mate ... they don't believe in it, I sure as hell won't.'

'What do you mean by that?'

'Girls are temptresses. They thrive off attention ... in a way that's all they've ever lived for ... think about it. What do you notice about all the women in Tolstoy, Dostoevsky, Balzac, Dickens, Hemingway, Fitzgerald ... they fall in "love" within a few minutes of meeting a man. It's all unrequited bollocks, all they want is to be subservient to men.'

'That's a narrow definition of authors you've got there. Was the 20th century just something that happened to other people to you? The suffragette movement just some momentary lapse in judgement? Oh my god, don't say such awful things!'

'How many single women are happy women? Why is it that when I swipe on tinder or bumble, girls won't reply to what I send them, but I will speak to every girl that sends me a message? They're rude, all they crave is someone who praises their beauty.'

'So that draws you somehow to the conclusion that love doesn't exist?'

'No, that's not what I mean.'

'What do you mean then?'

'I believe love is an emotion that exists in a temporary state … It only lasts as long as you see eye to eye. It is for the convenience of the moment … Sometimes I will love for the evening, sometimes a little longer, but it always ends.

'Put it this way, when you first start texting a girl or even a boy, both your lives can perfectly fit in with each other. It doesn't take much effort on either person's behalf to keep the relationship going. Then you meet up for a few dates, if there are no other suitors or other people you're interested in, for the convenience of the moment, there is nothing to hold you back. If the opportunity cost of going on a date with one person is going on a date with a more attractive person, then neither the girl nor boy would go on the date in the first place. Now let's say you've been on that date and things are going well and you start falling in "love" as you suggest. Well, there's likely to be support from your friends if you're dating someone, but what if they don't approve? Then you fall out of love just as quickly as you fell in love. In that case, you only see eye to eye because you are both able to maintain your friends and have sex with someone at the same time, that's an improvement on your previous situation of only friends and intermittent one-night stands. Now let's say you've been in a relationship for a year. The only way that a relationship remains is if you are in a stable position, able to afford the life you want, and neither partner wants a rapid change in any part of their lives.'

'That's a good thing though,' Gabriel interrupted.

'Is it? What on earth is so good about a constant. Life gets boring, beauty fades, the sex is the same, you've seen old couples in restaurants and pubs together, they don't even speak anymore.'

'No, but that's the point, their love is so strong that they don't need to speak in order to express what they're feeling.'

'You surely can't believe that rubbish. If I went on a date with someone and they didn't speak for half the date, I wouldn't go on a second date with them … why on earth would I not do the same if I'd been married for 30 years? … There must always be something that sparks your interest with each other.'

'But then you'd run out of things to talk about.'

'That's my point, if you've run out of things to talk about, then your love has expired and you no longer see eye to eye. You might as well move onto the next person who makes you feel interested.'

'But what about those couples who stay together for 60 years, are they not in love?'

'No, they're just very good friends, I sometimes wish my best male friends were girls because I love being around them, and I love spending time with them, the only issue is I can't release my sexual frustrations because I'm not attracted to them physically. That's what love is to me, friendship, it has fuck all to do with sex. Love is being best friends with someone, until you're no longer best friends with them.'

'But what if you find someone you're best friends with?'

'I mean theoretically sure, it's possible, but when will I now have the chance to see someone almost every day in the way that's needed to become best friends, like you would at school or university? My days of making new best friends are long behind me.'

Just then the front door opened and Charlie stumbled in, out of breath. He'd just come back from the gym in his tracksuits and had some sweat on his forehead, as if he'd been sprinting.

'Hey, guess who I just saw on my run back from the gym,' he said, panting quickly. 'It turns out to be great news for you,' he said, gesturing to Kevin.

'Why? Who'd you see?'

'So I saw Julia on the way outside the fruit store, and she told me there was a new girl from the agency next week to start at the kindergarten. She'd been meant to start with me after Chinese New Year but got delayed in South Africa or something. Anyway, Julia said they're shuffling around the classes and guess who's the lucky guy to get to be in Lily's class.'

'No way!' Kevin exclaimed, sitting up a little.

'Who's Julia?' Gabriel asked.

'The Deputy Headmistress,' Charlie explained.

'And what's so great about Lily's class?'

'The one with the fit mum,' Charlie replied.

'Ugh, boys,' Gabriel sighed, standing up to walk towards his room.

'Who's my other teacher?' Kevin asked, ignoring Gabriel.

'Errr, Emma, I think.'

'Did she say when the new schedule started?'

'Tomorrow.'

'Nice.'

The room was quiet again as the boys went about their Sunday routines. Charlie decided to play the PS4 whilst Gabriel studied Chinese on the dining table nearby, his notes taking up the whole table top. Kevin went into his room to relax and flicked through a dirty old English copy of Mao's little red book. As he sat on his bed, he pondered the next day; and a grin grew on his face.

5

'Sunshine,' Charlie mused at his desk as the other English teachers prepared to go to their respective classes, 'bit of a weird name, don't you think?'

He was looking over the memo that had been left on the door of their office alerting them to their reshuffle.

'It's because names in Chinese have meaning,' Daphne replied.

'But names in English don't.'

'It's quite common. There's a kid in my class called Apple.'

'Huh. Why do they pick them?'

'I don't know, maybe Sunshine likes the sun.'

'And Apple likes apples.'

'No, he spits them out whenever he eats them. Maybe his parents do though.'

Charlie enjoyed teaching, but he wasn't very good at it; his 150-hour TEFL course that he'd hoped would give him a grasp of how to teach had only taken him ten hours to complete online, and was focused on how to teach adults rather than young children. In fact, none of the foreign teachers in the school, who had also taken this multiple choice qualification, were very good at either controlling a class, or teaching them effectively.

The routine each day meant that the teachers arrived in the classroom at 09:00 where they proceeded to play with the children for about an hour. If the weather was good, they would bring the children outside, but if bad, they would stay within the classroom. At around 10:00, the teachers would return the children to the classroom to eat some snacks which had been prepared by the class *Ayi* – a middle-aged, little-educated but highly affectionate class nanny.

At 10:30, the hour long 'English time' began, which included throwing very basic vocabulary repeatedly at the class who then had to regurgitate it. If they were lucky and their English teacher was well organised, they participated in a game of snakes and ladders, roll the dice jump or pin the tail on the answer.

At 11:30, the children ate their lunch and once they'd finished, would be lulled into a nap on small army like beds. Their favourite nursery songs would be played in the background as they drifted into sleep after the tiring morning. The Chinese teachers, unable to leave the class at any-time during the day, would grab a spot on the sofa or a beanbag.

For the foreign teachers, lunchtime was a particular perk of the job alongside that of few actual teaching hours. From 11:30 to 14:30 they had a three-hour lunch break during which time they were free to do as they chose. Charlie and Kevin, for their part, had established a habit of going to the gym together for a quick workout before returning for the afternoon's lessons, refreshed and revitalised.

After 14:30 they moved to their second class of the day and proceeded to repeat the morning routine, finishing at 17:00.

Charlie sauntered into his morning class at 09:02 a.m.

'Charlie, where been?' Sunshine screeched.

'Sorry. Hi, I'm Charlie.'

'Yes, I know, where been?' she repeated.

'I just needed the toilet.'

'No, no, no, here nine clock. Now go, go, sit children.'

Sunshine tugged on Charlie's arm, pulling him towards a group of children sat around a knee-high table. They looked with puzzlement towards him.

'Go, go. Speak.'

'Speak?'

'Yes, speak.'

'Speak what?'

'English, English.'

'But they're eating.'

'No, no, sit and speak.'

Charlie took a seat next to a little boy who smiled at him.

'Hello,' he said awkwardly.

The boy laughed.

'Hello,' Charlie said again. 'What's your name?'

'Phhhhellooooo,' the boy returned before laughing once more.

The boy put his head beside his bowl, hiding his eyes from Charlie behind his forearm. Charlie looked around the table. Ten pairs of eyes stared back at him as they obediently ate their food in silence.

Just my luck to pick the idiot, he thought.

As the afternoon lessons drew to a close, it began to rain heavily outside. Charlie returned to the office to see the other foreign teachers staring glumly out onto the wet street below.

'Ugh again,' Daphne said. 'You know I don't know why the UK gets such a bad rep. This place is just as rainy.'

'At least it usually passes quickly,' someone replied.

'How were your classes, Charlie?' Daphne asked, noticing him enter.

'Average,' he said putting on his dark blue raincoat. 'I don't think Sunshine likes me much.'

'I don't think she likes anyone much.'

'Then why the hell is her name Sunshine?'

Daphne smirked.

'Are you waiting for Kevin again?'

'Yep, we've got salsa.'

'Ooh, OK, well, have fun,' she replied, grabbing her bike helmet.

She exited the classroom, soon followed by the other teachers.

Charlie looked at the large clock on the wall which had just gone 17:05. His mind turned to salsa.

He wondered if *she* would be there, whatever her name was. He took a deep breath before exhaling in one long blow. He smiled at the thought that one day he'd be good enough to buy her a drink.

He enjoyed the smooth rhythm of salsa. Its uncomplicated steps and universally known beat meant once he'd become good enough, he could easily dance at least ten times in a night. At least that's what Kevin had told him. The better he could become, Kevin had explained, the more drinks someone would allow him to buy.

Charlie remembered how he'd once tried salsa in the UK when he'd just turned 20. That first time was an embarrassment in execution, mentally scarring, but giving him the will to improve. He tripped all over the place, elbowed three people and stepped on the toes of a large man who gave him a frightening look.

There was, at the climax of the evening, a fat, mostly balding individual who'd danced as if he'd sold his soul to the devil. He had been able to dance with any partner of his choosing, and Charlie looked on in awe at the fast moves, quick feet and precision of timing.

Charlie looked at his watch, a cheap, plastic, replaceable object he'd been able to find online for US$1. It was already 17:20 and he was beginning to feel peckish, his stomach rumbling in short bursts. This is unlike Kevin to be so late, he thought. Then again, he didn't really follow anyone else's schedule.

He sent Kevin a WeChat message saying he was going to grab dinner in a nearby restaurant, and that he would wait for him there.

As he exited the building, the rain increased in its ferocity and he dashed for cover, finding solace under a small umbrella which normally covered a bored looking security guard. He cut through the business park at the back of the kindergarten to a little row of restaurants that seemed to have been there in perpetuity, their fronts crumbling. Despite the fact the business park could not be more than five years old, these eateries were designed to look like small rural abodes – open doorways sided by cracked outdoor wooden sinks used to wash dishes.

Behind him, a child screamed his name before saying something in Chinese to his mother along the lines of "Mummy, mummy, look it's my teacher". He turned around and waved a quick goodbye before continuing his journey under a hanger to avoid the rain. Once he'd reached the end of the hanger he stood for a moment under the open umbrella of a Starbucks, before eyeing a restaurant that sold fish noodles nearby. As he approached the neon-lighted front door, he squinted his eyes with effort in an attempt to look through the steamed-up glass, though from what he could see, the restaurant was near empty.

After entering the premises, he took a quick look at the pictures on the wall and pointed towards what he wanted using his limited Chinese to say 'this one'. The sullen man behind the counter, short, skin dark from exposure to the sun nodded with a grunt before disappearing behind a curtain to shout some orders at the chefs who looked like they could be his sons.

Sitting down, he took time to look around the restaurant – something he didn't normally do when he was with Kevin. The restaurant's tables mostly slanted a little towards the ground, whilst the mismatching chairs gave an almost artistic feel to the place. There were office chairs opposite fold out chairs, next to plastic stools with bits of them missing; one even had a bite mark in it.

The smell of spices and heat lingered in the steamy air, reminding Charlie of the time he'd visited India, where bazaars had the familiar stench of garlic. There were a few other people in the restaurant but they seemed absorbed in their phones, their eyes barely two inches away from their devices, checking emails, watching soap operas or playing video games. Most crouched over their tables like hunchbacks, fewer than a couple of inches from their bowl of rice, intently staring at their screens whilst poking at individual grains from time to time. On his table, there was a cup full of wooden chopsticks in packets, and a little jar next to it containing a red, oily substance.

The noodles he ordered were brought out in soup which he hadn't expected, but he didn't care to complain. He never complained because he knew he would never be understood. The steam covered his face as he took a big sniff of the bowl, its heat warming his chin. He added a generous amount of the red substance from the jar, expecting it to be chilli, before helping himself to a chunk of noodles with his chopsticks, the oil forming little pools around the surface of the broth. He still wasn't used to eating with chopsticks, spending most of the time stabbing aimlessly at his food, but as he was forced to use them on a daily basis, his instincts for survival kicked in.

The noodles were fluffy and filling, with a certain chewy texture. Charlie's nostrils flared as the food filled him with a much-needed warmth of spirit to compensate for a day of children screaming and climbing over him during playtime.

He pondered whether he actually liked his children. They could be so abrasive and abused him as if he were some plaything bought by mummy and daddy. He slurped some soup before wiping his chin. He never wanted to have kids.

Within a few minutes, his meal was gone and he took to his phone, scrolling aimlessly to kill time and wait for Kevin, who still hadn't replied to his message.

When the time reached 18:00, Charlie gave him a call. He hated impunctuality and it would take an hour by metro to get to the salsa class in the centre of town. As the phone rang, Charlie shook his leg in restlessness, tapping the table every few seconds. Finally, Kevin picked up, 'You alright mate?' he asked.

'Yeah, we doing salsa tonight or what?'

'Oh I completely forgot. No, not tonight, I'm busy but I'll catch you at home later. Trying to help out Yoyo by offering some free extra tuition if you get my drift.'

'Ahh, Yoyo's mother … Well alright, good luck. Don't do something I wouldn't,' with which he hung up, before looking at the receiver and sighing. He'll never learn, he thought.

Charlie hated to take the metro alone. On top of almost all his fellow passengers staring at him at some point during his journey, the dogs also looked at him with strange bemusement, as if even their animal senses could identify an Occidental gentleman when they came across one. They would nip at his ankles and sniff his crotch. Thankfully, Charlie thought, the locals did not do the same. He never felt entirely at ease on the metro but he tried to zone out by listening to some music. Having recently bought noise cancelling headphones for a bargain on Taobao, the cheaper Chinese equivalent of Amazon, he was able to close his eyes and be alone with his thoughts. In comparison to the tube in London, the ride of the metro was smoother and the train less noisy as it scuttled along the tracks. Hangzhou had been the location of a G20 summit less than two years before in 2016, so the metro was quite new. The seats weren't comfy, being designed for a seemingly smaller average sized individual, but the ride was fast.

As Charlie opened his eyes to see his stop fast approaching, an elderly man wearing a faded Mao jacket directly opposite him picked his nose.

'How lovely,' Charlie mumbled to himself.

As he exited the train, he held his head up to search for an exit sign; the same old man, now less than a metre behind him made a loud snort at such a velocity as to detach all the mucus he had in his nose and throat, plus his tongue and teeth by the sound of it. It reminded Charlie of his teenage years when he would make 'a snotter' on a rugby pitch before spitting it onto the floor. But when the old man did it, the sound was not only much louder, it was also much more disgusting than anything he'd remembered. Charlie shivered with revulsion. The inevitable spit came soon afterwards in all its coughing, spluttering glory, but Charlie tried to avoid turning around to see it. Unfortunately, as he walked up the stairs, he caught a glimpse of the man holding a plastic bag full of a bubbly liquid. There were dense green pieces floating in it; some little white bits too.

He reached the dance studio just in time as the music began to blare from the surround sound speakers, and a small lady at the front was in the process of taking the class through a warm-up of light movement and stretches. She was a very attractive Chinese lady, mid 30s, though like others in this part of the world, Charlie thought, looked in her late 20s at most. She was short, and for that reason had great control of her movements, which were at one with the intricacies of the music. Each beat and half beat caused a slight jerk or action which complimented everything that came before and gave all her dance routines a sense of fulfilment.

'Hi Scarlett,' Charlie screeched boyishly in passing before clearing his throat to sound more masculine.

Charlie, like all the boys in the studio, had a crush on her, but then again, so did all the girls too, who wanted to be her.

By the corner, selecting some music was her husband, Ray – one of the most fun and able teachers Charlie had ever had. Perhaps it was because it was dancing that allowed Ray to be as affable as he was, instead of being stuck to the confines of a classroom, but Charlie had a distinct impression this was not the case. Ray had energy, passion, stories and a great sense of humour. Kevin had told him he was a black guy from America who'd moved to China in 2008 after the financial crisis ruined his already tentative career as an extra in movies. He'd only started dancing at the age of 34 in pursuit of a girlfriend who had just left him, but by now, at the age of 50, he was a master of the craft and well renowned in Asia. His full-time job was at an international school as a sociology teacher, but his hobby meant he taught salsa, bachata and kizomba for two hours each night, five days a week.

'How's it going Ray?' Charlie cheered, patting him on the back.

'Hey brother,' Ray replied giving him a fist bump, 'good to see you again. No Kevin tonight?'

'Not tonight, not sure what he's up to.'

Charlie walked to a railing at the side of the studio and dumped his coat over it.

'Hey Charlie,' a middle-aged Chinese man said, 'how are you?'

'Robin! I'm good thanks, been a long day. The kids were very noisy.'

'Oh yes, you work at a kindergarten with Kevin, don't you?'

'That's right.'

'I remember when I was at university in Pennsylvania, they were always eager for me to talk with their children. It was as if they thought the kids would just absorb what I said in Chinese.'

'Exactly! Well, glad to hear it doesn't just happen here.'

'It happens a lot of places, I guess. My parents were both professors at the local university in Hunan as I grew up so I was lucky to have it more formalised.'

'Yes, well here the parents seem to think spending so much money on their children is all they need to do. Then they work their children to the bone outside of class with all these extra lessons. It's stupid. No offence.'

'Oh, none taken. For sure China has much to learn from other countries. Self-confidence most importantly, but I think you're right, you can't just throw money at some things, and expect them to improve. Then again, I haven't turned out too bad, I think,' he laughed.

'No. No, you're right,' Charlie smiled.

Ray called the class to attention and two lines of five people formed in front of the mirror.

'Alright, no new people tonight so let's carry on with the routine and we'll skip the basics.'

The rhythmical music started, and everyone soon shuffled the familiar pattern. Even Charlie's clunking feet couldn't be heard above the loudspeakers, placed at the four corners of the square room, but there was a certain military precision to everyone's timing. A slight breeze blew in through the open window, refreshing the studio after the humid rain of the afternoon.

To the shouts of Ray over the music, each followed the lead.

'Left right left … Right left right … Left right left … Right left right …' and so on.

Charlie could see the Korean girl in the corner. Despite still not knowing her name, he couldn't take his eyes off her reflection in the mirror, as every part of her moved in time to the beat. On her part, she didn't even notice him, instead staring intensely at her feet as if imploring them to move like Scarlett's.

During class, the ladies would rotate every two minutes as the pattern was repeated over and over again. Charlie realised as long as his hands weren't too sweaty, he didn't have anything to worry about. Most of the time, he would give the girls a quick smile, then look at his feet as he tried to get the steps right, but when the Korean girls circled to him, he froze.

'I guess this is the wonderful thing about salsa, isn't it?' Charlie said to the Korean.

'What is?'

'Err … That we can talk.'

'Hmmm,' she replied, nodding, before looking away.

Stupid idiot, he thought, what kind of opening line was that?

As 20:00 approached and the lesson for beginners finished, a couple of gruff men dressed in black knocked on the door to the studio. They looked like police. Scarlett went across to greet them but all the while they looked sinisterly behind her at the room of dancers. Ray ended the lesson soon after whilst Scarlett was still talking to the men. Students coming for the next lesson squeezed past their fat overbearing bodies as they hadn't bothered to step to the side.

'Hey Ray, what's going on there?' Charlie asked casually whilst picking up his coat from the side railing.

'Oh, just the police again. Some idiot downstairs keeps saying that I'm some illegal immigrant. Reckon he's just trying to get me deported cos he sees me walking around with Scarlett. Jealousy, right?' He looked a little hurt.

'Why, what's it to him?'

'Oh, locals get something like 500RMB from the police in reward for ratting on foreigners who are here working illegally. I mean I accept these extra checks on foreigners, this is their country. After some terrorist attacks a few years ago there was a line for foreigners at train stations which was separate from the rest, but I guess you gotta be extra careful whoever you are.'

'A bit excessive, no?'

'Naw, well at least I ain't ever had a gun pulled on me in China yet. Grew up in LA in the 70s man and I tell you what's wrong when they're treating their own people differently, let alone foreigners.'

'How long have you been here again?'

'Just gone ten years.'

'You must've seen a lot.'

'Yeah, it's awesome man, I love it, don't plan on ever going back to the US.'

'Really?'

'Naw, it's a perfect place. Look on the streets outside, there ain't no homeless people, they're wiping out poverty by 2020 and they treat everyone like human beings.'

'Is that all over China?'

'Oh yeah, definitely. Whenever you hear these stupid scare stories coming out of the West about Xinjiang slavery or something, it's like come on man, my ancestors worked on plantations, in China they get paid, that ain't slavery, that's lifting them out of poverty.'

'Not if they don't want do that job in the first place.'

'Look man,' Ray replied a little frustratedly, 'I been here for the best ten years of my life. I met Scarlett early on and I have a home here now. I ain't moving anytime soon, I've never suffered discrimination and nor does anyone else.'

'But the police?'

'That's just stupid shit man, that's one person with a small dick or something. Aint no worse than a white cracker in uniform in LA ...' he paused. 'Listen, let's not talk about this. I was broke when I came out here, trying to start a new life. China offered me a chance I never could've gotten in America.'

'Sorry,' Charlie stuttered, 'I ... I didn't mean to upset you.'

'I ain't upset. I just don't think you've been here long enough to understand. It's alright brother, have a safe trip home.'

After Charlie said his goodbyes, he took one last glance at the Korean before rushing to the lift and bounding out onto the streets below. Despite the March weather slowly beginning to show the hopes of spring, it was still cold as he traversed the pavements, puffer jacket zipped to the top to enclose his neck in its warmth.

The streets were filled with the smell of doughnut-like fried rolls which had suggestions of a wonderfully chewy texture, meat-filled pancakes dashed with pepper, and the standard noodle shops, whose windows it seemed, were constantly shrouded in condensation. Charlie sniffed the air and purchased one of the pancakes. Before he went down the escalator to the metro station below, he threw the paper wrapper in a public bin nearby.

There was a loud bang nearby as a car crashed into the railings of the pavement. Nobody was hurt but there was a motorcyclist who was a bit dazed at the sudden braking he was forced to do. There was a lot of shouting and pointing of fingers but Charlie hadn't heard the commotion. He'd already placed on his head the noise-cancelling headphones, turning up the volume of Freddie Mercury blaring out Radio Gaga at Live Aid 1985 as he descended the escalator.

6

The children screamed loudly as they chased Kevin through the playground outside the kindergarten. It was a large playground which had everything a three-to-five-year-old might want to explore. To the north side was a small basketball court, not that the children could even throw a ball higher than their own height, and next to that a small football pitch. Being situated away from the sun, this area became especially cold during the winter. However in the summer, it provided a cool getaway from the sharpness of the sun's rays.

To the west of the building was a large expanse of tarmac which had coloured lines drawn on it in the shape of a racetrack. About ten metres wide, this tarmac was adjacent to a grassy area which had a large climbing frame at the top of a small hill, complete with slides, obstacles and a tunnel which went underneath. If a child went into this tunnel they would usually come out the other side covered in mud and sand which had been dumped there by their schoolmates from the large sandpit situated halfway between the basketball court and the climbing frame. The sand pit had a terrible odour from the faeces buried in it, left by foxes and wild dogs that had found it a more convenient place for their business than the grassy grounds around the school. There was a metre's worth of allotment which hugged the inside of the fence following the perimeter the whole length of the playground.

When the weather was sunny, as it was this early April Tuesday morning, the children would go outside for their 9 a.m. playtime instead of staying inside, and this would entail a warm-up led by the English teachers. It was quite a sight to behold seeing 300 children line up in military precision following the exact movements of the teachers at the front directing them all. They went through the process stretch by stretch before being let loose on the playground for their own time. Usually to finish it off, the English teachers would run in different directions and their respective classes would follow them – it was pandemonium and often ended in a few tears as children inevitably ran into each other.

This morning, the children in Kevin's class chased him as usual, following Kevin like a swarm of bees, first around the football pitch, then around the basketball court before he sprinted to the top of the hill shouting 'you can't catch me, nah nah nah nah'. As Kevin started to tire, he slowed down to let the most eager children catch up with him. They were inevitably the oldest and tallest boys who wanted to show off their strength. As they grabbed Kevin, slowing him down, they held on tight until there were seven of them grabbing his trousers, hoodie, and one even trying to climb onto his back.

At that point Kevin screamed out in pain, 'AHHHHHH Fuck sake, little piece of shit!'

One of the children, as tall as Kevin's legs and in a bid to show he was the one who had truly caught the teacher, splayed his arms around Kevin's bum, one hand on each cheek and squeezed his face as hard as he could into Kevin's crotch. At the same time he had opened his mouth and bit down as hard as he could.

Kevin twisted and turned but the child wouldn't let go of his painful hold. He fell to the ground as the other English and Chinese teachers gathered around to see what the problem was. For about ten seconds he held his crotch with his right hand whilst he cursed under his breath. The adults, still unaware of what had happened, looked on bemusedly as they directed the children away from the scene of the incident. After Kevin stood up, still bending over every now and then in pain, he explained to the English teachers what had happened. Sympathetically, Bryn, Charlie and Elijah burst into fits of laughter.

As Daphne translated what happened for the good of the Chinese teachers, some of them couldn't hide their amusement either. Taking it upon herself to look after Kevin because it was her class he was teaching that morning, Emma helped walk him to the nurse's office. She took his arm with a firm grip and led him limping along, wincing with each step.

Just as they were about to reach the office, Kevin darted towards the bathroom. 'I just want to check something,' he blurted out.

'Kevin, where go?'

Not completely understanding English, Emma followed him into the unisex toilet.

Kevin, a little embarrassed, protested but at the same time felt a little comforted by this motherly figure helping him. All of the cubicles were squat toilets so he pushed on the first one before entering and locking the door behind him. He pulled down his pants and winced.

It wasn't a pretty sight – where two teeth had temporarily ingrained themselves, there were marks of blood, not streaming greatly, but the blood had clearly been spurting a little and there were small dark red stains on the inside of his underpants. He winced again as he reached for toilet paper only to remember the cubicles didn't contain any.

'Emma, two paper please,' he asked as politely as he could.

Was this not a little weird? he thought, shaking his head. Then again, together, they'd wiped all sorts of bodily fluids off children. There's nothing wrong with being professional. He assured himself she was simply showing her instinct to help.

Emma obediently passed two paper towels over the top of the cubicle door, saying in the little English she spoke, 'OK? Everything?'

'Errr no, bad,' Kevin laughed a little, 'blood.'

'Oh, no!' Emma said.

Out of instinct she tugged on the door.

'No, no, no!' Kevin exclaimed suddenly, relieved he'd remembered to lock it. 'Don't come in!'

'Is OK, I can help,' Emma replied reassuringly.

He ignored her but winced when he looked down again. The pain had gotten worse and the blood hadn't yet dried as he kept dabbing it gently. He kept breathing in short bursts, sucking air through his teeth, shuffling in pain as he touched it.

He became worried it might get infected.

'Kevin, let in,' Emma said again.

Kevin obediently opened the door. It'll be fine, he pondered, she's married and from what Daphne's said, she's madly in love with her husband. Besides, she was the one insisting on seeing it and that tone she has in her voice is the same she puts on when talking to the children.

Emma squeezed into the space. She was a small woman, about five feet tall, but as there was no seat in the cubicle, it gave it more room should a second person ever wish to use it as well. She looked down at his hand and gave a grimace.

'Oooooooh, painful ma?' she asked, looking up quickly at his face.

'Yeah … very,' Kevin replied quietly. His heartbeat quickened. Their heads were only a few inches away from each other and her perfume was strong. Each time he sucked air through his teeth, her scent was over-powering.

He looked at her for a time, trying to avoid thinking about the pain he was in. She in turn continued looking at the wound, trying to think of a way to help. He'd never noticed before how delicate her features were, but this was the first time he'd seen her so close up. Her hair was about shoulder length, but she had a cropped fringe which covered her forehead. Her wide-set eyes were large, brown and puppy-like. Her small, pointed nose complimented her wide mouth and sumptuous lips. He tried to avert his eyes but only succeeded landing on a necklace which dangled effortlessly on her breasts.

'Oww, oww, oww,' Kevin said.

She hadn't touched it but the attention she'd given had caused a stirring of pain. He pulled his pants up again and laughed awkwardly. Emma, unaware of what had happened, looked up at him.

'What do?' she asked, confusedly.

'It's OK now,' Kevin replied hurriedly, fiddling with the door's lock. He opened the door and jumped out. 'Err … shall we go back?' he said quickly.

'You not want see nurse?' Emma asked, still confused.

'No, no, no,' he replied, 'all better.'

He barged out of the bathroom, with Emma following soon after. At least no one was around, he thought.

As they walked down the corridor towards the playground, Kevin glanced at Emma every few moments. The well-proportioned structure of her features, her perfume scent just as overpowering during the walk as it had been in the cubicle. He wondered if she'd put some extra sprays of it on this morning because it was all that filled his nostrils. He opened the door for her when they reached the playground and she was immediately grabbed by one of the children in his class who she chased away.

While Kevin looked on after her, a little dazed, Charlie and Bryn shuffled up to his right, both still laughing.

'You alright buddy?' he asked.

'How bad is it?' Bryn asked.

'Errr … yeah, it's not great,' he said, losing sight of Emma as she went around the corner of the kindergarten building. He shifted his attention to Charlie, 'a bit of blood but nothing serious. It'll heal.'

'This whole time I've been cringing man,' Charlie stated.

'Cannot imagine what pain that must have been like. I'm gonna cover my balls every time a kid comes up to me from now on.'

'Yeah, not a bad idea,' Kevin said wistfully.

For the rest of their time outside, Kevin limped around the playground. He was still in pain but the throbbing wasn't as it had been before. The Chinese teachers had told the children to stay away from him for the morning.

As the sun rose higher in the sky, the heat climbed with it, exacerbated by the greenhouse-like atmosphere. At 10 a.m. there was a loud rush as the Chinese teachers shouted to get their children in lines so they could go back inside to have their morning snack. The foreigners, who most mornings when they were outside, stood in a small circle, walked to re-join their classes and helped guide them inside the building.

Kevin limped tentatively behind the children, but he might as well have been one of them – he was just as transfixed as they were on Emma who was facing them at the front of the queue. She had a comforting, wide smile on her face as she walked backwards, holding the hands of the two at the front. While they snaked into the building, she was reciting lines of a poem which the children were shouting back. She spoke with the same sweet, raised, child-like voice that she had spoken to Kevin within the cubicle of the bathroom. She was looking at the kids the whole way back to the classroom, even on the staircase, but Kevin couldn't take his eyes off her.

Back in the classroom, he sat with the kids and tried to engage as he normally did, playing with them and asking them what they were eating. The kids couldn't sense it – they were more focused on the apple and mango pieces they had in front of them – but Kevin kept looking towards Emma every few moments. He caught her eye during one of these glances, but she just smiled and continued talking to the *Ayi*. The

Ayi must not have been told about what happened to Kevin, because it looked like she was just giving off steam about something or other she didn't like. Always a gossip, these *Ayi*'s, he thought.

During the lesson, he was able to briefly refocus his mind on teaching whilst Emma went outside, but when she returned to sit at the edge of the class with the kids to make sure they weren't being disruptive, he found it hard to concentrate. She looked like the mother of the class. She was so good with the kids that they obediently did whatever she said. Even the usual troublemakers were quiet when she was around. One of them had even climbed onto her lap for a cuddle. Whilst he read the story of the day, he kept looking in the direction of Emma and smiling. She returned in kind and his heart raced.

At 11:30, he quickly packed up his things and, without saying goodbye, ran off. Coward, he thought to himself in the corridor outside, all she tried to do was help, don't be so awkward about it.

Back in the foreigners' office, he sat at his desk and scrolled through Instagram on his phone, trying to feign calmness. As the other foreign teachers came in, they asked how his wound was feeling and he acted like it didn't hurt anymore.

'It must have been weird having the nurse look at it?' Ellie pondered.

'No, no, she didn't, Emma just told her what had happened and she gave me a couple of paracetamol. No one looked at it but me,' he added hastily.

'Huh, interesting,' Charlie said.

'What, what, what! What's interesting?' Kevin retorted.

'Oh no, I wasn't talking about you, I was just looking at my computer, turns out there's a few roles in Shanghai my dad thinks I should apply to.'

'What? Already? You've only been here a month.'

'Yeah … but I told him I'm not really enjoying teaching. I don't care about breaking the contract I have here either if I can get a good job elsewhere in China. Anyway, now I'm in the country, I reckon it'll be a bit easier for me to find something I actually like.'

A little flustered, Kevin grabbed his gym bag and, not waiting for Charlie, headed out for his usual routine.

'What's his problem?' Daphne asked.

'Don't think you've ever been kicked in the balls before, have you

Daphne?'

'Er, don't think you've ever had a period before, have you Charlie?'

During his workout, Li Xiao Mei messaged Kevin, asking him to see her in her school office for a quick chat when he returned from the gym. Not wanting to allow himself to be in any more pain than he already was, he skipped going for his usual swim and slowly walked back to the kindergarten, enjoying the sunny day.

The streets were alive with the throng of office workers who'd ventured outside for lunch. As it was sunny, round tables were set out on the pavement in front of the restaurants with customers crowded round them on small plastic stools. At every restaurant, each of the frequenters had a bowl of rice, and each table had an array of dishes served on small plates. Kevin could smell the ever-present garlic and spices as he walked by. There were at least five to a table and if there were more, a larger table had been brought out. Kevin always had lunch by himself, but he liked the thought of doing something like this and wondered if he should ask the other foreign teachers to join him one day.

His gym workout had had a calming effect on him and he felt his usual self again. As he walked, it occurred to him that this was the first time Lesley had asked him to her office at the kindergarten. Had she heard about what had happened to him in the morning and wanted to talk about it? Did someone see Emma and him entering and exiting the bathroom together? He became nervous at the thought but decided it would be best to simply tell her the same story he had told the others. She wouldn't know, would she? Lesley barely even spoke with her staff at the school, leaving the day to day running of it to the headmistress Diana. No, he didn't have any idea what the conversation would be about.

He returned to the kindergarten at around 13:30 and dropped off his bags in the half-empty foreigners' office. As he bounded up the stairs to Lesley's office on the fourth floor he could hear laughter. When he'd reached the top of the stairs he saw her office door was open and realised the laughter was coming from within. He tentatively walked to the open door and knocked to get Lesley's attention.

'Ahh, Kevin!' Lesley exclaimed from behind her big wooden desk which faced the door. The room had a large window at the back that overlooked the playground below. 'Come in.'

Sat in front of the desk was a young lady who looked remarkably similar to Lesley, except she didn't have the mole next to her eye. She didn't bother to rise like Lesley when Kevin came in, but she turned around and gave him a big smile. She had smooth black straightened hair which had been placed neatly behind her ears, and big brown eyes the colour of chestnuts. They gave her wrinkle-free face an even younger look. She was in a summery dress in contrast to Lesley's formal attire – Kevin had only ever seen her wear suits – and the vivid colours made her stand out in the blandness of the minimalist but grand office. Kevin thought she must have been about 20 years old but had known better than to guess someone's age in China.

'Err hell–' he cleared his throat, 'Hello.'

Suddenly, all the pain in his crotch had disappeared and he had forgotten why he felt so nervous.

'This is my daughter Li Xiao Tai,' Lesley said, 'she's just come back from New York for the Easter holidays.'

'How do you do?' she said in perfect English with no hint of a Chinese accent. 'Please call me Sophia.'

Kevin took her hand briefly as they linked eyes, holding each other's gaze for a moment. After a few seconds he let go and calmly sat down in the chair next to her, leaning back into the soft cushion.

'I asked you to come here Kevin because I wanted to discuss the renewal of your contract.'

'Oh, maybe we shouldn't discuss this in front of Sophia,' he replied. 'It would bore her.'

'No, no, don't worry.' Lesley continued, 'She do accountancy in New York, she will one day take over from me, this is good experience for her. Besides, I think you two should get to know each other. I think you should go on date.' She smiled.

Well, that's a new one, Kevin thought, pimping out your daughter.

'How old are you Kevin?' Sophia asked.

'29,' he said. He opened his mouth to ask her the same but thought better of it. Sophia, sensing his apprehensiveness, filled in the blanks for him.

'I'm 23,' she replied sweetly. 'Maybe we *could* go on a date,' she smiled. Kevin grinned stupidly.

'And about your contract,' Lesley continued. 'I think you've done great job while you been here for six months. I have big plans in the area and will need experience teachers like you to stay on for many years. I have talked to the agency that hired you and have agreed a pay increase of 2000RMB per month if you sign this three-year contract, effective immediately.'

'Can I think about it for a bit?' Kevin pondered.

'Ooooh, agency say they treating you special this way,' she lied. 'Must have decision today or the contract is null and void. You must keep quiet about it too.'

'It would be ever so nice to have you around,' Sophia interjected. 'I'm finishing my studies this summer and would love to get to know you better once I return to Hangzhou for good.'

'Hmmm,' her mother agreed, 'she'll be with me most of the time in the main office building across the river you've been to once … not far at all.'

'Maybe we can go for a date this weekend. What are you up to?' Sophia asked.

Kevin sat in silence for a few moments. Looking first to Lesley before darting his eyes to Sophia then back to Lesley.

What the hell is this? he thought. He shifted in his seat slightly, the leather beneath felt uncomfortable.

Then again, he pondered, he didn't have plans to go anywhere for a while. Life here was particularly easy and he enjoyed it, but a three year contract would lock him in until he was 32. He didn't want to stay in China forever. But then again, he struggled to think what would be there for him in the UK.

He looked across at the smiling Sophia. Maybe it will be worth it, he continued, imagine that, going on a date with someone who will one day inherit millions and millions, maybe even billions by the time Lesley passes on the mantle. He could definitely do worse, besides she wouldn't know what he got up to on weekends if he was discreet. What the hell, maybe this was a sign.

'OK,' he said abruptly, looking up at Lesley, 'I'll do it.'

'Wonderful,' she replied.

As he read through the contract, mother and daughter spoke in Chinese briefly. He didn't know what they were saying but Lesley kept flicking her arm from left to right.

'My mother said she'd pay for our first date together. She said she'll book her favourite table at the Four Seasons next to West Lake,' Sophia explained.

'That's kind of you,' he said.

Is she barmy? He thought, maybe this really wasn't a dirty trick after all.

After he'd signed the contract, Sophia turned to him in her chair. She was clutching her phone and gesturing to add him on WeChat. She told him to message her later in order to set the time and date of the reconvening. As he got up to go, he smiled at Sophia, then smiled at Lesley.

He walked out of the office, and then down the stairs where he could see some of the children in the classrooms on the third floor had already woken up. When he reached the foreigners' office he remembered he hadn't yet eaten lunch and felt his stomach rumble in hunger. He ran to the lift and impatiently tapped the button to call it.

7

The next morning, it rained heavily and the ground swelled with water. The downpour started just as Kevin and Charlie left their flat for the kindergarten, and in their boldness, they had failed to wear raincoats. When they arrived, Charlie went to one of the classrooms to ask to use a hairdryer – the *Ayi* smirked as she handed over the device.

Half-naked with the wet t-shirts laid flat across the same desk, they stood by each other slowly tilting the dryer from left to right. Whilst Charlie inspected his t-shirt from time to time, tentatively pressing it with his forefinger, Kevin jerked the dryer from left to right. Due to the weather, they knew there was no chance they would be going out to the playground that morning, so once their t-shirts had a semblance of dryness again, they pulled them back on and rushed to their classes.

As Kevin entered his classroom, Emma gave him her usual beguiling smile, full of warmth and affection, and he smiled back. As he filled his water bottle at the filter next to the tap, she tentatively approached, arms folded, tucked inside her elbows to her body. She wore a white shirt which seemed to radiate with light.

'OK now?' she asked, raising her finger but pointing downwards in a hushed tone.

'Yeah, yeah,' Kevin replied. 'Thank you for helping.'

'It's OK,' she giggled, 'but I want ask you something.'

'OK.'

'Next week is class play in errrr … you know for all school …' she pinched the fingers on her right hand together, searching for the right word.

'Assembly?' Kevin suggested.

'Yes, yes, assembly,' she said, eyes lighting up. 'I need to make errr …' She flailed her arms in the air and kept laughing as she couldn't find the right word.

'Chair? Caterpillar?'

'No, no, no!' She laughed, lifting her hand to cover her mouth.

'Oh, like a design, like background,' he took out his phone to translate and show her what he thought she meant. He was shaking a little, so it took him a while to type it out properly.

'Yes, yes!' she exclaimed 'my English so bad.'

'Very rubbish,' he winked.

She laughed loudly.

'Back-round,' she said slowly. 'Maybe help me make?' she asked.

'Sure, what is it?' he replied.

'Chinese Great Wall.'

'Oh right.'

'You know?'

'Of course, one of the less well-known attractions of China.'

This attempt at humour was lost on her.

'After school today?' she continued. 'Maybe tomorrow too? I don't know how long take.'

'Yeah, sure. I'd be happy to.'

She smiled at him. He smiled back and stared into her big brown eyes. They were so charming and beautiful, he thought, and she seemed so embarrassed by her inability to speak English, but he liked that.

A child walked up behind Emma before tugging her leg. She bent over, causing Kevin to turn away in embarrassment. He noticed the *Ayi* smirking as she wiped a table across the room. He quickly grabbed a seat beside a child who was eating a bowl of porridge.

Whilst this was going on, Charlie struggled to get along with his teacher. Sunshine had put him to work pretty quickly and he found it boring. Her English was good, but she used it to mostly issue orders and expected them to be followed. Despite what her name would suggest, she did not have a sunny disposition. She had a constant frown on her face, and Charlie often wondered if she even enjoyed teaching. Daphne sometimes spoke to Sunshine in the playground, having taught her class before Charlie arrived, but she said all Sunshine did was complain about the children. Daphne had even once suggested to Sunshine she get a job elsewhere. It made sense because a kindergarten teacher earned about as much per month as a McDonald's employee, or a food delivery driver. Perhaps the only reason she hadn't already taken the jump was that she'd gone to university for four years to study towards an Education Degree. It would be tough to turn her back on four years of her life.

He sat and pondered this whilst the children ate their morning snack. It's not a huge surprise, he thought, why would anybody want to work under someone like Lesley? He couldn't imagine their grievances were taken seriously, if even aired to begin with. Then again why wouldn't Sunshine apply somewhere else? Or are all kindergartens like this? But surely, no kindergarten can be as bad as this.

Instead of interactive whiteboards, they used projectors and a screen. Instead of enough workbooks to go around for each student, the teachers had to photocopy all their exercises from one scruffy book which hadn't been replaced since the school opened. The photocopier was always in use, constantly broke down and yet Lesley would not invest in another one despite the long-term benefits. Finally, and perhaps worst of all, it seemed that education was secondary to the looks of the place. Every day, Sunshine sent photos of the children from the day's activities to the parents' WeChat group. It was a constant striving to meet every whim of the parents, however outlandish they were. Sometimes, during the English lesson, Sunshine would interrupt and tell both Charlie and the child to hold a pose for a few seconds so she could get the best angle for the picture. On top of this, the teacher was at the beck and call of parents at all hours of the day. Sometimes, Charlie would look in the group chat and see parents had sent a message at 10 p.m. for something that was relevant the next day and needed a reply.

He wondered how proud Sunshine's parents must have been when she first told them about her job at the kindergarten. Sat around the family table, she would've announced happily she'd finally found a well-paying role. At least well-paying by rural standards since her parents were most probably farmers. A nice stable job in a city notorious for its rich people. They must have imagined she'd meet someone famous. Maybe that's why she hadn't moved jobs. Maybe she was afraid she'd have to live with her parents again or admit that this wasn't the job for her.

On the whole, the foreign teachers felt sorry for the Chinese teachers. They knew the native teachers were aware that foreigners were paid more and didn't have to achieve similarly rigorous teaching qualifications. They even knew how farcical the Teaching English as a Foreign Language qualification had been. The questions asked in the multiple question exams were more about common sense than teaching procedure. Instead of complex English grammar and roundtable discussions with switched on professionals, Charlie was now teaching one word a day, and doing more dancing with the children than actual teaching. Whereas a Chinese teacher who had made it their profession was earning 5,000RMB or about £570 a month to begin with, this would only rise to 10,000RMB per month by the age of 30, and Charlie was earning double that at the age of 22, just out of a university.

This sometimes led to a tension between the foreigners and the Chinese teachers, a fact he'd heard was common at every school but particularly where grievances could not be taken to the boss. The Chinese would gossip that the foreigners were lazy, whilst the foreigners would say they couldn't believe they were paid so much more. Not that it stopped them pocketing the proceeds with no real complaints against the main culprit at the top. They had travelled half the world to take a job which still paid less than an average job in the UK, why shouldn't they take what they could?

Regardless of this, Charlie still felt it was wrong. Whilst at university, he had been part of the student union and participated in many demonstrations. He knew that it was the only way to get things done. You had to stand up for yourself, he thought, even without unions, you still have to stand up for yourself.

Daphne had told him that despite the outward look of a Communist country, workers had remarkably fewer rights than those in the West. They were afforded five days of annual leave compared to 20+ afforded those in Europe. Their weekends were expendable and did not lead to any extra pay if they had to work on them. From experience, Charlie knew teachers unions in the UK were strong and spoke with one voice. In China, no such voice existed. They considered any criticism of the system a criticism of the Communist Party, and thereby a criticism of China itself.

It had been only six weeks since Charlie arrived in China, but he often considered a change in profession. It was easy being a teacher, he thought to himself, but your mind could go to slush, only working for two hours per day and spending the rest of the time as a punch-bag for bawdy four-year-old boys, or as a doll for their girl counterparts. Worst, what if he became what he'd seen in Ray or what he'd seen in Elijah's friends. Continuing as a teacher, he might become blind to the problems of China, or worse, an oaf.

The email he'd received from his father the previous day had set him in a philosophical mood, and he wondered if he should already pursue a different life. The only perk of his current role was the prospect of a six-week summer holiday where he could travel around China, but he could always delay the start date of the next job if he wanted that time to travel.

The sorts of jobs he was interested in were all in Shanghai. He'd seen one about legal professionals in a multinational, another about salesmen for an international brand – surprisingly it wasn't a prerequisite to speak Chinese. The one that had caught his eye most, however, was to become a research assistant at a political risk firm. The website for the firm was bland, but the description of what it did had interested him. On top of business analytics and research on the political climate in a country, the firm also conducted due diligence on companies all over Asia. Charlie had read somewhere that there were dodgy businesses in China, but he was fascinated to see how they operated.

Over Christmas he'd read an article about a supermarket chain's Christmas cards selection having a hidden message inside asking the reader to send help for people stuck in a prison near Guangzhou. There was temporary outrage on a diplomatic level, but nothing had been done about it as far as Charlie could see. Ever since, he'd been fascinated at how a reputable UK chain could hire a company in China that subcontracted work to prisons that effectively used slave labour.

Once the clock reached 11:25, Charlie grabbed his things and darted upstairs before Sunshine could call after him. Sitting down at his desk, he opened his laptop and went to the firm's website.

'You're in early,' Elijah stated as he walked in five minutes later.

'So are you,' Charlie said bluntly.

The other foreign teachers came in and sat down, they already looked exhausted. When it was raining outside and they were forced to stay with the children indoors, it was particularly hard work as the children turned their attention to the teachers more often. Kevin came in without saying a word, grabbed his gym bag and disappeared from the scene.

Charlie remained sat at his desk, waiting for quiet to descend in the office. He found it hard to concentrate with any background noise. With a blank page in front of him, he tried to think of something he could write, but struggled.

After a while, he gave up and wrote the only thing that was on his mind. 'All Chinese firms are crooks, I want to investigate them.' No that's too blunt, he mumbled. He needed something punchy, he thought, but less direct. Then he thought of Lesley. She hadn't given him the best first impression of the way Chinese schools functioned, with her interpretation of the profit motive as it related to education. What this could mean for other businesses around China, and what their motives were, was anyone's guess. He tapped the keys on his mac and strung one word after another, without any idea where he would finish.

It took the whole of lunch for him to write a draft that he was happy with. His law education had given him a certain eye for detail and a patience with text, so he put it to one side and promised himself he'd check it again the next day.

The afternoon's lesson passed relatively slowly for Kevin. Excited to have some time alone with Emma, he frequently glanced at the clock on the wall, willing the minute hand to move faster.

When the time came, he grabbed his things and rushed out of the door, not even noticing Yoyo's mother as he ducked and dived through the parents standing outside waiting for their children. Some of them looked after him, muttering 'silly foreigner'.

In the foreigners' office, he told Charlie would head to their salsa class by himself as he had some things to do beforehand. Charlie didn't even bother to ask what he meant by 'things', knowing it could mean anything in Kevin's vocabulary, so he proceeded to pack his belongings and left the room. With the office to himself, Kevin grabbed some cologne from inside a drawer and liberally sprayed himself to such an extent that it brought a tear to his eye. After a quick look in the bathroom mirror where he swept his blond hair up a little, he bounded downstairs, hopping two steps at a time.

As he entered Emma's classroom, he saw her on her hands and knees shuffling across the floor besides a large piece of brown cardboard. He stopped and stared towards her, still unnoticed, his pupils dilated and his heartbeat quickened. He had a tingly feeling in his chest. Still on her hands and knees, Emma saw his reflection in the window and swung her head backwards. She smiled and called him over. 'Here take, I need draw round.' she said.

Kevin walked toward her as she threw an apron on a chair nearby. After he put it on, he shuffled up next to her, also on hands and knees, and caught the same scent he'd been overpowered by in the bathroom cubicle.

They looked at each other briefly. She had evidently caught his musk as well. 'You smell nice,' she said quickly.

'Er … thanks,' he replied, smiling.

He let her hold his hand and guide it to where she wanted it placed. Then she drew a large circle around it before guiding his other hand to a different part of the cardboard where she drew a second large circle around it. As if in a game of twister, their limbs overlapped and thighs brushed.

'OK, now same other side.'

As they crawled and climbed over each other, seeking to readjust the cardboard, they giggled. Feeling a little playful, Kevin placed his hand on one corner of the cardboard only to remove it when Emma approached to circle it. She laughed. He put it down again, then grabbed the pen from her. She reached to grab it but her arms were too short. He stood up, her following in sync, still stretching as far as she could. Her body pressed against his as she reached up to try and get his raised hands. Kevin caught the scent of the coconut oil in her hair and felt the delicate touch of her hand grabbing his torso as she struggled to reach. He could feel her bosom against his stomach and her other hand pushing on his firm chest. They jostled a little while longer before she gave up and hugged him, her arms reaching around his back. She gave a small moan as she squeezed him gently.

'No fair,' she whispered.

He slowly brought down his hand and dropped the pen on the floor before wrapping his arms around her. As he tried to draw himself away, she held on tight. He looked down at her face as she looked up at his. There were tears in her eyes as she held his gaze.

The room was still. Everything went quiet. His blue eyes stared into her large brown ones. He knew the look she was giving him. He'd seen it hundreds of times before and knew what to do when he read it in someone's face. He leaned in and pressed his lips to hers. She silently accepted the kiss, relaxing into his arms obediently.

A door crashed in the corridor outside and they hurriedly gasped, letting go of each other in the process. They stepped away and shuffled awkwardly before smiling once again. Emma pointed towards her lips, insinuating some of her lipstick was now on Kevin's face. He wiped his mouth ungracefully with the palm of his hand but Emma shook her head before taking a tissue out of her pocket and stepping closer to finish the job. She bit her bottom lip as she held Kevin's jaw steady.

'Emma, err … I'm sorry.'

'It is OK. I want to do,' she replied softly.

'But, your husband?' he said, confused.

Emma sighed. She stepped back and turned away, angling towards the sofa, a large grey one with two seats covered in toys. She swatted the toys onto the floor before sitting down and patting the seat next to her. He perched himself on the arm of the sofa, keeping his distance in case someone were to walk by outside.

'I don't love my husband … Actually, no, I do, he be good man. But not …' She gestured her whole figure up and down, 'With body … you understand?'

'I think so,' Kevin replied.

'He care for me … and give me money to shop … but he always so … busy …'

She expected Kevin to reply but he stayed silent, staring intensely at the floor instead.

'I sometimes wonder, what if not marry him? You understand?'

'Why did you marry him?' he finally said.

'My family say to.'

'Your family?'

'Yes, they say, "Emma, you don't want be left behind. Choose this man as husband".'

'Oh, you were scared of being leftover.'

'Yes. I turn 30, and mother tell me next day to go on date with my husband.'

'Only him?'

'Yes. Why someone else?'

'But if you didn't like him, what then?'

'Why that matter?'

'Isn't marriage meant to be about love?'

'Maybe. But he love me.'

'Don't you love him?'

'No ... yes, ooooh,' she placed her hands over her eyes, 'I don't know. He give me home, of course I love him.'

'That's not love.'

'No?'

'No!'

'What is love?'

Kevin laughed awkwardly. 'I don't know. Wanting to spend time with him. Wanting to make him happy.'

'But I do want make him happy.'

'That's not what I mean.'

'What do mean?'

'It's hard to explain. You wouldn't understand.'

'No ... I guess not.'

'I didn't mean it like that, my views are complicated.'

'Com-poo-li-ca-ted?' she said slowly.

'Like ... hard to say.'

'Oh ...' she paused for a moment and stared out the window in thought. 'Anyway,' she finally said, 'I just wanted to feel another man once ... Thank you give me.'

She looked away from him and stood up before walking back to the cardboard where she proceeded to cut holes into the circles they'd made together. Kevin looked on disappointedly. Was that all she'd wanted?

He stood up and walked across to help her continue cutting. They didn't speak much, he followed her directions and helped her adjust the cardboard when she asked him to. By the time they'd finished this first part of the process, it was 18:00 and Kevin's mind turned to salsa. He wasn't sure how to say goodbye, so he waited for her to take the lead. She asked him to come back the next afternoon after school and on Friday afternoon at the same time. There was no more mention of the kiss, and her near coldness confused him.

He promised he would be there and then left the classroom. Turning around at the doorway, he smiled, but she was too absorbed in her work to notice. He sighed before running down the stairs and toward the exit.

8

The clock ticked silently with its slow, incessant rhythm. Kevin stared at it while the setting sun cast a golden light across the classroom. As some children played with their toys on the hard wooden floor by his feet, others sat on a sofa nearby, looking wondrously at picture books filled with dinosaurs and robots.

He reflected on the morning's class. Emma had acted distant – as if nothing of any great importance had taken place between them. Kevin had been disappointed at her coldness, in a way made worse by the sensation that he had done something wrong. Had he? He thought. Did he not kiss her for long enough? Did she expect him to say something? These questions played on his mind as the clock ticked past 16:50. He wouldn't normally give a woman much thought. Perhaps had she shown more attention that morning he wouldn't feel as he did.

At precisely 16:55, he couldn't bear it any longer and left the class. Again he brushed past Yoyo's mother, who gave him a smile he didn't even acknowledge.

Before the other foreign teachers returned, he grabbed his belongings and made it look like he'd gone home for the day – Charlie would get the message. He was about to dart out into the corridor when a Chinese man's frame blocked the door. He was about five feet tall with a small round belly. He had a horribly receding hairline which he'd attempted to cover up with a streaky combover. He must have been climbing the stairs because he had a sweaty forehead and his glasses looked moist, a droplet of water forming on their rim.

'Er … excuse me,' Kevin asked as politely as he could.

'You is Kevin?' the man grumbled in a deep voice, barely moving his lips.

'Yes, that's me,' he smiled.

'You know my wife.'

'I … I do?' Kevin replied, a little hesitantly.

'Yes! … Do you know who I am?'

'No …' he replied, worried. Could it be? He thought to himself. Did Emma already tell him? Was that why she hadn't talked to him today? He balked at the thought he'd shared a kiss with someone who kissed this man standing before him now.

'I am Yoyo's father! My wife and he love you! Say Daddy, go say hello Kevin!'

'Oh thank goodness,' he sighed.

'Thanks for what?'

'Oh nothing, nothing. Sorry my mind was on something else. Anyway … uh … hello!'

'I want give you small present.'

'Oh no, you don't have to do …'

'I want to,' the man cut off.

'OK.'

Yoyo's father took out a small box of chocolates.

'This for you.'

'Oh … Thank you, I guess.'

'We get from Switzerland, we go last year, skiing.'

'Oh wow, I've never been skiing.'

'You must go. Very good fun, maybe Yoyo can teach you.'

'Yoyo?'

'Yes, we go again next winter. Maybe you can come?'

'Maybe.'

There was a moment of silence.

'Err … Yoyo says you are from England, correct?'

'That's right.'

'I have been four times,' he said showing the digits on his right hand before continuing, 'Cheers!'

'Yes, ha, cheers!'

Kevin made a step forward as if to suggest he considered the conversation over.

'You have been in China long?' the father continued, either ignoring or failing to notice Kevin's intimations.

'Yes. Seven years.'

'Wow, seven years! So long. Do you speak Chinese?'

'No.'

'Oh … well, that's OK, you're still very welcome in China I think. At least you stay so long so you must like very much.'

'Yes, yes, I do.'

There was another silence between them. Still blocked in the room, Kevin feigned interest in the father's background.

'Oh, I am from Hangzhou, yes. I have lived here my whole life. My wife is from Beijing and join me here. I now work for Huawei, we have office not too far away.'

'That's nice.'

'Unnn,' the father replied and, content at having shared something of himself to Kevin continued, 'Anyway, maybe you can give Yoyo some more English lessons? I mean outside of school.'

'I'm not really allowed to do that.'

'You don't have to tell anyone, I pay you well.'

'I'm not so sure …'

'How about 500RMB for one hour?'

Kevin struggled to hide his excitement, but his eyes widened at the thought of a day's salary for very little effort. He finally angled his body towards Yoyo's father.

'OK … Then yes, that's fine, when would you like me to start?'

'I give you my WeChat, we can discuss later when is best.'

After exchanging details, Kevin said goodbye and finally squeezed himself into the corridor. He dived into a bathroom before locking himself in a cubicle. There was someone in the cubicle next to him with what sounded like irritable bowels, so he rapidly placed his earphones in their place and turned the music volume up.

After about five minutes he removed one of the earplugs and gently opened the door. The person in the next cubicle was still there, but the kindergarten seemed quieter. Shrieks came through the window of children on the street below, but these were slowly fading. Walking to the bathroom door, he opened it silently and popped his head out into an empty hallway. Satisfied they'd be alone, he exited the bathroom and strolled effortlessly to Emma's classroom. Upon entering, he saw her in an apron again on her hands and knees, with some paintbrushes in her colourfully stained hands. Her limbs moved gracefully over the cardboard, leaving streaks of paint. She was so focused on her work that she didn't notice Kevin entering the room.

He approached cautiously, eager not to disturb the picture of serenity in front of him. The light streamed through the windows, casting the room in a warm yellow glow and long shadows from the books and toys still left messily on the floor. The dust, caught by light rays, seemed blissfully suspended in the air moving slowly around each other as leaves swirling in a breeze. In that moment, when Emma looked up at him with a smile, she looked like an artist at work, full of energy and passion.

'Come, join,' she said excitedly.

'Oh, OK.' He grabbed an apron she was holding up for him, 'what should I do?'

'Umm …' she thought out-loud, 'here, follow my lead.'

She grabbed his hand whilst he was still standing and guided it downwards. He kneeled beside her and followed her direction. She pulled his hand to the canvas and gently pushed it in a figure of eight. Almost cheek to cheek, he looked at her face, barely an inch away from his and took a deep breath. She laughed slightly as he tensed his hand.

'I think I have the hang of it,' he whispered.

She returned to her work less than a metre away, her bum angled towards Kevin. He frequently stopped to ask for her opinion on his work, to which she gleefully turned around before returning once again.

As time went on, their conversation varied from one topic to another. From areas of China they'd both visited to their dreams for the future. Every so often, one of their hands would softly brush the other's hand as they reached for the paint at the same time. Emma had smooth, delicate, feminine fingers which held gracefully to the paintbrush, making her strokes look effortless.

Emma's English wasn't fluent, Kevin thought, but she knew how to get her point across – no doubt a result of her kindergarten teaching experience, where children responded better to actions than they did to words. Kevin spoke a little slower than his usual pace, but he had the impression she must have been taught by a foreigner when she was at school, because she understood his accent well, not often asking him to repeat what he said.

The dusk outside turned to night by the time they had completed the first bit of painting. Emma looked at the clock on the wall.

'Kevin, I need to go home … Cook for husband.'

'Oh,' he replied dejectedly, 'I see.'

'I see you tomorrow?'

'Yes. Yes, of course.'

The next evening, Kevin, although conscious that he had a date with Sophia later that evening, eagerly hurried to Emma's classroom once again. He hadn't experienced the highs and lows of this sort of lust for at least five years, but as it returned, it felt like a whole new adventure.

He reflected on his luck as he exited the foreigners' office. Just as he had signed a new contract with the school, he felt something along the lines of a love he'd never believed in. And yet, here he was, giggling like a teenage schoolboy at the thought of a married female co-worker choosing him over her husband. Charlie had summarised his situation the previous evening.

'You know you only want her as a power thing.'

'That's not true, I really feel something for her.'

'No, you don't. You just want to prove something to yourself and others that you can have any girl you want, even married ones. That's what makes it exciting for you. You've done it before with married women, and now you're doing it again.'

'But that was different.'

'In what way?'

'I mean, sure, in that case I wanted to prove to myself I was better than these rich husbands who could send their over privileged kids to these schools as some sort of token of prestige, but like I say this is different. Emma doesn't have a rich husband. At least not an inordinately rich one. I really like her.'

'Saying it again and again doesn't make it true. If anything, to me it seems you're trying to convince yourself it's true … What do you want her for anyway? Aren't you going on a date with Sophia tomorrow?'

'I don't know. Why can't I have both for the time being?'

'Oh, I give up.'

He smiled as he entered Emma's classroom, the light once again romantically golden. He wondered if Charlie was in any way jealous. It was clear he didn't enjoy his time at the kindergarten, but that might be for a number of reasons. He just might not like China in general. Or perhaps he'd struggled with the ladies himself and couldn't take another person being successful. Or maybe he fancied Emma himself. In any case, he was wrong.

After Emma and Kevin had put on their aprons, they continued where they'd left off the previous day in both painting and conversation. It seemed strange to Kevin that she acted so differently depending on the room they were in and who they were with. When they were alone after school, she was so much more open, but when the *Ayi* or the kids were around, all of whom struggled to speak and understand English anyway, she acted as if they were simply colleagues and not very interested in each other at that. Then again, there were moments of great intimacy, and he imagined she didn't speak like that with anyone except her husband.

As 18:00 approached again, a tinge of sadness overcame him at the thought of not seeing her for the whole weekend. Besides this, given they'd now completed the background set for next week's play, they didn't have an excuse to spend more time together.

They both laboured their movements as they took off their aprons. Each expected the other to break the silence first. Neither started talking, so Emma led them out of the classroom quietly. As they walked out of the corridor and down the stairs in silence, Kevin noticed Emma's eyes were red.

'Are you OK?' he asked tentatively.

'Yes, yes …' she said, 'thank you for help … have nice weekend.'

She turned and walked quickly away.

'Well fuck me …' he exclaimed aloud when she was a suitable distance away so as not to hear 'What the hell does she want from me?'

He turned towards home and considered what he might wear for his date with Sophia.

9

Kevin leaped up the stairs at Fengqi Lu station in the centre of town, bypassing everyone ahead of him. Thinking it was a famous actor trying to avoid people stopping him for a chat, some other passengers took out phones to record him. The attention would have seemed far-fetched had he not been wearing an expensive looking black suit with gold lining. Within this, he wore a pristine white shirt and a pocket square he'd been keeping for such an occasion. His hair, slightly greased and slicked upwards, gently rocked as one bulk from side to side as he dodged people. One strand fell down from the rest and landed halfway down his forehead, giving him a dishevelled look, like a West End dancer who had just finished a number. Not that he meant to look dishevelled, he was simply running late.

As he rushed through the crowds, heading in one direction like sheep towards the vast expanse of West Lake, he looked at his watch; it was 20:13. The plan had been that he meet Sophia at 19:30 so they could have a quick cocktail on the roof lounge of the hotel followed by their dinner reservation at 20:00. Sophia had texted it was a charming little romantic spot and that she knew one of the barmaids well.

At the entrance to the hotel's restaurant, he could see Sophia waiting impatiently, scrolling through her phone and tapping her right foot on the ground. 'Not the best way to start a future relationship,' he muttered to himself. After apologising, he gave her a kiss on the cheek and opened the door to the restaurant for her. Inside was immaculate. The smooth, rich, red interior opened out onto a Cantonese-style restaurant with waitresses dressed in fetching cheongsams, and waiters dressed in smart black tie.

The restaurant seemed designed for the social elite of Hangzhou. Men in suits on one side discussed business and would sometimes burst into loud fits of laughter, whilst women on the other celebrated birthdays and marriages around lavish circular tables with Lazy Susan's rotating piles of food. There were tables of rich young families too, clothed to the hilt in designer products. Of all the frequenters, this type seemed most out of place for they ate loudly and what seemed like without enjoyment. Whilst the father watched a video on his phone and the mother looked wistfully towards the group of ladies, Kevin wondered if they were only there for the appearance of being seen at a place like this, as if some magic prestige was attached to it.

They were led along a corridor into a smaller, more intimate room with tables for two. There were young couples and elderly gentlemen with suspiciously young and well-groomed ladies sitting opposite each other. The chatter was quiet and civilised, at odds to the raucous feeling of the restaurant they had just walked through. By the open window which looked out onto the well-manicured lawn, there was an empty table with a reserved block placed on it. Kevin took one of the seats out from under the table and invited Sophia to sit. She sat down elegantly and thanked him in a soft, hushed voice. As he pushed the seat in, the gleam of the silk dress shimmered effortlessly. He looked out of the window toward the shore of West Lake and a vast expansive view of the hills behind,

'So,' Kevin started, clearing his throat as he sat down, 'you come here often?'

'Only with mother. She comes here almost weekly with my father.'

The waiter arrived and presented the wine list and menu to Kevin, before disappearing to another table that had a raised hand.

'What's the ... err shall I give this to you?' he said intimating at the wine list.

'Don't you want wine?'

'I've realised when someone else is paying for something, I shouldn't get too greedy.'

'Oh, don't worry about that, mother doesn't mind. Besides we're not paying a bill tonight, they just add it to mother's tab.'

'Oh, well, anyway, I'll just get whatever's cheapest.'

'You're not very good at this are you?'

'What? Of course I am, why do you say that?' he said, almost affronted.

'You don't need to get defensive.'

'I wasn't!'

'Anyway ...' she continued, 'I'll have a look at it if you won't.'

He threw the list across the table which caused the glasses to shudder slightly. Sophia paused before picking up the menu.

'Sorry, I don't like being told I'm wrong.'

'Don't worry, it's OK. You're just used to Asian girls who agree with you on everything, aren't you?' she laughed.

'No, that's not true.'

'I can see right through you. Not all of us are submissive objects of your sexual desires.'

Kevin coughed awkwardly.

'Well then er …' he shuffled in his seat, 'tell me more about yourself. I guess we are here for a date.'

Sophia explained she'd had an education typical of the English upper classes, whom she said rich Chinese people take as their inspiration. She'd been sent to boarding school in Brighton at the age of seven, only returning during the summer holidays to spend limited amounts of time with her mother. At the age of 18 she enrolled in a Bachelors in Economics at the London School of Economics, before going on to complete a two year Masters in Accountancy at New York University. Her co-curricular interests were serious if not very varied. She had taken part in numerous debating competitions and was well up to date with current affairs.

Kevin tried to turn the subject to more familiar fields.

'So, do you dance?'

'I wish I could, but I can never find the time to learn.'

'Have you ever tried salsa?' he asked.

'I haven't no, then again when I was in New York I always wanted someone to ask me to dance but no one ever would.'

Not surprising, he thought. She's terrifying.

Some starters arrived, spring rolls alongside dumplings of various stuffings. Sophia lifted one expertly with her chopsticks before gracefully placing it in her mouth. Kevin, expecting her to ask about him, struggled to think of what to say next.

'So do you like the theatre?' he blurted out.

'It depends, I like Noël Coward but find Shakespeare *such* a bore. Nobody falls in love like that Romeo and Juliet, get over yourselves. Noël Coward's ability to mock anything and everything is so much more worthwhile.'

'Music?' Kevin asked tentatively.

'Maybe a little bit of classical music but I find Mozart far too dull. Only Wagner and Mahler know anything about the human soul.'

'Sports?'

'Yes, I play golf, do you?'

'No,' he sighed.

'Is this all you want to talk about?'

'What do you mean?'

'Well … I was expecting something a bit more from you. Like, what's your view on what's going on in the world at the moment? What do you think of China? Why have you stayed here for so long?'

'Uh, I don't really know what to say.'

'The attention?' she asked.

'No! ...' before correcting himself, 'I mean, yes but no.'

'The energy?'

'Yes, I guess you could say that.'

'Well, why didn't you just go to London?'

'I don't know, I just wanted to stay here you know. Let's talk about something else.'

Sophia laughed as the main course of BBQ duck arrived.

'Alright ... We'll leave that there.'

While Kevin and Sophia were at the restaurant, Charlie prepared for his own night out. Every Friday night, the salsa club Charlie and Kevin attended held a party at a bar in the university area of the city, just north of West Lake. Here, from 10 p.m. each Friday, almost all of Hangzhou's, and even some of Shanghai's salsa tribes would meet and party until the early hours of the morning. The venue was perfect for the style of dance. It was a rooftop bar of a one storey building, among the trees of the natural scenery around the lake. About 70 individuals showed up on an average night, and when there were more, they would overflow onto the streets below – it was like a scene from Ray's native Los Angeles. This particular evening promised to be pleasant as the air was still humid with the day's heat and the void-like empty sky assured that there would be no rain.

After Charlie had finished the noodles he'd ordered to go from the Uyghur restaurant, he took a shower and walked around the flat naked, pondering what he should wear. Every so often he would stop by the mirror and flick his hair whilst pouting his lips. After going with a standard combination of black jeans and a black shirt, he liberally doused himself in deodorant, almost suffocating in the process before he opened the window, coughing and spluttering. At 21:30, he looked at himself in the mirror once more and ordered a taxi on his phone.

As the map in the app indicated he'd have about five minutes to wait, he slowly meandered outside, making sure to double lock the door as he left. At the bottom of his building, he waved toward a security guard on his break nearby who waved back with a large grin on his face, teeth interlaced with grains of rice. Charlie chuckled as he walked towards the gate.

'Good evening,' another security guard said slowly in English as he opened the gate for Charlie.

'Good evening, how are you?' Charlie replied.

'Good, thank you.'

'You get very good Chen!'

Chen blushed as he laughed. 'Thank you, thank you,' he repeated.

As the taxi arrived, a white sedan with a small dent on the side, Charlie turned around and waved at Chen.

'Have fun!' Chen called after him, before returning to his colleagues under an umbrella nearby.

During the taxi ride, Charlie went over what he might say to the Korean girl. So far when in lessons, they would laugh together over how bad he was at salsa but he never enjoyed self-effacing pity. He also had the impression only British people understood that it wasn't always meant to sound sincere. Instead of coming across as modest, he instead must've sounded completely lacking in confidence.

At the bar, the party had already started, the music was loud and the smell of cigarettes, sweat and alcohol lingered in the air. All the better-known dancers from the group had turned up for the night. Simba, Chris and Ray were doing the rounds it seemed, dancing one song with one girl, then as soon as it finished, offering their hand to another. Pedro, Laurence and Sanchez too. Even a man affectionately called Old Stuart, for he was in his 70s but still able to dance well, seemed active on the floor. There were all shapes and sizes dancing. No matter how large or small, ugly or handsome, anyone with energy could make themselves dominate the floor in front of them.

Charlie, still a beginner, and still without a decision on how to approach the Korean girl, froze when he saw her alone by the bar. He took a deep breath, clenched his fists, and started in her direction. It'll come, he thought, whatever needs to be said, it'll come. As he strode over in a direct line to her, he got within two metres before a suave Frenchman by the name of Pierre jumped in from her left and grabbed her first. Trying to avoid embarrassment, Charlie turned around as quickly as possible, only to knock a drink out of the hand of a large gentleman by the name of Cecil. Cecil looked down at him with a dirty look, which was tough because Charlie was himself pretty tall. Charlie apologised profusely before proceeding to buy his first drink of the night and passing it directly to the large man.

Reassessing the situation, Charlie grabbed a chair at the bar and tried to look like he was busy checking messages on his phone. Every so often, he looked behind him to see if there was anyone he knew well enough to dance with without suffering embarrassment. With the knowledge of only one routine, he feared he could only dance for at most one minute before repetition set in. He ventured he could try and make up moves but then shook his head, expecting this would upset the balance of the dancing. Nor could he expect whoever he danced with to know what he was attempting to do.

As he scoured the dance floor, eager to find his first dance partner for the night, he could see Scarlett moving through the crowd towards him. Scarlett! Of course! He thought. As a teacher who knew how much he'd already learned, she was unlikely to laugh at his inabilities, and secondly, she could teach him something while they were dancing that would make it look like he was better than he actually was. God bless her.

He took her hand and led her to the dance floor as the next song started. OK here we go, he thought. Left right left, right left right. Left right left, right left right. Look at her eyes … wait no don't do that, they're too pretty … look down, no, you're staring at her boobs … look above her eyes … He attempted turning her by raising her arm and drawing a small circle above her head. Nice one, he thought, OK here it goes, let's try a movement and twist at the same time. With surprising confidence, he started the move and Scarlett followed. However, at this moment Charlie made the mistake of an amateur and hadn't looked behind him at the layers of people who were there. Scarlett, following his lead, ended up bashing into the back of a large gentleman behind. The large gentleman turned around to show a familiar face. Dammit Cecil, out the way, Charlie thought.

'Sorry Cecil,' he said.

One minute into the song, he started to struggle. As he had worried, he'd run out of moves. Just then, Scarlett, sensing his nervousness and knowing him to be a beginner, started spinning herself and using his hands as leverage to complete a movement. This only required Charlie to stay balanced as he continued the basic step. A smug smile came across Charlie's face as he looked around the dance floor, hoping someone could see him doing these moves. As no one was, he soon returned to staring at Scarlett's forehead with the same intensity as before. But then he remembered if he was going to impress the Korean girl, he would have to do these moves that he didn't know all over again. He started to pay closer attention to what Scarlett was doing with his hands.

At the end of the song, Scarlett somehow managed to wrap herself using his arms into such an intricate position that even Charlie was able to read that all he had to do was drop one shoulder and he would have the perfect dip. He dropped his right shoulder, put his hand under her back and … 'oh no!'

'Oh god, I'm so sorry Scarlett!' he exclaimed suddenly, loud enough to be heard by some of those around him.

He'd forgotten to place his hand under her neck. Instead of a smooth ending, Scarlett threw her head back, bringing on a self-induced whiplash. As Charlie raised her back up to standing position, she rubbed her neck and assured him everyone did this their first time. With that she sauntered off to find some ice at the bar.

Charlie, embarrassed and a little dazed by what had happened, grabbed his drink from the table and sat at a stool on the edge of the venue which overlooked a pond below.

'Charlie,' Robin shouted from across the bar as he moved towards him, 'you dance so well!'

'Are you joking? I was terrible.'

'Everyone's bad to start, I wouldn't worry. Just keep going.'

'Thanks,' Charlie mumbled, as Robin offered his hand to a nearby girl as another song started.

As he sipped the drink, he kept going through the moves Scarlett had just done with him in his head, and tried to remember what the cues were for each twist and turn. As the next song ended, he felt a tap on the shoulder, and turned around. The Korean girl smiled at him, eyes glistening, and stretched her hand out towards his.

Charlie rose from his chair and followed the Korean girl to the centre of the dance floor just as another song began. They started the routine they'd both been learning in the last few weeks. All was going well, she followed his lead and he'd gained a little bit of confidence from his dance with Scarlett. As the song approached one minute, he pushed his chest up and started to move his hands in the way Scarlett had directed them. The Korean girl followed dutifully and let him continue his lead.

Two minutes passed and he was impressed by how well he'd done thus far. He hadn't repeated a major move yet. As he continued his steps, he saw Ray in the corner of his eye swing his girl's arms down, then anticlockwise upwards as they both followed and turned a full 360 to face each other again, but this time not holding hands. Ray then proceeded to dance by himself and so did the girl he was with, their moves out of sync. That's it! Charlie thought, do that and he wouldn't need to look like a fool not knowing what he was doing.

As he continued to step in the usual pattern, he boldly lifted both his and the Korean girl's arms up. She looked at him in a confused manner as if to suggest she had no confidence in his ability to do what he was about to attempt. He thought to himself, 'OK … here we go,' and completely out of time with the music, flung their hands down, then anticlockwise as he'd seen Ray do. He turned, just as Ray had done, then fell to the ground just as Ray hadn't done.

In his eagerness to show off, he hadn't taken into account that, when turning, it was important to keep your balance and, when flinging your whole body weight one way, letting go of the person who had helped keep you balanced was likely to send you flailing. The Korean, having anticipated this was going to happen, hadn't bothered to turn, and now offered him a hand up. Some of the others in the vicinity of the dance floor stopped to help him get up too.

'Are you hurt?' the Korean girl asked.

'Only my pride,' he joked.

'That's a relief.'

'Hey, I've never actually asked you your name. What is it?' he asked.

'It's Areum,' she said holding out her hand for him to shake. 'Nice to meet you.'

'Nice to meet you too,' he said.

Before he could even ask her if she wanted a drink, Cecil had come across and offered her his hand which, out of politeness she took. Fucking Cecil, he thought to himself.

As Charlie wallowed in his misery, a little annoyed that he'd not only

made a fool of himself dancing, but hadn't succeeded in learning anything about Areum, he saw Kevin approaching him through the crowd.
He looked bitter, and had a can of beer in his hand he'd bought from a
shop nearby.

'You alright mate? How was your date?' Charlie asked.

'Not amazing to be honest,' Kevin replied, having a long glug of beer
before taking another can out of his jacket pocket and opening it. He
chucked the empty can over the edge of the bar and it landed somewhere
amongst the trees below.

'How come? What did you get up to?'

'I mean the food was nice, the setting was good … but she wasn't
what I imagined she'd be. She seemed to disagree with me on most
things and we have such different opinions.'

'That can be a good thing?' Charlie said hopefully.

'True, but this was different, like if she wasn't loaded and if I'd paid
for everything I probably wouldn't have organised to have another date
with her.'

'So you've already decided on another date? … Sounds like love to
me,' Charlie joked.

'Yeah, when I walked her to her taxi, she said we should meet up
again so I thought, "yeah why not". We're going to have a drink next
weekend at West Lake.'

'What are you on about? That sounds proper nice,' Charlie exclaimed.

'You weren't there man, it just wasn't the date I imagined it would be
… it wasn't the disagreements that annoyed me, it was the air she carried
herself with. She's obviously been treated like a princess from a young
age and believes herself to be one. She spoke in big words and of heavy
subjects.'

'But you used to love that stuff, didn't you?'

'Right up until I realised none of it matters.'

'Are you going to be like this all night?'

'What do you fancy doing later?' Kevin finally asked, ignoring him.

'How about, stay here a bit longer, then head to Basement?' Charlie
replied.

Kevin nodded at the suggestion.

It was just coming up to midnight, and since they had some time
before Basement would liven up, Kevin grabbed the girl closest to him

and pulled her to the dance floor. Charlie, not quite over the embarrassment he'd caused himself, stayed in his place until Scarlett came over
again to drag him into another dance.

At about half past one, and after the effects of alcohol on their dancing
had passed the point of confidence to sloppiness, they made a start for
Basement. Hangzhou, even the university quarter, felt strange at night. It
was no London or New York centre. The streets were empty and there
was no congregation of bars, only watering holes at large intervals
between each other. The roads were empty other than a few taxis
ferrying people around. Both boys swayed a little as they walked the 15
minutes through the still evening air. Their stomachs hurt, but they were
intent on drinking more by the time they reached their destination.

When they arrived, there were a couple of large, beefy locals acting as
bouncers outside the front door – at least as tall as Kevin but twice his
width with fat. They didn't ask to check IDs, but upturned the boys'
pockets instead, for which they didn't even bother to say why. Up close,
the two bouncers were hideous. One had a scar on his face from what
looked like the slice of a knife, it followed the curve of his cheek before
ending just to the inside of his ear. The other had shaved his head so
awfully, that patches of hair stuck out in tufts across his head.

After the bouncers grunted, as if to say the search was over, Kevin
led the way through the door and immediately down a staircase that
smelled strongly of urine. The music pulsated through the concrete walls
as they jolted down, barely able to keep balance as they held onto the
balustrade. There was a pile of vomit in the corner at the bottom of the
first flight of stairs, and beside this an empty bottle of Tsingtao beer.
Charlie turned as if to shout towards the bouncers that it should be
cleaned up, before deciding against it.

Inside, the bar was packed from wall to wall, and so noisy that Charlie
immediately placed his hands to his ears in an attempt to protect them.
Unlike other bars, this place wasn't only for the expat population. This
was one of the few bars which had a sizable Chinese contingent, and the
place prided itself on being run by some people who had grown up in
Hong Kong, which they thought gave it an element of legitimacy.

Kevin, now in a much better mood, recognised a few faces and went
to pat their shoulders and jostle with them while Charlie went to the bar

to buy them both a drink. When Charlie returned with the drinks, they grabbed a table near the large crowd in front of the DJs and glanced around the audience.

'She'd get it,' Kevin shouted.

Ugh, Charlie thought, not this.

'She'd get it,' Kevin shouted again at a different girl, 'and her. And her. And her. Charlie pal, aren't you in heaven right now?'

Charlie grimaced and lifted the bottle as if in agreement.

At this point, he saw two Chinese girls sitting by themselves at a large table with some empty drinks around them. As if to play along with Kevin's game, he nudged him, who then turned to look in the direction Charlie was looking. The two ladies were in an alcove, on a semi-circular bench, chatting whilst nursing some near-empty cocktails. There was just enough space next to the one on the left for one of them to squeeze in whilst the one on the right had enough space for three to four people next to her.

'OK, which one do you want?' Kevin said.

'I don't really care.'

'OK, you take the left, I'll take the right,' Kevin proclaimed before abruptly standing up and striding towards the two women.

'Good evening beautiful ladies,' Kevin said in basic Chinese before reverting back to English. 'How are you doing tonight? My name's Kevin, my friend Charlie and I were wondering if we could get you a drink.'

'Ohh ha ha … no, zank you,' she said in an awkward laugh.

Kevin didn't lose steam.

'Well, how about we come and sit with you?'

He pushed Charlie towards the girl and gestured at him to sit down whilst he took a seat next to the other one, taking up a large space with his legs wide open.

'Are you from the university?' Kevin continued.

'Yes.'

'Oh, that's nice. What do you study?' he asked.

'None of business,' she replied.

'That's a little rude … how about you give me a kiss on the cheek to make up for it?'

As he leaned his cheek across, he felt a tapping on his shoulder. At first he gave it no notice but as he held his cheek in place, the girl still not leaning in to give him a kiss, he was slapped on the back of the head. Kevin turned around and stood up ferociously, the alcohol making his eyes light up.

'Oi, what do you think you're doing dickhead?' he shouted.

Standing by the table were five guys, all locals, dressed in black jumpers staring at him with angry faces. The one closest to Kevin shouted. 'That's my girlfriend faggot.'

He was at least four inches shorter than Kevin, so when Kevin stood tall and puffed his chest a little, he almost dwarfed him. The tallest Chinese person at the back, about an inch taller than Kevin, pushed himself forward to square up to him, but he was skinny underneath his loose jumper and wore glasses. Kevin turned to look at Charlie and laughed before turning to face off the tallest of the friends again.

'What are you gonna do?' Kevin jeered.

Charlie had risen at this point, hardly hiding his fear and tugged on Kevin, willing him to let it go. Some people at other tables nearby had turned to see what the shouting had been about. When they saw it was foreigner against Chinese, they took sides, and started shouting obscenities in Chinese at Kevin, not that he understood them. The short one whose girlfriend it had been threw a punch at Kevin from behind the safety of his tall compatriot only to miss his face by an inch – Kevin felt the rush of wind as it went by. Kevin returned the favour with a jab which hit the boyfriend in the jaw. The tall friend in front grabbed Kevin's shirt with two hands from the front, only to have Kevin head-butt his nose which immediately began to stream blood. The girls behind him screamed as Charlie tugged on his back harder. 'Mate let's go,' he said into his ear. 'It's not worth it.'

Kevin wasn't finished. 'Fucking yellow cunts,' he shouted, before throwing some more punches.

The commotion had come to the attention of the bar, and they called security to come down from the door. There were punches being thrown at Kevin from all sides now. Even the girlfriend behind him was slapping his back. Four of the Chinese were trying to get him, but they weren't connecting with his head, only his arms, which he brushed off with ease. The tallest one with the broken nose was kneeling over nearby, wailing as he held his nose in place, blood gushing. Finally, realising this was not a good place to be, and seeing three beefy security guards pushing their way through the crowd towards him, he jumped out of the way and made a line for the fire exit which Charlie had been pulling him towards. As people, some foreigners included but mostly Chinese, jeered and shouted at him, he pushed through to the fire exit. Neither Charlie nor Kevin knew where it would lead, so followed the stairs as far as they could.

Unfortunately, knowing the venue much better than they did, the security guard with the scar on his face had foreseen they might head up this way and stood at the top of the flight of stairs with a baton in his hand. He whacked it a few times into his palm and shouted something in Chinese. Kevin had been in scraps before, and knew that it was best for the two of them to charge this solitary figure, even if they got a few bumps and bruises in the process. He predicted if they were caught by the three security guards behind them, they'd get a kicking anyway before being released.

'OK, follow me Charlie, trust me, trust me,' he said.

He put his hands up as if surrendering about three steps from the top and Charlie copied him. The bouncer moved slowly towards them.

Then, as the doors of the fire exit down the flight of stairs crashed open, he edged closer, baton still grasped firmly in his hand. Kevin prepared himself and whispered calmly.

'Three … Two … One.'

At one, he jumped up and tackled the bouncer in his midriff, pushing him to one side as the bouncer began to hit his back with the baton. Charlie dived through the space behind before shouting he was through.

Kevin, struggling with the bouncer, tried to get his head out of a headlock. He stamped on the large man's toes and threw a punch at his genitalia. Just as the other three bouncers turned the corner, he bit the bouncer's hand which made him yelp before finally releasing his grip. The other three bouncers reached out to grab him, one of them managing to grip the sleeve of his jacket. Kevin sacrificed the jacket before jumping up again and through the door to Charlie waiting outside. Turning left into the darkness they ran as fast as their legs could carry them.

They thought that would be it, but they turned around and saw three of the bouncers chasing after them, batons in hand.

'I think we'll easily be able to lose them,' Kevin puffed.

They were much faster, and unsurprisingly fitter than the three large men. They continued running even though the prospect of being caught was slowly becoming less great. At the end of the road, they turned the corner at top speed heading towards West Lake, but Charlie didn't notice a hole in the ground. Tripping up, he tried to correct himself but placed his foot on an uneven tile. He rolled his ankle and fell to the ground, shouting briefly in pain. Kevin, who was about 10 metres ahead, turned around to see his flatmate writhing in agony. He ran back to help him up, constantly looking around the corner to see if the bouncers were coming.

'Charlie come on mate get up, we have to keep running.'

'No mate, they're not coming.'

'Yes, they are mate, keep running.'

About 100 metres away, he saw the bouncers still in pursuit of them. He pulled Charlie up and tried to help him walk but it was too hard, Charlie tentatively limped and hissed whenever he stood on his right foot. The road was empty, bar a few taxis. He tried to flag one down but they were already taken. The bouncers were now about 40 metres away and gaining on the corner quickly. Charlie sat on the bench, trying not to moan from the pain, and sucked air through his teeth. Kevin frantically looked around, trying to think up a way they could hide before noticing that there was a hedge with a small ditch of water behind the bench. They could now hear the shouts of the bouncers within range. Before Charlie could complain, Kevin grabbed him by the jumper and dragged him behind the bench, placing him under the hedge.

'Roll underneath it! Roll underneath it!' he hissed.

Kevin pushed Charlie as far as he could into the muddy undergrowth, and then dived next to him. The hedge was still shaking as the bouncers turned the corner and looked at the empty road ahead of them. The wind picked up, making the trees around them rustle. The three Chinese men stopped to catch their breath and said something along the lines of 'they're gone'.

As one of them sat on the bench, panting, Kevin held his hand over Charlie's mouth. The largest of the three bouncers looked ahead towards West Lake and pointed towards it. 'Maybe they went that way,' he intimated. 'Give up already,' another one panted, 'we're not going to get them … God damned fucking foreigners.'

After about a minute of rest, the bouncers seemed to have recuperated some of their energy and turned back towards the bar. Charlie, eyes closed, winced silently underneath Kevin's hand.

Once the bouncers had turned the corner, Kevin waited about half a minute longer before crawling out from beneath the hedge. His trousers and shirt were ruined, and he had a small cut to his face where one of the punches had skimmed him, but he was OK.

'Charlie, are you alright?' he asked, brushing himself off.

'My ankle is killing me,' he moaned.

Charlie slowly crawled out from the space, clothes equally as muddy as Kevin's, and used the bench to pull himself up to his feet. Using his hands, he guided himself around to the front and threw himself ungracefully on the seat.

'I think I have to go to hospital.'

'Are you sure?' Kevin replied. 'Maybe just put some ice on it.'

'No, this is bad … Honestly I think we have to go, I can feel the swelling already.'

'Alright, alright …' Kevin said, almost panicking, 'Calm down … I'll try and find someone to call an ambulance.'

As Kevin went off in search of someone, Charlie looked at his mangled shoes. The mud was drying on his bare arm and he wiped off as much as he still could. He groaned at the sharp pain that shot up his leg when he tried to put some weight on his foot. As he saw Kevin in the distance gesturing to a Chinese man what had happened and pointing towards his foot and to Charlie, a mosquito buzzed around his head. It landed on his ear, and Charlie felt a little prick as it drew blood. The adrenaline from the chase had worn off and he was too tired to flick it off. As the mosquito buzzed away, Charlie closed his eyes. The throbbing in his ankle grew.

10

Charlie and Kevin arrived back at the apartment at 8 a.m. Their visit to the hospital had gone better than expected. The empty corridors suggested that the Chinese either didn't get ill or had a high tolerance of pain and disease. Either way, it didn't take too long for Charlie to be diagnosed with a broken ankle. His foot was placed in a cast and he was given a number of drugs, none of which he understood when to take. During the half hour taxi trip back, they both fell asleep and had to be shaken awake by the taxi driver.

As they slowly waddled up to their residential block, the security guards in the neighbourhood stared at them with bewilderment. Foreigners, usually respected educators with families of their own within the neighbourhood, didn't often come back caked in mud and bruises. Gabriel looked equally shocked as they came through the doorway, battered and bruised. They both went to bed and fell asleep.

When Charlie awoke at 6 p.m., groggy and in pain, he hopped out to the living room and encountered Kevin on the PS4, playing football with Gabriel. They were staring intently at the screen mid-match and didn't even notice their injured flatmate. On the whole, Kevin was by far the best at the game, and Gabriel, having grown up in a place that refers to football as a game where hands were used, struggled to put up much of a fight. They were mid conversation.

'Yeah, well I'm sorry to hear the date didn't go great,' Gabriel said.

'I mean no date ever goes to plan, does it?' Kevin replied, 'maybe the next one will be good.'

'You're going to meet up with her again?' Gabriel asked.

'Yeah … look man, I'm almost 30. This could be the one. She's got money and looks. Doesn't matter if we don't have the same interests now … those will grow.'

Gabriel looked at him, confused, but thought better than to engage further.

'And how's Sleeping Beauty over there?' noticing Charlie.

'Not great,' Charlie replied. 'My foot is killing me.'

'Sounded painful … why didn't you call the police?' Gabriel said, turning to Kevin.

'You think they'd be on our side? They're not gonna help a foreigner if there's a Chinese person involved.' He continued, 'Besides, the bouncers didn't actually do much to us, it was this idiot who decided to trip himself up,' he said winking at Charlie.

Charlie stared at him blankly, his eyes betraying his anger.

'How long did the doctor say you'd be in a cast?' Gabriel asked.

'Four weeks, but it's not too bad, I've been in a cast before.'

Charlie took a seat on the sofa next to Gabriel and was about to reach for a puff to raise his leg onto when Gabriel jumped up.

'Take the whole sofa, I'm going to the gym.'

He grabbed his swimming trunks which were hanging on the laundry line above the balcony, and left the others sat in silence. With the doors to the balcony open, fresh air blew into the room, and there was a bird cawing outside in the darkness. Charlie pushed himself across to the section of the sofa Gabriel had been playing the game from, still warm, and winced as he bent down to take Gabriel's controller from the coffee table. After picking two teams to play with, Charlie a Premiership side, Kevin a non-league side, they started the game.

The gentle breeze from the window did little to alleviate the air of awkwardness. Neither wanted to speak first, and by the time they reached half-time, Charlie had almost decided he'd rather go back to bed than do this all evening.

'How are you feeling?' Kevin finally asked.

'Not great … but the paracetamol helps.'

There was a little more silence between them. The air was still as the second half started.

'Look … I'm sorry that this happened. I should've calmed down or taken on the bouncers myself, instead I dragged you into it.'

'Honestly it's fine,' Charlie quietly replied. He didn't mean it and Kevin could tell.

'Look … I just signed a three-year contract to stay at the school. The last thing I wanted to do was call the police or get into trouble with the bar, so I just ran. I've been fired from other areas of the country before for lesser things, so I don't want it to happen again. I really like this city and could potentially see a future here. You know what I mean?'

'I guess,' Charlie mumbled.

Kevin offered his hand in peace, and Charlie shook it.

The bastard, Charlie thought to himself. The insolent bastard. Used to getting everything he wants. You couldn't trust a man like that. Not unless you knew something about him.

'You know, Gabriel said you'd been fired lots of times before. How come?'

'I've been fired a few times, yeah.'

'Once a year?'

'I get into bad habits, I guess.'

'But I thought you came out here for a gap year to start? Why didn't you just go back after you'd been fired?'

'You really want to know?' Kevin said, taking a moment to look across at him.

Charlie nodded before resuming his concentration on the game. He was holding his own at only 2-1 down.

'First lemme grab a beer, it's a long story. You want one?' Kevin asked

'Already? No, I'm good.'

Kevin stood up slowly and slumbered across to the kitchen. He was in his silk dressing gown, but this time he'd tied it up. The door to the kitchen creaked open, and after Kevin took a can of Tsingtao out of the fridge, he sat back down on the sofa and had a long sip. He gasped as he took the can away from his lips.

'That hits the spot,' he said before turning slightly towards Charlie 'So, where to begin, well ... I first came out in 2011, fresh faced, whatever you might call it, eager to see the mysteries of China, see all the big sights. I mean you know what it's like growing up in the UK, we celebrate Chinese New Year and maybe do a project in primary school but our history lessons are so focused on WWI and WWII, it's like China doesn't even exist. How can a country with over 3,000 years of history not make it into our textbooks?'

'I know what you mean.'

'Anyway, I came out with my books, my guitar. I wanted to learn Chinese, learn something new every week, do my own exploration. I mean I was studious back then. I'd just got a First at uni and was even considering a career in academia, perhaps specialising in Human Geography. Regardless, I wanted this gap year to think things over and add something to the CV. I've always found the best way to educate yourself is to get some practical experience on the ground, whatever it is.'

Charlie nodded silently.

'I guess it started alright. I'd escaped Sally, my ex, missed her but would sometimes send her a text just to see how she was. Anyway, two months go by, maybe I'm still too focused on Sally and spending all my time trying to study but I hadn't met anyone new other than my co-workers. I guess over time I realised it was all truly over between me and my ex and I block her on everything, I kept hearing rumours about what she got up to and it upset me.'

'But weren't you doing the same here?'

'Not back then, I was innocent,' he laughed. 'The ways of China hadn't spoiled me. I mean, I had seen sleazy guys in some of the Sanlitun bars, and from the local American Football club but I didn't hang out with them, like I said I was here to learn, not drink all the time.'

He took a long sip of his beer.

'After I'd settled down a bit, became familiar with my surroundings and had a bit of cash in the bank I started to get a bit lonely. I mean, I loved talking to locals, trying to get them to teach me Chinese but it seemed all they wanted was a photo. They were super nice, I even went on a few dates with a Chinese girl, but she wasn't keen on doing anything serious, she told me she wanted to wait until marriage, which back then, I was fine with. But it was after a few dates she basically broke up with me saying she'd told her parents she was dating a foreigner and they didn't like it.'

'Why not?'

'I don't know, whatever the reason she said she didn't want to disappoint them so she broke it off. Anyway, that night was the first night I went out properly. Like I mean, out out. I'd been to bars but most of the time I headed home around midnight. But that night I was out until 10 a.m. I had the best night of my life, honestly, maybe my drinks were laced with something but I didn't feel tired or nothing. I found some Chinese guys who were eager to take me somewhere, so I just followed them. We end up in a KTV bar but they find me a prostitute who takes me to our own room and I tell you, that was the best damn sex I've had in my life. Anyway, guess how much it cost?'

'How much?'

'Like £50.'

'Was she uhh … clean?'

'Oh yeah definitely, I've realised most of the girls here are.'

Charlie remained silent and stared blankly ahead at the paused game on the TV.

'So after that, I started hanging out with these guys more. I mean I had the money, and they seemed to know all the best places. After a few weeks though, I realised why did I need to pay in the first place? I mean the amount of people who stop me and ask for a photo in the street as if I'm some celebrity, the amount of people calling me handsome, surely I could just go to a bar and pick up a girl. So that's what I started doing.'

He took another long sip of beer.

'Honestly it was the easiest thing, I mean this was about five months in by now, I'd given up Chinese, it was too damn difficult, all the girls I slept with spoke English so it didn't matter. I stopped reading on weekends, I'd seen most of the tourist sights. Anyway, China wasn't as mysterious as I'd initially been led to believe, the people no more different than the ones I'd met in Chinatown before, I might as well have stayed in Bristol and read Wikipedia if I'd really wanted to explore Chinese culture more.'

'So how did you get fired?'

'Oh, right, yeah, that's what you asked. Basically I kept this up on Friday and Saturday nights for months, but around November time when my contract was up for renewal I started going out on weekdays too. Life as a teacher was so meaningless, I was tired of wiping snot off kid's faces, none of the kids seemed to be learning anything, and I hated Monday to Fridays. I started living for the weekend. Long story short, I got shitfaced one Monday night and came into work stinking of alcohol and swaying from side to side. They told me not to come in again.'

'Jesus, how did you find work after that?'

'Oh mate, as a teacher in China? Come on it's easy, you saw how you were hired, one five-minute interview. Do you speak English? Yep. Do you have a degree? Yep. Cool, welcome aboard.'

'So that was what happened every year?'

'Not every year, I think Gabriel was exaggerating. I mean I did sleep with two mums of kids, but that was at the same school and that was after I'd been there for two years. That was a weird school, literally all the husbands were ugly rich guys and all the wives were models.'

'So what's the worst thing you've done to get fired?'

Kevin sighed. 'You really want to know?' he asked again.

'Yes.'

'Alright, alright,' he huffed, 'let me get another beer.'

He stood up, darted to the fridge again and returned with another can of Tsingtao.

'Look man, I'm only telling this because I like you and I feel sorry for what I did. But you can't tell *anyone*. Alright?'

Charlie nodded in agreement.

'Well, I was Shenyang, you know, the city up in the north-east. This was about two and a half years ago, after I'd been fired from that school because of the two mums. Basically, I'd given up on kindergartens and thought, with four years of experience I could get a university job. It paid less but that didn't matter, I was already well off enough. I tell you, I loved it. Honestly, I had the easiest shifts ever. All they wanted you to do was speak in class, that was it ... literally I didn't need to prepare any lessons. I would turn up, half-drunk from the night before, set them having a few conversations with each other, then saunter off to another part of campus and chill. Most of my lessons didn't start until 11 a.m. anyway, and given they were university students I hung out with them outside of hours too. I'd gone to that part of China with no friends and suddenly everyone wanted to be my friend.

'There were two other English teachers at the school who'd just graduated from university and they were degenerate as hell. Within a few weeks, we all realised the girls would sleep with us for some extra tuition. We didn't exactly complain, you see I thought of it a little like a transaction. We weren't forcing them into it. Sex for tuition – like trading cards as a kid. About eight months in, my contract came up for renewal, and I gladly signed it. The others did too. They wanted more of what was going on. The only problem is that it was at this stage that one of the girls, an ugly one who none of us had cared to sleep with, along with the boys of the classes complained that we had favourites and that we were sleeping with the better looking girls who naturally had higher grades. I know this all sounds bad, but I didn't feel at the time that it was wrong.

'Anyway, the faculty wouldn't fire us unless they had proof that we were sleeping with them, none of which they had. About a month later, one of the two other English teachers got found hiring prostitutes in Beijing on a weekend with some mates who had come across from the UK to see him. The idiots had been naïve enough to think that the staff at their hotel wouldn't inform the police what was going on. I'd even told him "whatever you do, don't bring them back to your hotel, only fuck them in the brothels". I got a text from him which woke me up in the middle of the night saying that the hotel staff had knocked on their door saying the police were coming and they were busted. I was in shock and didn't really know what to do with this information. But then it dawned on me.'

Kevin paused.

'I mean I don't want to tell you this next part because it makes me seem like an arsehole.'

He paused again, taking a sip of beer, he didn't even look at Charlie. Beads of sweat appeared on his forehead and his breathing became slightly faster.

'But what if they took his phone? I didn't know what the privacy laws were in China or if they needed a warrant to check his phone. Who *does* know what the Chinese can pull you up and arrest you on? Even after a few years I was still clueless. I told you I'd given up keeping up to date with current affairs and doing research and shit so I was in a bubble, not knowing any of the recently passed laws or announcements. Most of the people here self-censor because they live in fear that they'll be put in jail for any comment they make. Nobody knows what the red lines are – only the courts do and believe me, if you're ever pulled up in front of them, there's no point hoping they'll be lenient. You don't get a fair trial or nothing. Basically, I knew that some of the files on his phone were pornographic. In China it's a big no no, you're not allowed to share or distribute porn.'

'How did you know that?' Charlie interrupted.

'Because I was the one who sent them to him,' Kevin said. 'This whole time, I'd filmed every time I'd had sex with a girl and sent the video to him. There must have been at least 20 videos. I don't know why I did it but I felt like I should prove I was sleeping with the most girls in the little competition we were having between us. I was genuinely quite worried that if they did check through his phone, he would tell them they weren't actually his, but that they were mine and that I had sent them to him.'

Kevin stopped talking and swallowed the rest of his beer. He then turned to look at Charlie, the whites of his eyes bulging.

'Anyway, like I say I was scared he would tell them it was me. But, I realised that I could get out of this if they were proved to be his. I knew his laptop password because we'd shared some lesson plans to each other before. It was a simple password, his birthday. I logged onto his laptop and hoped to God that he used the same password for his Weibo account.'

'Oh no,' Charlie said.

'Yeah ... so I logged onto his account, transferred all the videos from my phone to his laptop and uploaded them to his Weibo account. Then logged out and deleted the videos from my phone.'

'Jesus Christ, what happened to the guy?' Charlie asked.

Kevin was silent, staring into Charlie's eyes. He turned away and looked out into the darkness.

'Turned out,' he choked, 'they never actually checked his phone when they got to the premises. He would've been given a fine, and told to leave the country for soliciting a prostitute but he wouldn't have been imprisoned. But, because his account had all the porn on it for all the university to see, he was charged with sharing obscene material and sentenced to two years in prison, before being deported back to the UK. I'm told he protested his innocence and said they were my videos but it was his social media account and they were uploaded before the police arrived to deal with the prostitute incident. Despite the fact the story was completely fishy and it was obvious it can't have been him, to anyone with a sane mind, they had proof from his account, and I guess the Chinese wanted to make an example out of him.'

Charlie sat forward and put his hand on Kevin's back.

'So why did you leave the school?'

'I decided to pack up there and then and started looking for another job. The school didn't suspect anything but I knew the girls in the class knew most of the videos would've been from me and I didn't want to take a chance, nor see them again. I guess the university had expected me to resign because they accepted quickly and seemed to be happy to get rid of me. I then moved to Guangzhou, the other side of the country, as far away as I could be from Shenyang, but still in China, before coming here last year. It's crazy that I could escape that past and still live in China but I did.'

'How many people have you told this?' Charlie asked.

'You're the first.'

'Have you talked to the guy since?'

'No … no,' he said pondering in silence. 'What exactly can I do? "Sorry for what happened mate, let's get even"?'

Kevin wiped his eyes and looked at Charlie.

'Don't worry man, those days are long past me, I wouldn't do that to you.'

Charlie looked out into the darkness beyond the window. Kevin silently sipped on his can of beer before picking up his remote and indicating they should finish the game. Pressing triangle, one of Charlie's players outmanoeuvred one of Kevin's players with a chip over his head. Just as Charlie's player was about to get to the ball again and be through on goal, Kevin pressed square and committed his player to a slide tackle from behind. Charlie's player went tumbling and had to be taken off, injured. Kevin's player was given a red card, but the goal was saved.

11

The following Monday, Kevin rushed to school, almost skipping as he dashed across the final zebra crossing to reach the front gate. Charlie, confused by this sudden display of enthusiasm, enquired about its source.

'Emma messaged me!' Kevin shouted.

Charlie, expecting something more, remained silent before realising Kevin had finished.

'Oh … Is … is that it?'

'Yeah.'

With a teenage like thrill, Kevin bounded ahead of the limping Charlie before realising he should wait for his ailing flatmate.

'Well, what did you talk about?' Charlie asked.

'Oh, nothing in particular, but don't you see what this means?'

'I know you're going to tell me anyway so I …'

'It means,' Kevin said, cutting him off, 'that I still have a chance.'

Charlie sighed but nodded in agreement.

'Yes, I suppose it does.'

It's all a game to him, Charlie thought. Explore the levels of infidelity in a woman, then move onto the next. What's the use? There's no point confronting him about it.

After they'd reached the kindergarten, Kevin ran to the playground before any of the other foreign teachers had a chance to greet them. The weather was pristine and the sun shone in rays around patches of cloud, casting morning shadows on the grass as children jostled to get the best tools for digging up the sand pit. In the corner of the playground, Emma crouched down to help children onto the trampoline, lifting them in with a surprising amount of strength for someone so thin. Her back was turned to Kevin, so he cautiously approached.

'Good morning,' he said excitedly.

'Good morning,' she beamed back.

They stood for a few moments, watching the children jumping on the trampoline, bumping into each other as they did. The other foreign teachers came out to the playground, surprised to see Kevin engaged in anything other than kicking a football around, which he did most mornings with a few of the older children who had sports lessons outside of the school.

'I liked talking to you last night,' he finally said.

'I do too,' she replied, giving him the usual smile.

There was more silence. Kevin shuffled awkwardly, only then realising this was a very open space, and he was acting very differently to how he usually would. Enough to arouse suspicions, he thought. The children on the trampoline screamed for Kevin to look at them as they somersaulted and jumped on each other. He feigned laughter, but hoped something would inspire conversation from Emma.

'When's the assembly play?' he asked.

'On Friday,' she said.

'Do you think the children will be ready?'

'Yes.'

Like trying to draw blood from a stone, he thought.

'Kevin ...' she asked shyly, 'you want see movie with me?'

Kevin's heart quickened and a warm feeling filled his cheeks.

'I would love to,' he giggled, barely suppressing the excitement in his voice, 'when?'

'Ermm ... Tonight?' she asked tentatively.

'Sure!' he replied.

The air of awkwardness lifted, and with the confidence of a confirmed time and location set in stone, they relaxed into lighter conversation. They stood, chatting and smiling until 10 a.m., shielding their eyes from the sun as they took more interest in each other than they did in the children running and screaming around them.

A tree rustled in the playground as the day darkened. The screams and shouts of children lessened as they filtered onto the surrounding streets with their parents in tow. One of the school's security guards, slouched and dragging his feet, shuffled around the school, glancing in each classroom before laboriously switching off the lights.

When he reached the foreign teachers' office, he saw Kevin still at work and cursed under his breath that he'd have to return later to switch the light off. Kevin looked up and smiled at the glum faced guard before returning to his phone, awaiting Emma's signal that she was ready to see him.

Kevin immediately jumped up at 5:32 p.m. when Emma sent the signal and dashed out of the room, forgetting to switch off the light. He bounded out of the front door as the old security man huffed. As the air became cooler, darkness grew, and the dusk settled into night, they embraced in the glow of the nearby lampposts, which cast their shadows in four directions. The scent of Emma alone was enough to excite Kevin for the promise of what lay ahead. He looked at her for a brief moment and smiled.

The local area contained an abundance of cinemas, but Emma insisted they shouldn't take the chance of bumping into anyone they might know, so they took a twenty-minute taxi to another part of Hangzhou. The ride across was silent, as if Emma was having second thoughts. Kevin, nervous like a teenager might have been, peered out into the clear night. Even for a Monday, the roads were fairly full.

Once they reached the cinema, they took a seat on a filthy couch next to a bathroom in the cold lobby and looked at the schedule on Emma's phone. Leaning in, Kevin experienced the same sensation of the toilet cubicle when they'd first been physically close.

'What about *Black Panther*?' Kevin suggested.

'Oh no,' Emma replied, 'too … erm, black. Maybe we have to sit next to black people in cinema.'

'What?' he spluttered the water he was drinking. 'What's wrong with that?'

She giggled awkwardly. 'OK, we can if you want.'

'I don't care. But what's wrong with sitting in same cinema with a black person?' he asked, confused.

'They big and scary,' she laughed.

'Emma, don't be …' he paused before continuing, 'anyway, what else is on?'

'Erm …' she said in thought as she scrolled through the list of films 'maybe *Tomb Raider*?'

'Yes, that's fine.'

After buying the tickets and a box of large salted popcorn, they entered the screening room.

The theatre wasn't big, housing perhaps 30 seats. The place was completely empty apart from a few eager teenagers at the front who were absorbed in their phones waiting for the film to start. Kevin had seen a few before and was thankful there were no adverts, nor indeed a national anthem as was the case when he'd visited Thailand.

Upon taking their seats at the back of the cinema, they sat awkwardly among some empty paper cups and popcorn boxes. Emma shuffled in her seat whilst Kevin sat still, wondering why this felt like he was a 14-year-old on his first ever date. He kicked the litter out of the way, and stretched his legs. She angled her legs towards his, her knee gently brushing his thigh.

As the film started, the room darkened. Kevin tentatively placed his arm on the rest in between them, his hand in line with her left hand, which was tightly clasped around her knee. In response, she moved her hand slightly towards his. It was agonising for both of them, each in their own mind willing the other to make the first move.

After ten minutes, during which neither had been focusing on the film, Kevin felt Emma's little finger brush his. He took his cue and moved his hand over hers, turning to her and smiling at the same time. She relaxed her grip on her knee and turned her hand around, clasping his outstretched hand. She stroked his palm with her fingers.

About halfway through the film he moved his hand to her leg and she moved hers to his. She brushed his thigh with the tips of her fingers, which made him sit up slightly. The higher her nimble fingers hovered up his thigh, the less he could control his lust. She angled her hand closer and closer until she was touching the outline of his crotch. She laughed a little and moved her face closer to his, her cheek brushing against his. By now, neither had the slightest hint of the plot of the movie. Kevin leaned in to kiss her and she whimpered. As the kissing became more aggressive, Kevin moved his hand higher up her leg. He picked her up and placed her on his lap, lips still tightly sealed around hers.

He pulled her closer to him as she slid her hands inside his underpants. Quickly turning around to glance her eyes over the near empty cinema, she tugged at his trousers.

'I want you have me every night,' she whispered into his ear.

They went to the same cinema the next evening. A couple sat next to them at the back of the screening room and they were silent throughout the whole film.

The night after, they chose a different cinema, but the room was busier and they could only hold hands. Even when they attempted a kiss, one of the couples turned around and asked them to be quiet.

After these experiences, Kevin insisted dates to the cinema were no longer enough and that they needed privacy.

'What about your house?' he whispered during Thursday morning's playtime as they stood by the trampoline together.

'But my husband,' she shot back quietly.

'You said he's never around?'

'He come home at 8. No, too hard.'

They stared at the children in front of them, jumping up and down.

'Is your husband always around on weekends?'

'Yes ... his next trip not until May.'

'Trip?'

'For work yes.'

'Dammit. That's too long away. I want to see you this weekend.'

'But how?'

Kevin pondered for a few moments as they both stared blankly ahead of them.

'Well ... Charlie already knows.'

'What?!' she almost yelped.

'Yes. But he's fine with it.'

'No, no. I can't see you then.'

'You don't have to worry about him, he doesn't care.'

He quickly grabbed her hand soothe her but she snatched it away.

'Not here,' she hissed.

'It'll be OK. You're just scared that this is too ... real,' he whispered. 'That you ... love ... me.'

She looked up into his eyes, angry at first, but soon softening to acceptance.

'OK,' she finally said 'tomorrow after school. But make sure Charlie not around.'

'Deal.'

Back at the flat that evening, Kevin told Gabriel that he planned to bring a girl back the next night. Gabriel, bemused at this politeness in advance, quizzically looked at him in a 'so what' fashion. Seeing his bemusement, Kevin explained.

'It's the teacher I work with,' he said. 'That's why I'm telling you. It would be great if, er, you know, er, you weren't around.'

'Oh, for God's sakes. Fine. Just don't get fired again,' Gabriel responded.

'Fired for what?' Charlie said, neither of them had heard him come through the front door.

'Kevin's bringing a girl back to the flat tomorrow. Old enough to be a married colleague. In fact, she is a married colleague.'

'Emma? Already? Cool ... I guess. So what?' Charlie replied.

'I knew it! God, Emma is being so wet about this. She seems to think the whole world will collapse if you know about it.'

'Kevin, have you ever thought what it must be like in her shoes?' Gabriel sighed.

'No, why?'

'I mean ... she is a married woman. This isn't some fling for her. This could mean the end of her marriage.'

'But don't worry,' Charlie butted in. 'I think every single person at the school still thinks Emma is happily married to her husband. Whatever you do with her, keep it a secret. Like we should be the only two you tell.'

'Well, I can tell the foreign teachers.'

'No!' Gabriel and Charlie said at once.

'Seriously, Kevin,' Gabriel flustered. 'Don't do this again. Take your ego out of it. Don't do it for kudos or because you want to make some point. Do it because you like her.'

Besides, aren't you dating Lesley's daughter anyway?' Charlie said.

'Yeah ... yeah. But ... you know. I don't want to put all my eggs in one basket.'

He thought this the most diplomatic thing to say.

Gabriel sighed again.

'Anyway,' Kevin continued, ignoring Gabriel's displays. 'She's coming round tomorrow after school. Is there any chance you two could be sparse?'

'Fine …' Gabriel rolled his eyes. 'I'll go to the gym.'

'Thanks,' Kevin said before turning abruptly to Charlie in the hope of a similar answer.

'Well, I'll go for a run, shall I?' Charlie said, pointing to his casted ankle.

'Please mate,' Kevin pleaded, 'just this once.'

'Alright,' Charlie huffed. 'I'll go to the cinema or something … but you owe us one,' he added.

After school the next day, as usual, Kevin waited in the office to work on his 'lesson plans'. As he pretended to type on his computer, the office went quiet, then the school went quiet. He kept checking his phone for the message that would mean it was time.

Anytime now, he was thinking, and she'll be ready for me. She knows what she's doing, more than anyone I've ever dated previously. I bet she's sat in there, stopping herself from texting me to build up my lust. Older women always know. Well, I've had enough of her games. I know what I want. She knows what I want. Why won't she get on with it?

A notification pinged on his phone and he jolted. He jumped up quickly, not even bothering to check if it was Emma.

But why this sudden desire? He thought. Within two weeks, I've gone from indifference to this, whatever it is. Maybe I'm afraid of getting older. No, turning 30 is just a part of ageing. There's nothing different about it. It's just another day in life. What about the thought of settling down with a millionaire's daughter? Not that it mattered if she liked him or he liked her, he thought, this was as good as an arranged marriage. If that's the case, Emma must be a last gasp. A last expression of my 20s.

He meandered down the stairs and out into the street, avoiding anyone's eyesight.

But then if Gabriel's right, and she breaks off her marriage, then that suggests she wants to marry me. But I can't marry her – can I? I don't really love her, I just love being with her. But at the same time I do love her. Stuck as she is in a dead-end marriage, I can save her.

He stopped at their usual spot and waited, eyes set on the doorway to the kindergarten.

But do I want to save her? Can I save her? What kind of life will I have if I do save her? I have three choices, he thought, down one path I take the easy option with Sophia. But then I would probably be unhappy. There's something different about her. She seems more independent than most Asian girls I've met. OK, let's scratch that. Option number two, I keep things going with Emma, and see what happens. I'm hardly under an obligation to marry her even if I feel compelled to. Finally, I continue with life as it has been until now. But I don't want to do this for the rest of my life, surely?

After five minutes, Emma walked out of the kindergarten, and gestured from afar for him to walk ahead and she would follow. For a moment, Kevin stood confusedly, but then saw a few of the parents from Emma's class exiting the building behind her.

Kevin paced away, trying to avoid being noticed by the children. As he turned the corner of the building, he had to swerve to avoid being hit by someone wheeling a motorcycle out of the car park. The person shouted obscenities in Chinese at him before putting the key to the motorbike into the ignition. He continued to walk, crossing the car park and reaching the main road. There, he turned around to see Emma 30 metres behind him, gesturing for him to keep going. He kept walking, this time a little slower, but she refused to catch up, acting like a tiger which didn't pounce until the moment is right. He became agitated. He'd been looking forward to this all day, and suddenly she didn't want to be seen with him.

Was she not as excited to be with him as he was to be with her? He thought. Maybe she wasn't. Maybe I've misjudged that woman.

After five minutes of walking, he looked behind and saw her typing something into her phone about 40 metres away. He felt his phone vibrate in his pocket and took it out to read her message. It said, 'u wait at end of road by river'. The river was a further 400 metres ahead. Once he got there, he looked over the bank into the vast darkness of the water below, before looking up at the outline of the dark hills on the other side of the embankment.

I can't spend the rest of my life chasing girls, he thought. Maybe this isn't for me.

As she sidled up next to him, she hugged his arm, tightly and with affection. All the anger he'd felt vanished and he lifted her chin to meet his lips in a kiss.

His mind suddenly burned with desire and he could only think of one thing he wanted to do.

They didn't talk as he turned around to lead her toward his flat. Only when they reached within a stone's throw of his neighbourhood did she let go of his hand – not that it stopped the security guards staring. One of them spat in disgust on the ground, as they always did when Kevin brought a Chinese girl back.

In the lift up to the apartment, as soon as the doors shut, he grabbed her waist and pushed her against the side, breaking the plastic of an advertising board. For the short ride, they passionately kissed, she groaned as he held her arms at her side.

They sidled into the apartment, still kissing. He grabbed her bag and chucked it on the floor. Before she could even take her shoes off, he pulled her into his room. When they were there, he let her go. After closing the large curtains of the window to prevent prying eyes, he turned around to see her with her shoes off, standing motionless in the middle of the room. She had an innocent look on her face.

12

'The weather in China is most pleasant in the spring and the autumn, when the climate is welcoming and invites a spirit of outdoor activity. As April turns to May and the air fills with heat, the cicadas' chorus of clicks fills the air with vibrations of energy. The hotter it gets, the more the cold days of winter are longed for, and the harder they become to remember as people look at the buildings shimmering in heat, slumbered on their chairs. The first week of May every year is a week of celebration and holiday. As a communist country, May Day is specially celebrated, and everyone gets five days holiday. Unfortunately, when approximately 1.5 billion people get five days off at the same time, they all want to travel, which makes the act particularly unpleasant. The trains are stuffed, the hotels overpriced, and the tourist sights crammed – even the mountain tops have queues … What do you think?'

'Sound like you're trying to write a novel,' Charlie remarked.

'It's terrible, isn't it?' Gabriel replied.

'I didn't say that.'

'I can tell by the tone of your voice you did.'

'Don't be silly, I'm trying to be supportive.'

They were on their way to Hangzhou railway station via the metro. Charlie, lacking money and still struggling with his ankle, had decided that for the May Day holiday and with Gabriel as guide, he would join his flatmate on one of his trips to Shanghai. Gabriel, very well plugged into the expat community, had noticed there was a beer festival on in the gardens of a hotel in the centre of the French Concession. It was a chance to get drunk and enjoy the sunshine, so they decided on finding a place nearby to stay, and then spend the afternoon lazily drinking beer before heading back the next day. Kevin, who took this opportunity to have the flat alone with Emma, readily declined, insisting they spend a second night and, if they really insisted, he would pay for their third night.

Throughout the month of April, Kevin and Emma's passionate love affair had quickened in pace and now encompassed even more of their lives outside of school. All of the foreign teachers were aware of it, but for Emma's sake, didn't speak of it unless exclusively amongst themselves. Not that this would have mattered much. The lives of the locals and expats barely intertwined. The language barrier being all too much for most people. However, one slip of the tongue at the wrong moment and it was likely Emma would be fired. Now the initial awkwardness was gone, Emma and Kevin spent every weekday evening together – her husband in complete ignorance of events.

Emma had chosen to tell Kevin who had in turn told the foreign teachers – not that they wanted to know – all the reasons why she was having an affair on her husband. When she had turned 30, only two years before, she had been told that her days to find a rich, attractive husband were over. Her parents insisted she should instead find someone who would provide and care for her, and to do it before she aged any further. They'd known her now husband for a few years as a prosperous, hard-working man they had met at a family friend's wedding, and pushed her to accept his offer of a date. She'd reluctantly accepted and, about a week after her 30th birthday, went with him to the nicest restaurant in Ningbo, the town where she had grown up. From there, a form of friendship developed. Within a few months they were married and she moved to his home town of Hangzhou to start a new life.

Emma explained there was no physical attraction. She found her husband's body repulsive and had seized up on the night of their wedding, subjecting herself without emotion to his advances. He was out of shape, with balding hair and bad teeth. He also snored 'loud enough to shake the ceiling', and she found it hard to sleep in the same bed as him at night. He was seven years older than her too, but she suspected he'd never been with anyone else.

However, she insisted he had some redeeming qualities. For example, a kind heart that forgave Emma any wrongdoing. As far as Kevin could see, Emma was a terrible wife for what she was doing, but her husband was a terrible husband for allowing it to happen in the first place. He'd remarked to the other foreign teachers that, 'A wife is not a possession, but a man who kowtows to his wife is no man at all – how he could not suspect her after she returned smelling of another man with her hair and make up slightly frazzled, is a mystery to me'. Not that he thought he should change his behaviour as a result.

For Charlie and Gabriel, his long suffering and discreet flatmates, the tiptoeing around the subject was at times incredibly frustrating. They hated that Kevin was pulling a marriage apart, but knowing where their friendships and loyalties lay, brushed aside the issue and gave him their support. This May Day holiday could not have come sooner – they looked forward to getting out of the house and away from the drama of the affair.

Hangzhou East railway station, like all railway stations in China, Gabriel explained, was more like an airport than a train station. The security to get through to the near 30 platforms was as rigorous as that at JFK airport. The ceiling, dome shaped and composed of frosted glass, was at least 80 metres tall, but when it rained, not a sound could be heard on the concourse below. The concourse itself was at least 200 metres long, and took a few minutes to cover by foot. Elevators led up to a row of restaurants, whose smell drifted below and filled the noses of hungry passengers.

Gabriel, knowing the state of Chinese transportation during holidays, and with Charlie still on crutches, insisted they get there at least an hour early. They were happy they did. As soon as they stepped off the metro at the station, they were swamped by a moving mass of Chinese bodies. From the metro station platform to the ticket office three floors up, they weren't able to speak, nor breathe without being pushed into by a fellow passenger. At the ticket office, every line for a ticket booth stretched 20 metres back, but some people didn't think any of the rules of queueing applied to them.

'Oh, for fuck's sake. Another one,' Charlie huffed. 'Honestly, it's crazy that for a country with advanced methods of payment, and high-speed trains, they still haven't been able to sort out the state of their stupid ticketing.'

'Yeah, I don't know why they don't just allow you to show a train ticket on your phone.'

'How much longer do you think we'll have to wait?'

'A few more years.'

'I was talking about the queue.'

'So was I.'

Charlie watched the pack of people with near disgust as his foot began to ache from standing on it for too long.

After they'd received their tickets, they joined the concourse of the main train station, getting to their platform just in time for boarding.

The train slowly built up speed, and pretty soon, Charlie was over-awed. The countryside around them blurred into one as they shot through the air at over 200km/h, defying the hilly terrain around them. The ride was smooth and the seats spacious despite their usual patron being an Asian of a small frame.

A small boy in the seat in front of them spent the entire hour-long journey propped up on his seat, staring at them – whenever Gabriel tried to engage him in conversation he jumped down and laughed before returning to his position of looking at them like they were zoo animals. Once they'd arrived in Shanghai, they were again swamped until they reached South Shanxi Road Metro Station where they disembarked, to their relief, onto an almost empty platform.

The French Concession reminded Charlie of Paris. The avenues of trees, the neoclassical structures of colonial times; ruined by years of neglect but their essence still alive in the buildings. The air was pleasant as they walked the streets towards the festival, neither too hot, nor too cold. It allowed you to be fashionable without being excessive, and both the boys, having travelled to Shanghai for leisure, had dressed to impress. They wore silk shirts with luscious patterns, and matching white summer trousers which Charlie had cut slightly to allow his casted foot to fit through. As the clothing was from Taobao, his entire get up was inexpensive and easily replaceable.

When they reached the venue, they were impressed by the array of food and the beer selection. This being Shanghai, many of the world's largest brewers had paid for a tent, and they were handing out vast quantities of free samples to eager punters. The largest tent was reserved for the home-grown beer of choice, Tsingtao, crammed with foreigners and locals alike. The venue itself – the garden of a 1920's colonial club that had been converted into a hotel – was a rare green space in the sprawling metropolis of Shanghai.

Gabriel and Charlie were in a familiar heaven. Within an hour they'd sampled every free beer before stumbling onto the lawn and unfurling a picnic mat Gabriel had brought. The smell of freshly cut grass alongside the background murmur of crowds induced Charlie to drift in and out of sleep, tired from hobbling on his crutches since the morning. Next to him, Gabriel vigorously flicked through Tinder. After he'd established that one of his matches was also at the beer festival, he shook Charlie awake and told him he'd be back in a while. Charlie grunted in approval before closing his eyes again and drifting into partial sleep once more.

Some time later, Charlie was again awoken, this time by a child sticking their finger up his nose. Charlie snorted and sat upright immediately. He wanted to shout but the little boy had run back to his mother. 'Little shit,' he muttered, at the same time smiling at the mother.

Now wide awake, he yawned before standing up for a stretch and looking at his watch. He had been asleep for over an hour. Picking up his crutches, he surveyed the immediate area. The oak trees, a rarity in China, were strewn around the grounds of the hotel, enabling festival goers to saunter out of the heat and lay in their cool shadows. Most people had picnic mats out and were dining on sandwiches, fruit and little snacks easily bought in corner shops. Whereas the foreigners in the garden were munching on muesli bars, the locals gorged on chicken feet, crunchy with a hint of salt. The main area of the festival was at the far end of the garden, and enclosed a stage with live music. There was a party atmosphere in the air and the music, loud to the point of blurring, drew everyone into its vicinity. Charlie packed up the picnic mat, put it in his bag then slung it around his back. He hobbled towards the music stage, passing inebriated people urinating behind the food stands, their owners too busy to care.

When he'd reached the edge of the main area, he hopped onto the side of a food van to try and get a better look. All he could see was a sea of heads, bopping, swerving, and ducking to the music. He heard someone call his name but couldn't quite see who it was, the crowd being thick with people who all wore the same style of clothing. About ten heads in front he saw Gabriel with a few other men who all had their shirts opened to expose their chests. Each had a little necklace, wore the same sorts of sunglasses, and had identical haircuts. Charlie piled through the crowd towards them, apologising as his crutches stood on reveller's bare feet. They turned round aggressively before apologising when they saw the reason.

'Charlie, come meet my new friends!' Gabriel shouted over the music when he saw his injured friend approach.

'Hello,' Charlie said awkwardly.

'Hello handsome,' one of the new friends said.

'Oh no, he's not gay,' Gabriel interrupted.

'He doesn't need to be … he's still handsome.'

'He's new to China,' Gabriel responded. 'Charlie, this is Wayne, Wayne, Charlie.'

'No way! What do you think?' an excited Wayne shouted over the sound of the music.

'I love it. So friendly.'

'Yes we are.'

Wayne's Hawaiian shirt clung loosely to his shoulders as he bopped in time to the music.

'How do you know Gabriel?' Wayne shouted in his ear.

'We're flatmates.'

'He's my flatmate for tonight,' Wayne laughed.

Wayne's friends looked towards Charlie and Wayne talking with envy. One of them whispered something in Wayne's ear.

'My friend wants to know if you're really straight … or just a little bi-curious.'

'No, I'm really straight,' Charlie replied quickly, almost aggressively.

'No need to be so scared honey, we're not going to bite.'

As the afternoon wore on, the light turned to darkness and the families began to filter out. Gabriel said he was heading with his new friends to a gay bar on the other side of town and invited Charlie to join them. Initially hesitant, all the gays insisted there would be girls there too despite the emphasis of the place – besides, the crutches would get him sympathy from everyone. Not wanting to spend the night alone on his first trip to Shanghai, he accepted their invitation and joined them as they crowded into taxis on the streets outside the venue.

During the taxi journey he politely declined an advance by one of the troupe who slid his hand onto his knee. Gabriel noticed and began a conversation in Chinese that seemed to interest the guy more.

They swooped into the nightclub in one large group, and immediately Charlie was hit by a wall of heat and sweat, which flared his nostrils and stung his eyes. Most of the patrons had their tops off and stepped from side to side, in beat with the heavy music, more at home in Berlin than the gay bars Charlie had heard of. As he waddled through the crowd staying as close as he could to Gabriel, people pinched his cheeks and slapped his arse, violating his personal space and giving him new cause to become a feminist. One highly inebriated person grabbed one of his crutches to the chagrin of Gabriel in front who wrestled it back from him.

When they'd reached the seats at the edge of the venue, Charlie sat down for a rest, exhausted from the sun of the afternoon and the heat of the dark club.

'Hey, is this seat taken?' an attractive girl asked.

'No! Come sit down,' he shouted back.

'Hi, I'm Sally,' she slurred into his ear.

'Hi, Charlie.'

'No, I said Sally ha ha,' she swayed from side to side.

'Oh no I said … never mind. Where are your friends?'

'Wayne's my friend, he sent me over for some reason.'

'Is that so …' Charlie wondered aloud, looking across to see Wayne, beside Gabriel, raising a glass at him from the middle of the dance floor.

'You don't seem very talkative,' Sally said drunkenly.

'Oh no, I'm just tired, I guess. And this music is too loud.'

'You want to go for a smoke?'

'Can't you smoke in here?' he replied, immediately regretting it.

'Yes, I guess,' she said disappointedly.

The night wore on and, as the beer of earlier in the day wore off, his ankle started to throb in short bursts of sharp pain. The girl, bored of his company and unsure of his sexuality, left him without saying goodbye. Not seeing Gabriel anywhere, he decided to leave and limped embarrassedly towards the exit, trying his best to ignore the pinches and slaps that once again started.

Once outside the club, he hailed a taxi and said 'Bund' in a loud clear accent. The taxi driver nodded his head before switching on his meter. The driver tried to engage in conversation in Chinese, but Charlie shrugged, saying one of the few phrases he knew how to say, 'I don't understand'. This only induced the driver to continue until he realised this was the one phrase his passenger knew.

Throughout the journey, Charlie sat in silence as the car drove past the still thronging streets, alive with the energy of young people.

This is so much better than Hangzhou, he thought to himself. At least places are open past 10 p.m. It feels like New York, or London – a city of history and a city of the future wrapped into one.

The highways, suspended mid-air over the streets below, gave expansive views of the skyline, stretching out into the distance. There were rows and rows of apartment buildings all around, each at least 20 storeys in height. Interspersed at regular intervals, were representations of the old Shanghai – grand, colonial buildings, often with the Communist Party emblem proudly displayed at their top from the time they were commandeered in the late 1940s. It was hard not to stare in awe at the beauty of this chaotic spectacle.

Arriving at the Bund, Charlie hopped out of the car, and smiled at the taxi driver who waved in appreciation. Turning around as the car sped away, he hobbled onto the platform which overlooked the river's edge. It was 2 a.m., yet the platform still had many couples, arm in arm taking photos with the well-known Pearl Tower backdrop – the surrounding buildings ablaze with light.

Behind him, facing the river, stood many old buildings that reminded Charlie of the City of London – short in height but dignified in nature and appearance. Like elsewhere dotted around Shanghai, they were European colonial in design and adorned with statues of Roman gods. On the other side of the river stood a seemingly endless backdrop of skyscrapers reaching taller the further back they were built from the river's edge. He sat down on a nearby flower bank and stared at this image of China's future – the brightness of the shining displays; the chaos of skyscrapers competing for the skyline; the inadequateness of the colonial buildings behind him in the face of it.

In the morning, Charlie woke up to the sight of an empty bed next to his in the Airbnb. He checked his phone and saw a message from Gabriel which said he'd meet him at the train station at 3 p.m. This left Charlie with the morning and some of the afternoon to pass, and he was thrilled to get a chance to see Shanghai in the full glory of this sunny spring day. As he hurriedly grabbed his crutches, he planned what he would try to see. Firstly, he thought, he wanted to view the streets of the French Concession and drink a proper coffee for the first time in the three months since he'd left home. He wanted to explore the financial district, and window shop on the famous Nanjing Road. He hired a taxi through the app on his phone and selected the address of a coffee shop Gabriel had mentioned the day before on the streets of the French Concession.

He knew he'd arrived when the scenery outside the taxi windows changed from apartment buildings to leafy European avenues. The boutique clothing stores and bakeries, together with restaurants and antique shops incited a nostalgia for London. Once he'd arrived at the café, he shuffled eagerly to a table outside. After ordering a Cappuccino and Danish, he slumped himself into a chair and observed the elegance of the people around him.

The streets were alive with the throng of young, fashionable, good looking people. The style of the West transposed onto the energy of the East. The street was a melting pot of all cultures and ways of life which reminded Charlie of the time he'd visited Hong Kong with his parents many years before. The same chaotic narrow streets, the same dress sense of its people, and the same level of English overheard from passing locals.

After he'd finished his coffee and Danish, he jumped in another taxi and arrived in time for lunch at Nanjing Road. A now pedestrianised commercial road, there were department stores alongside eateries as far as the eye could see. The street was filled with a sea of people, eating sticks of meat and carrying multiple bags of shopping. All the big chains were on this road, and some of the older ones of Shanghai's past. Initially part of the International Concession in Shanghai, there were still flickers of the 1920s. Some mannequins in shop windows displayed the bobbed haircut with patterned blouses and skirts of the time. There were post-cards of old Shanghai at some of the tourist shops too. Charlie picked one up which joked, 'The International Settlement is about as interna-tional as the Tower of London'.

After buying himself a couple of sticks of meat at a street food stall, he found a bench and sat down. The meat was salty and Charlie had asked for extra spice which made him quickly thirst for a drink. Knowing he was on a deadline, he shoved it into his mouth till his cheeks were bursting, and washed it down with a bottle of water he'd taken from the Airbnb that morning, now lukewarm and crinkled. The day was heating up quickly and the sun felt harsh on his skin, bringing out spots of prickly heat.

In the taxi again, he typed in the financial district as his destination and showed it to the driver who looked behind him bemusedly. He checked his watch to see it was almost 1 p.m. Knowing how bad the ticket queues had been in Hangzhou, he told himself to be at the station at 2 p.m., which gave him 20 minutes to explore the streets on the other side of the river. When he arrived, he hopped around as fast as he could, trying to absorb the atmosphere of the roads despite the fact it was a weekend, and the streets were almost empty, bar a few which led to shopping malls. Everywhere he craned his neck to look at had tall spires pointing to heaven. He imagined the energy it must have on a normal working day and was jealous he could not be a part of it.

Noticing the time, he reluctantly hailed his final taxi and asked to go to the train station. As the taxi crossed the river over a bridge, he looked back at the skyscrapers and sighed. He was convinced this magical city was the place for him, and knew he wanted to see it many more times in the years to come. He opened his phone and found where he saved his cover letter.

Gabriel was already waiting with the tickets at the train station.

'Where've you been? It leaves in five minutes,' he exclaimed.

'Sorry, the traffic was bad.'

They rushed down the escalator and jumped on the train just as it was about to leave. As it exited the station, they found their seats and, panting heavily, sat down. Gabriel, confident that nobody would understand him, told Charlie in graphic detail what he'd been up to the night before.

'So, will you see him again?' Charlie asked innocently.

'Hell to the no!' Gabriel replied. 'His dick was way too small.'

'Does that really matter?'

'You're very young, aren't you?'

'No, I'm not, but surely a dick's just a dick?'

'What! Don't make me laugh.'

The train passed through some fields as it picked up more speed.

'When did you realise you were gay?' Charlie asked.

'Oh, I was young. I think like 12 or 13, and I remember going to watch my big brother play in the local schools' football final and I couldn't take my eyes off their quarterback, he was so dreamy. Since then, I kinda knew I was more attracted to guys than girls. I just couldn't tell anyone. I was from a Catholic family in Texas, ya don't get much more conservative than that.'

'Did your parents care?'

'Well … my dad did … my mom said she still loved me but I knew she was disappointed.'

'Jesus.'

Charlie shuffled in his place, regretful that he'd broached the subject to begin with.

'Er … do you speak to your parents anymore?'

'Not my dad, but I have brothers and sisters I speak to.'

'Oh, that's good, at least there were others.'

'What do you mean by that?'

'Oh shit, no, sorry I didn't mean to be offensive, I just thought that if there are brothers and sisters, surely that whole thing about having to be the man in the house as a son doesn't really matter as much.'

'You'd think,' Gabriel said bitterly, staring out the window. 'but … I don't know, I just wish he'd said *I love you son* once more after that.'

'Maybe he still will?'

'I don't know … My brother says he took down my school photos after I moved to California. Basically acts like he never had me.'

'When was the last time you went home?'

'I dropped off my car at the house before I came to China a few years ago but he'd gone out shooting or something, only mom and my brothers and sisters came to say goodbye.'

'I'm sorry.'

'For what?'

'For bringing the topic up, I shouldn't have.'

'No, it's OK … you didn't know.'

When they arrived at Hangzhou, they got on the metro and chatted some more about their love of Shanghai. Gabriel said he tried to go once a fortnight if he could because it was the best place for a foreigner, but at the same time he found the city too lively for his Texas country boy heart.

'It's tough. I love my home, but I love the thrill of the city. At the same time, I hate my home, and I feel scared in big cities. Do you know what I mean?'

Charlie silently nodded, more out of politeness than agreement. Gabriel continued, 'It's just … I can't go back. No … I won't go back. If I go back, what's the use? What can I do back home I can't do here? I guess I could become a yoga instructor or something, or become an English teacher, but I can do that here, and I'm already set up. I might as well stay,' he concluded, though by this time he wasn't even looking at Charlie for a response.

When they reached their neighbourhood, Gabriel stopped in the middle of the street, and stared ahead of him.

'What are they doing here?' he exclaimed.

Charlie, who had continued hopping, turned around a few metres ahead.

'Who are where?' he asked.

'The Iranians,' Gabriel pointed.

Ahead of them at the gate to their neighbourhood stood a man and woman of brown complexion, smoking cigarettes and talking to each other. He had short dark hair in the style of a young Elvis Presley, with wide set eyes and a clean-shaven face, whilst she had curly brown hair, dyed in an ombre style, with a face scarred by teenage acne. They looked strangely familiar to Charlie. He couldn't place his finger on it but he felt he'd seen them before.

Gabriel grabbed Charlie and pushed him in another direction towards the other entrance to the neighbourhood, but not before they'd been noticed. The man waved at them with a smile and jogged across, his wife close behind him.

'Gabriel!' he said in a thick Persian accent, 'how are you, my friend?'

'Heyyyy,' Gabriel grimaced. 'Gooood.'

They stared at each other for a few moments, Gabriel trying his best to make it clear he was in no mood to talk. The Iranian didn't catch on, and continued. 'My friend, you didn't reply to my messages. 'Why not?'

'You know …' Gabriel said only for Charlie to interject.

'He's been super busy.'

He held out his hand for the man to shake. The Iranian took it but kept looking at Gabriel. 'Maybe we can have a talk upstairs?'

Gabriel, never one to say no in a situation, even to an unwanted guest, for fear of creating a sour atmosphere, agreed.

As they awkwardly walked through the gate to the community in silence, the man's wife tried to help Charlie. He politely declined but she insisted she carry his backpack.

In the lift, Charlie felt her hand touch his bottom, but didn't complain, assuring himself it was only because the lift was small in size. As they opened the door to the flat, it suddenly occurred to Charlie that Emma would be there. He quickly held the handle to the door and whispered to Gabriel that maybe they should knock first. Gabriel's eyes widened as he realised what a terrible mistake he had made.

'You know what guys …' he said, turning around to face the two Iranians 'er … the flat's so dirty. I'm so embarrassed, you shouldn't come in.'

Inside, something crashed to the floor while there was a patter of feet, it was clear Emma and Kevin had heard the dialogue at the door and escaped to his room. The Iranians, short on temper stormed into the flat.

'Hey what are you doing?' Gabriel protested.

'Listen,' the Iranian said, turning in the middle of the room. 'Why haven't you replied? I thought we were friends? And you upset my wife very much by your actions.'

'Get out of my flat!'

'Not until you explain what happened!'

At that point, the Iranian noticed Kevin's lesson plan book on the table. It was bound in red leather and had the kindergarten's crest on it.

'Hey, our son goes there,' he said pointing at the book. He turned to his wife. 'Honey, that's Ardi's school isn't it?'

'Yes,' she said obediently.

'Of course!' Charlie thought. He'd seen them at the kindergarten before. He didn't know what class their son was in but he'd given a polite nod and smile to them.

There was another notebook next to Kevin's, almost identical, but this one had notes written in Chinese stuffed messily inside. The Iranian walked across and picked it up.

'What are these doing here? Did you steal them?' he asked seriously.

'No of course not,' Gabriel said. 'They're Kevin and Charlie's. They both work at the kindergarten.'

'Oh of course!' the Iranian exclaimed. 'I recognise you yes … but these are in Chinese. You speak Chinese Charlie?'

'No,' he replied.

The room filled with silence. Emma and Kevin must've been in the middle of a movie because Kevin's laptop was stood open on the sofa, power still on with the screen paused. Their half eaten lunch stood cold on the coffee table in front of them, chopsticks suspended in the rice.

'What are these?' the wife asked, pointing at Emma's small, fur coat on the hanger, it had her perfume scent emanating from it. 'You wear this?' she said looking at Charlie.

'No, no, no … er Kevin's girlfriend's,' he added hastily.

'Look, I think it's time you left,' Gabriel said.

'But we haven't finished!' the man protested.

'Yes we have,' Gabriel said firmly, surprised by the authority in his voice.

Charlie didn't notice if it was hatred, tiredness, or embarrassment at the situation he'd got them into, but a sudden strength came to Gabriel as he swept the Iranians out of the door before slamming it shut. He turned with an exasperated look towards Charlie. 'God I wish I'd never spoken to that guy.'

Charlie laughed before smiling admiringly at the person he had come to know over the previous two days.

Kevin tentatively peaked his head around the door. 'Coast clear?' he asked, his own observations reaching the conclusion without the need for it to be answered. He opened the door further and Emma popped out with him, wearing one of Kevin's t-shirts which didn't hide the fact she was naked underneath.

'Who were they?' he asked.

'Ugh the Iranians … turns out their son goes to the kindergarten.'

Emma's face went white.

'What?' Kevin exclaimed, 'Shit!'

'Don't worry. I told them your girlfriend was here. I don't think they suspect anything.'

13

Kevin paced along the waterfront at West Lake. The evening, though a little cloudy and with a strong breeze, was pleasant, and the edge of the lake was a throng of people, even in the relatively bad weather. Every inch of pavement seemed to be taken up by someone's foot. He checked his watch every few moments to make sure he wasn't late. Arriving ten minutes before the 7 p.m. agreed time, he loitered for a few seconds before finding a flower bank to sit on. He looked at the water lapping on the side of the lake, slowly eroding the stone as it had done for over a millennia. Further along the water's edge, he saw a light show beginning with a fairly substantial crowd gathered, cameras out, craning their necks to get the best view they could. Kevin smiled. Bunch of ants, he thought to himself.

'Are you still dating her?' Charlie had asked as he'd been getting ready earlier.

'Yes of course. Why do you ask?'

'I mean … you're spending every waking moment with Emma.'

'Her husband's at home tonight, she can't go out.'

'And you don't feel any … how shall I say … you know … double crossingness?'

'No, why should I?'

'Kevin, how long are you going to keep this up?' Charlie had scoffed.

'As long as I bloody want.'

'Alright, alright … what do you even still see in Sophia? You obviously prefer someone else.'

'I don't know man, the dates are so damn boring. She has a view on everything that seems to divide the world into right and wrong. It's like she's already in her 40s or something.'

'Isn't that what you want? To settle down?'

'I do but not with a bore.'

'From what I can tell she's not a bore at all. She just won't agree with you on everything.'

'Well yeah, but that's beside …'

'Does Emma agree with you on everything?' Charlie cut in.

'No … She sometimes wants to watch different movies.'

Charlie laughed. 'Oh Kevin … Come on … Don't be so disingenuous, you know what I mean.'

'Well, I don't want to spend all my time arguing with someone.'

'It doesn't sound like you're arguing at all, just disagreeing on some things which is part of intellectual conversation. From what you told me, had you met someone like Sophia when you first came out to China, you would've really enjoyed her company.'

Kevin pondered this as he sat on the flower bank overlooking West Lake. Had he really changed that much in the intervening years? He thought. It didn't feel like it. What even is beauty? The intellect has something to do with it. Competence more so. Do I really only care about looks? Nonsense, there was something more to Emma. Wasn't there?

Someone tapped his shoulder. Deep in thought he hadn't seen Sophia approach in her elegant blue dress, silk lapping over one side of her shoulder and down as far as her knees, with a generous slit that showed off her right thigh. She looked stunning in the moonlight, its white shining off her dark eyes, and her hair shimmering. She offered her cheek for him to softly brush with his lips.

'You're late,' he said.

'Sorry,' she replied. 'I had to finish packing my bag for tomorrow's flight. I have to get up at 6 a.m.!'

'Where are you going?'

'I told you, back to New York for a few months. Did you forget?'

Kevin laughed awkwardly before grabbing her hand.

'Hang on, let me put my coat back on.'

She put on her black trench coat, then grabbed his left arm with both of hers. She crouched a little toward him, trying to use his body and coat to shield herself from the wind. As they walked, they talked about what they'd been getting up to during the week. Kevin lied and said he'd gone to Shanghai with the others whilst she had spent most of it helping her mother look over financial records.

'How fun,' he replied drearily.

The crystal moon's reflection could be seen in the clean water, still like a sheet of paper, so calm it mirrored each crevice and crater on the moon's surface. The hills on the other side of the lake loomed dark, encircling the lake in its own little world, giving it a foreboding, surreal feeling. Walking around its edge, the branches and leaves of trees above cast shadows of moonlight onto the ground. Around the lake, couples walked arm in arm, stopping every so often to kiss, each in their own little world. There was a truly magic feeling to this place which made Kevin wish he was there at that moment with Emma instead of Sophia.

After they found their lakeside bar, situated in an old 1930's house, they sat inside at a table which overlooked the lake below. He ordered a bloody mary whilst she opted for a gin and tonic. They sat in silence for a few minutes appreciating the view outside, the little bubble they were in still unbroken. When the drinks arrived, Kevin took one gulp which drained about half of the glass, then set it down and leant forward.

'So, what are your plans for the future?' Sophia finally asked.

'I'm not sure. What about you?'

'I'd like to move to America in the long run, after spending a few years here.'

'America? Why would you want to go there, when you could live here?'

'Freedom.'

Alright, let's see where this goes, he thought. Charlie said I should engage in more intellectual conversation.

'Freedom? It's run by a fascist at the moment. What freedom can you have there that you can't get here?'

'Fascist? Only someone who doesn't understand authoritarianism would call Donald Trump a fascist. I don't like him but thankfully the American constitution prevents him from doing too much wrong in the world.'

'Why do you even like America? You're Chinese,' Kevin said with surprising bitterness.

'I think America is one of the greatest countries in the world.'

'What are you on about? They committed war crimes in Vietnam and Cambodia, topple governments they don't like, and treat black people in their country appallingly … just like second class citizens.'

'And yet, despite all their faults, they are still a shining beacon that all should follow.'

'Ugh, go on then, explain,' he said, leaning back.

'Nations hold America to a much tougher standard than they hold any other country. It is a measure of their success and their failings that they hold such a sway on everyone's psyche – everyone has an opinion one way or another, often because of the soft power they hold through cinema and the fact the English language is almost universally known. Think about it, when America does something wrong, the whole world moans at it because their leaders are so often on a moral high horse that we all laugh when they fall off – it is our hatred at their belief in the universality of democracy that brings it about. But think about it, it is also our jealousy at their wealth and confidence. We want to be like them and that's why we hate them, we hate what we can't have. But why can't we be like them? Because our leaders won't allow our constitutions to be based on theirs. Instead of starting from democratic first principles, a lot of nations start from authoritarian principles because that means the people in charge can reserve wealth for the top. There can be no social mobility unless you bring down your fellow man, either through corruption or downright exploitation. So long as you effectively pay off the people at the top, either through bribes or silence to their wrongdoings, you can reach the top. Under democracy it is the opposite, you can only reach the top by helping your fellow man. The second you do something bad to your fellow man, you are ostracized because your actions are transparent. When they are caught out and it's published in the news, it is not hypocrisy that it happens in America, it is actually an example of the system working, because only in America could they be found out.'

'But like I said, America treats some of its own people like second class citizens. They can't reach the top.'

'The only reason you know about that is because America has a free press due to its democratic principles. The only reason you don't hear very much about how ethnic minorities in China are treated awfully is because China controls what people can and can't say. Just look at the protests in Hong Kong in 2014, they happened because the one place in China that can speak up against Communist Party rule, ultimately did. I hope to God nothing ever changes Hong Kong's ability to stand up to the mainland because that will be the first warning bell. What's that poem again? First they came for the Jews, and I said nothing ... then they came for me, and there was no one to speak on my behalf, or something like that.'

'You're the least Chinese, Chinese person I've ever met.'

'I take that as a compliment. You should visit Taiwan, they're more like me.'

'But you still haven't convinced me why America has to be overseas. Why are they in Asia at all? Why can't they leave foreign countries alone? It's because all they want to do is exploit these countries ... it's neo-colonialism.'

'Because fledgling countries around the world are too weak. Think about it, after the American War of Independence, it took a century before America was finally strong enough to enter the world. Due to its geographic isolation, it *could* be left alone without the colonialist Europeans forcing their will on America. Because of the lack of technology at the time, America existed in a perfect vacuum where no power could intervene. Now look at these African and Asian countries that are also fledgling. If America wasn't present, who would fill the vacuum? The only country rich enough to fill the vacuum is China, and they haven't left these African countries alone. These fledgling democracies will ultimately turn to totalitarianism on the China model, because the second they become democracies, they will stand up to China. China's incentive is to make sure they remain authoritarian, hence why they support Venezuela, Iran, all these places where the lives of ordinary people don't matter.'

Kevin, flustered, fidgeted in his seat. There was something about her fierce independence of mind he didn't like. He didn't like that she wouldn't just agree with him – why wouldn't she just agree? Surely if her initial intention was to find a potential husband, she should just agree with whatever he said, not go about saying what felt like the contrary the whole time.

'Kevin!' a shout came from across the bar.

Kevin, who was about to make a point about the improvement of the current Iranian regime over what had existed before under the Shah's, looked up.

'Oh shit,' he whispered before hiding his face.

'What's wrong?' Sophia responded, turning around to see who it was. An attractive local girl in her 20s was striding across. She was similarly attired to Sophia but it was clear the clothing quality was cheaper.

'Sophia, whatever she says, it's a lie.'

'I'll be the judge of that,' she responded.

'Kevin!' the girl repeated as she approached the table, 'where have you been, why haven't you texted me back?'

'Chanel, it's been a long time since I saw you.'

'No it hasn't, you only saw me in March.'

'Well, yeah, but I haven't seen you since.'

'Why were you still texting me then?'

'No ... I didn't do that.'

Chanel took her phone out

'Yes you were, April 18th ... "Hey, want to meet up this weekend?" "Sure", April 20th "Hey, what time tonight?" and you never replied. April 29th "Hey I missed my period, can we meet up?"'

Sophia's eyes widened.

'You never sent me that, what are you on about?'

'Who's this?' Chanel pointed accusingly at Sophia. 'Is this that *teacher* you've been sleeping with I heard about. Kevin, I could be pregnant and you're out with another girl.'

'I don't even know you,' Kevin protested loudly. 'Besides what the hell are you doing in a bar if you're pregnant?'

By now people at other tables had noticed the commotion and watched Kevin shuffle in his seat, half grimacing, half chuckling in embarrassment. Sophia, composed, leaned back and picked up her drink before draining its contents.

'Sophia, I can explain,' he said turning pleadingly towards her.

'Well go on then,' she calmly replied.

'Yeah, go on,' Chanel exclaimed, standing by the table with her arms folded.

'Well ... I knew this girl before I met you ... and she and I well ... you know ... anyway, I haven't met up with her since I've known you.'

Sophia leaned forward before looking up at Chanel.

'Chanel, it is Chanel, isn't it? Come sit down, are you OK?'

She grabbed a chair from the table behind and placed it in front of her. Chanel sat in it, wiping at her eyes as if on the verge of tears. By now the whole bar was staring at the table.

'What are you all looking at?' Kevin shouted aggressively.

Sophia rubbed Chanel's back and took a tissue from her purse. Kevin looked out of the window at the lake. The wind had picked up while they'd been in the bar and with it the calm serenity of the lake disappeared – small waves hit into each other and the moon looked distorted in its reflection on the water's surface.

'Kevin, I think it's time you left,' Sophia finally said calmly.

'No,' he muttered under his breath. 'I'm not going to …' but then he realised this was his only way out, he simply hadn't liked to listen to someone telling him what to do.

He stood up laboriously then walked a few paces before turning around, lifting up a 100 RMB note and showing it to the bar as he placed it on the table over Chanel's shoulder. Chanel whimpered slightly as Sophia continued to rub her back. He strode quickly towards the door, stumbling into a chair. He continued to walk fast once he was outside before looking back to see the whole bar was still looking at him through the window.

'Bloody girls,' he muttered under his breath as he took out his phone to order a taxi. 'I don't fucking need them anyway, I have Emma.'

14

The light of the evening faded as Kevin and Emma lay naked in bed, the thin duvet stretched lightly across their legs. It was only seven o'clock but they'd come to Kevin's flat an hour before, just after they'd finished work for the day.

It was now June and the previous weeks had seen the heat become nearly intolerable. Kevin even left the A/C on during the day when he was at school to the chagrin of both Gabriel and Charlie. The humidity was unbearable at times, and the shade provided little respite from its all-encompassing reach.

Kevin had not heard from Sophia since their date, but had noticed Lesley avoiding his gaze whenever she walked past the foreigners' office. His relationship with Emma, however, had become serious very quickly in the aftermath. Apart from on weekends, when her husband was at home, she would spend as much time with Kevin as possible. Despite their incoherence in each other's languages, they spoke of marriage, children and a home with artwork, books, and gnomes with little hats guarding their balcony.

'What time?' she asked with her eyes closed, head resting on his chest.

'Er … seven.'

'I should go soon, husband back early tonight. I cook dinner.'

'No, Emma. Remember, we have to make call tonight.'

'I said that when we first arrived and you just wanted sex,' she protested.

'Well, let's do it now then.'

'No, I'm not in the mood.'

'But Emma, you told me we needed them to know … We need them to know and then you can get a divorce from your husband.'

'Oh Kevin, not so simple. We need my parents to agree is good idea.'

'But you love me, don't you?' Kevin asked, agitated.

'Yes.'

'And you want to live the rest of your life with me?'

'Yes.'

'And we can have little children running around our living room. You want that, don't you?'

'Yes,' she laughed.

'Half Chinese, half English,' Kevin chuckled, sliding down so their faces were next to each other, 'running around our flat, in our neighbourhood of Shanghai.'

'Yes,' she smiled.

'We can teach at the same kindergarten and put all our money towards the future. Every day we could walk in together, every night we could walk home together … Emma, don't you want that?'

'Yes, I do.'

'Say that you love me.'

'I love you.'

'Then we need to do this now,' he said, reaching for her phone on his bedside table.

She looked at it in his hand, then looked into his bright blue eyes.

'Do you love me?' she asked.

'Yes.'

'Say it.'

'Say what?'

'That you love me. All your heart.'

'I love you.'

Emma sat up and took her phone. Kevin shifted himself behind her and began to lightly stroke her back with his fingertips. She opened her phone and found her father's number. She turned around and they shared a glance that confirmed to each other this is what they wanted.

'Remember what to say ...' he whispered, 'you don't love him, you love me instead. I have money, I can look after you and you want to raise a family with me. I'm tall and handsome and can speak a little bit of Chinese.'

'But you can't.'

'That doesn't matter. Just say and I will learn ... or not, it doesn't matter. All that's needed is you tell them you love me.'

She nodded and, after a deep breath, pressed 'call'.

The phone rang a few times before a high-pitched wail responded on the other end of the line. Whilst she spoke to them in their local Ningbo dialect, Kevin lay on his back, and stared at the ceiling. Emma seemed like she was shouting into the phone, but Kevin had come to realise over the years that shouting over the phone was what Chinese people did all the time. He closed his eyes and dreamt of their future again – he pictured them walking arm in arm together along the Bund, then imagined them sitting in a café together staring at each other lovingly as a waitress brought them brunch. He knew she was the one for him. It had only been since Sophia had embarrassed him that he'd realised, but she didn't matter anymore, only Emma mattered. Charlie might have suggested she was simply a rebound, a way for him to feel wanted again after so public a humiliation, but he told himself that can't have been true. He hadn't felt this way since his ex-girlfriend, from all those years ago before he came out to China, and he'd been prepared to marry her.

So intense was he in thought that he hadn't realised Emma had been silent for about two minutes and when Kevin finally sat up, he noticed tears in her eyes as a man's voice blared at her from the other end of the line. She was simply saying "Hao" in response. He grabbed her free hand and started to rub her back again.

After about ten minutes, she put the phone down and stared into space. Kevin didn't even bother to ask what they'd said. He held her in his arms, gently kissing her forehead.

'We must go together, tonight,' she said.

Kevin hesitated for a moment, unsure if she knew what she was saying. 'What do you mean?'

'I mean go tonight. Live elsewhere,' she replied.

'No we can't,' he said. 'We have no job in Shanghai yet, no flat. My visa is tied to the school, so if we go I get kicked out of the country.'

She put her hands to cover her face and screamed into them. She said something in Chinese before turning to Kevin again. 'OK, my parents said to leave you and they will not tell my husband what happened. They said they would want me to share my location on WeChat every night to make sure I'm with my husband. We can still keep this going for now.'

Kevin nodded. 'OK,' he said, 'let's not worry about it … There is no rush … Maybe in a few months your parents will realise you actually love me and this is not just an affair. Now get dressed, I'll walk you home.'

The streets were empty bar a few lonely figures as they slumbered along them, holding hands. The night was warm and the air pleasant, but neither of them felt it. The people, seeing a foreigner holding the hand of a local, stopped and stared. They walked past the kindergarten in the direction of Emma's home, diving right down a small canal. On the edge of the canal, a few individuals sat on stools, watching their rods in the calm water, waiting for the nibble of a fish. Ahead was a man carrying a large rucksack, waddling home for the evening.

'Maybe he's got a big fish in there,' Kevin whispered to Emma.

She laughed, and he felt positive for the first time since the call. He liked it when she laughed.

The canal was far from the main road, and it was a pleasant setting. They continued to walk and talk until Emma had forgotten the reason she'd been upset in the first place. At the end of the canal was the entrance to her neighbourhood. Even from far away the community looked incredibly grand – the main residential building at its centre about 30 storeys high and designed to look like a castle. It was gimmicky and lacked taste, but it was imposing. About 20 metres from the gate, they stopped and looked into each other's eyes. They were about to lean in for a kiss when they heard a voice shouting in front of them. They turned towards the voice and Emma's face went white. Kevin looked from her to the man shouting and gulped. He turned Emma towards him.

'Baby, it doesn't matter,' he whispered quickly as her husband bounded to them. 'Tell him the truth and leave him tonight. Tell him you don't love him. Live with me.'

Emma remained silent. She didn't even acknowledge what Kevin was saying, she only looked in the direction of her husband.

When the husband came within five metres of the two of them, Kevin let go of Emma and looked at him. He nudged Emma again.

'Tell him,' he said, before saying it again more aggressively. 'Tell him!'

'Fuck off, Laowai!' the husband shouted.

There was sweat on the top of the husband's forehead beneath his dishevelled hair. He looked with a mixture of anger and cowardice at Kevin. It was clear a part of him wanted to take a swing, but the other half, the half that Emma had taken advantage of this whole time, was holding him back.

Kevin clenched his fists. His eyes burned with hatred as he thought about how pathetic a specimen this man in front of him looked. Not even willing to hit me, he thought, what kind of cuck is this?

'Do it,' he whispered, 'hit me. I know you want to.'

'Kevin stop,' Emma shrieked.

'Do it,' Kevin said again.

He took a step toward the husband, who recoiled before regaining his stance.

'Fuck off, Laowai!' he repeated.

'She doesn't love you,' Kevin said, taking another step forward, 'she never has.'

'Fuck off, Laowai! I call police.'

'Do it. I dare you.'

The husband fumbled for his phone. 'Stay back,' he shouted.

The security guards at the gate, having heard the commotion, looked on from inside. One opened the door and looked like he was about to rush forward with a baton. Kevin, noticing this, placed his hands up and laughed. 'I was just kidding,' he said.

Emma's husband grabbed her hand and pulled her in the direction of the gate. Kevin watched on, helpless as two security guards opened it obediently and guided them through. Once the gate was closed they looked towards him with glowering eyes. They could tell what had happened.

The following morning was wet and dreary. The streets were soaked through with the previous night's showers yet, despite this, it was still uncomfortably hot. Kevin and Charlie sauntered to school slowly, the conversation stunted.

'What do you think will happen?' Kevin asked Charlie as they exited their neighbourhood.

'I don't know,' Charlie replied. 'From what you told me last night … maybe nothing … you often overthink things you know … maybe it will be OK.'

'I don't know man. It seemed bad … She texted me this morning to say she won't be coming in.'

'Was that it? No explanation? Nothing?'

'Yeah.'

A homeless dog crossed the pathway in front of them, shaggy fur soaked through.

'I really don't know,' Charlie repeated. 'I'm still surprised the husband didn't whack you.'

Once they arrived at the school, Kevin slumbered up the stairs towards the foreigners' office, sighing with each step. Time moved very slowly for him, and he was scared of what might happen. At his desk, while the other foreign teachers talked, he kept looking at his phone, hoping she might send him another message. He pretended to get on with some lesson plans.

His phone flashed and he grabbed it quickly. He unlocked it and opened his messages to see Lesley had requested his attendance in her office. His heart jumped. Did she already know? He thought.

When he arrived, she was sat on a chair opposite Emma's husband. The two men exchanged a look of hate filled anger. The husband looked far less contemptible in the light of day. Wearing an expensive suit and perched coolly on the edge of a sofa, he watched the boy enter the room and stand awkwardly by the open door. This time, unlike the night before, he was unafraid. He remained still as the boy took a step forward.

'Where's Emma?' Kevin asked tentatively.

'None of business,' her husband said in a thick Chinese accent, barely moving.

'Emma is not going to join us today,' Lesley said. 'In fact, I have now agreed with her husband, she is no longer a teacher at this school. She will be let go.'

'Wait, what?' Kevin said, surprised. 'You can't be serious.'

'Yes. My school, my rules.'

'What reason do you have to fire her?' he burst out.

'Because of what she did,' her husband said calmly.

'What does that have to do with the school!' Kevin shouted back, still standing. 'Maybe if you treated her right she wouldn't have cheated on you!'

'Enough!' Lesley said sternly. 'The decision has been made.'

The husband sat back, satisfied that he had won.

'Then I leave with her,' Kevin said, taking a stride forward as if about to attack.

'No. You won't,' Lesley replied, looking directly into his eyes. 'I own your work permit. The second I cancel it, you have one week to leave the country. In your contract it states you cannot find work at any other school in China for two years if you quit from the school. You have to finish your contract or I will alert the authorities and you will be deported for breaking my contract. You will never be allowed back into China again. Do you understand me?'

Kevin stared at her. He tried to speak but when he opened his mouth, all that came out was a gargling noise.

'Do you understand me?' she said again firmly.

'Yes,' he said meekly.

'What will you do with Emma?' he asked, turning to her husband.

'None of business,' the husband said serenely, flicking the boy away as he picked up his small saucer of tea which had been placed by Lesley on the table beside him.

The same anger rose in Kevin as it had the night before, but instead of contempt, its cause was fear. He had thought of Emma's husband as a coward when he'd seen him in the darkness, but now, as he sat nonchalantly on the couch in front of him, posture relaxed, as if dismissing an underling, Kevin felt intimidated.

He turned around, shoulders hunched, and walked slowly to the door, stopping at it to look towards Lesley and Emma's husband. 'You know, you're a terrible mother,' he shrieked, 'and you're a terrible husband.'

He ran out of the door and towards the stairs. He paced about inside the foreigners' office, considering his options. As his forehead glazed with sweat, all he could think about was whether the future he'd dreamed about with Emma was now gone. He took out his phone and tried to ring her. He tried again, and again until on his seventh attempt, she finally answered. 'Hello,' she said sniffling.

'Emma … Emma … What's going on? Why have you been fired?'

'Because of affair,' she replied.

'Emma … an affair is nothing to do with the school. Emma I thought you loved me?'

'I did. But you lied to me. Why did you date Lesley's daughter and not tell me?' she said, bursting into tears on the other end of the phone.

Kevin gawped, and for the second time that day didn't have a response.

'Emma … I … I …would never want to hurt you … We planned to go away together … Why did you allow your husband to do this?'

'What do you mean allow? He told me to stay indoors. It is a wife's duty to be devoted to her husband.'

'Then why did you allow Lesley to do this? Stand up to her! Say you want your job back!' he said, almost in tears himself.

'Lesley means well,' she said. 'She doesn't want the school to … er to … you know … be bad name.'

'Baby … we can still make it work. You don't have to listen to them. Who cares what they think? You don't have to be obedient to your husband nor a slave to Lesley. What kind of fucking country is this where you have to do whatever you're told?' he said.

'Don't say that!' she shouted down the receiver before composing herself. 'You don't know anything about China … Goodbye Kevin,' she finally said before hanging up the phone.

15

Whilst Kevin had been in the office with Lesley and Emma's husband, Charlie received an email from a company in Shanghai he'd applied to work for. He hadn't had much success so far, but he'd not given up. In fact, the application he'd put most effort into was for a research assistant role at the political risk consultancy. He'd interviewed the weekend before at their HQ when he'd gone on a quick afternoon trip to Shanghai, and it had gone very well. His background as a law student meant he had a good eye for discrepancies in the detail and could read long documents and absorb them. In addition, the more research he'd done into the role, the more he loved it. This company operated fairly secretly and would do research on high profile Chinese companies, finding out who they were cheating and if their management was trustworthy.

He tentatively opened the email and skimmed the top. By the time he read 'congratulations', he threw his hand into the air before awkwardly returning them to his desk. The other foreign teachers, a little confused, asked what happened. After he'd explained he'd got the job they seemed even more confused.

'So, are you quitting here then?' Daphne asked.

'Yes, I'll give my one month's notice,' he replied.

'But you can't go to another employer in China, can you?' she asked, puzzled.

'Yes I can. As long as it's not another school. Contract specifically says.'

'Lesley will fight you on it.'

'No she won't. I've made sure of it. She might try but all you need to do is hold your ground I think … in fact once Kevin comes back, I'll head up to tell her.'

When it reached 9 a.m. and Kevin still hadn't returned to the office, Charlie decided to head upstairs himself. He darted into the bathroom for a quick wee but could hear shouting emanating from Lesley's office. He washed his hands and heard the door slam. Drying his hands with a paper towel, he peaked out to see the back of Kevin's head descend down the stairs. That can't be good, Charlie thought. Maybe I should approach her later. As he walked in the direction of the stairs, he doubled back, thinking aloud, 'There'll never be a good time to do this anyway,' before turning around and making a line for her door.

He knocked on it but there was no response. He knocked again, and Lesley opened it abruptly, her figure blocking Charlie's view.

'Yes, what is it?' she snapped.

'Erm …' Charlie hesitated, perhaps it wasn't the best time. 'I'd like to speak with you, if that's OK?'

'Come back at lunch,' she thundered before slamming the door.

Wow, he thought. After he walked down the stairs and heard Kevin crying over the phone, he rolled his eyes and dashed to his classroom.

After the morning lesson, Charlie returned to the office and news that Kevin had disappeared, nor had anyone heard from him since he'd gone to Lesley's office. Charlie was certain it had something to do with Emma, but he had important business of his own to attend to. He promised he'd go home to check if Kevin was there after he'd told Lesley his own news.

He ran up the stairs, this time determined that he should say what he had to say. At the top of the stairs, he stopped and felt some trepidation. What would this woman do? Maybe she could have him arrested?

Charlie shook his head. No, don't be silly, he thought, how could she? Then again, who does she know? Shanghai is a big export hub and Lesley must have lots of connections within that area of the world. With all her millions, she might seek a vendetta against someone. But is she that petty? She's just one person.

He felt fear, not at the prospect of being told no, but that he didn't know what could happen. It was the lack of understanding that made him afraid, a total lack of the ability to see the future. By crossing her this way now, could she do something in return to ruin him later on?

As Charlie mulled this over in his head, he thought about how Kevin had been similarly paranoid all those years before when his friend had been arrested in Beijing. No wonder nobody ever stood up against bad employers, or against the government. They never had the courage to do it themselves for fear of the unknown consequences. At least the worst that could happen to Charlie was deportation, or was it?

Charlie stopped at the top of the stairs, then went down a few steps, then back up, before diving into the bathroom. He looked at himself in the mirror. There was a bead of sweat on his forehead and his cheeks were flush. He took a tissue from beside the sink, ran it under the tap before wiping his face lightly.

'You're just being paranoid,' he said to himself. 'She can't do anything against you.' After he'd plucked up his courage, he walked to her door and knocked on it.

'Enter,' came a shout from the other side.

Charlie had never been in her kindergarten office before. It wasn't too dissimilar to her office in the tower she'd built, but the proportions were smaller. Instead of artwork on her walls, she had pictures of her other businesses laid atop a map of China. Most of the businesses seemed to be located in Shanghai, Jiangsu, and Zhejiang, but there were some photos in Guangzhou and some in Chongqing, towards the west of China. There were three even further west though Charlie didn't know if they were located in Xinjiang or Tibet. A few pictures stood out in particular, for next to three of them were pictures of Lesley at the New York Stock Exchange opening bell.

'Oh wow!' Charlie exclaimed. 'I never knew your companies were listed in America.'

'Oh those,' Lesley replied. 'Yes, only a few, I made over 100 million dollars from them,' she said tastelessly. Before quickly changing the subject, 'so you wanted to see me?'

'Er … yes,' he replied awkwardly.

Charlie shuffled in his seat. The feeling of fear had returned and gnawed at him from within. His head felt light and he struggled to find the right words to say.

'I wanted to let you know that I have accepted a job offer in Shanghai and I am starting there at the end of July. I will work for the rest of the school year until mid-July, but after that I won't be returning in September.'

'Uh huh,' Lesley said, narrowing her eyes. 'You know you can't do that.'

'Yes I can. In my contract it says I can't work for another school, but it says nothing about another company.'

'You're not going to another school?' she said.

'No.'

'What kind of company are you going to?' she probed.

'Respectfully, I don't have to tell you,' he said. 'All I need from you is a document releasing me from the school. As long as I am not going to another school, the new work permit will be approved. You can trust the system.'

'Hmmm. I don't,' she said before leaning back in her chair and announcing with a sigh. 'No, I will not allow you to leave.'

'What?'

'I said I will not allow you to leave. I need you to stay, and I will not provide the release letter even if you quit. The contract says you can only leave with mutual agreement, but I do not agree to it. Yes, you can quit, but I will not release you, meaning you will have to go back to UK and start visa process all over again in eight months' time when the school contract runs out.'

Charlie sat in silence. He clenched his hands into the chair and a rage built up inside him. He no longer felt fear now he was face to face with Lesley, but a contempt bordering on anger. This woman would rather he not enjoy his job for eight months, or send him home, than help him move along in his life.

'Lesley … Mrs Li, surely if a teacher says they want to leave, you can see the decision had not been taken lightly. You have been very successful in business, but why keep someone on who doesn't want to be here? Do you need me to help find you a replacement?'

'You know if you were one of the other teachers I would fire you for coming up here and wasting my time.'

'Well yes, but that's because there are lots of Chinese teachers and very few foreign ones. I want to help you find that replacement.'

'How dare you … What do you want?' she said abruptly. 'More money?'

'No, that's not what I came here for.'

She leaned forward. 'Then get out, I am not releasing you from your contract.'

Charlie composed himself, looked at her with a blank expression, then stood up. 'Thank you for your time,' he said as he exited the door.

Heading down the stairs he pondered if he might be able to find another way to leave the school. Back in the office, he emailed the company, outlining his predicament. Then, remembering that Kevin had missed the morning's lessons, he walked back to the flat.

The dining table lay on its side. Kevin's books, strewn on the floor, had been ripped in a fit of rage. There was a large rectangle of dust now where the sofa had previously been, which itself had been moved to the balcony outside. The gentle breeze drafted through the flat towards the open door where Charlie stood, mouth agasp. The kitchen door had a crack in it, and the bathroom sink tap was on.

As Charlie meandered around the upturned furniture to turn the tap off, he looked towards Kevin's bedroom and could see the inside of it hadn't fared much better. The bright sunlight outdoors penetrated the half-open curtains and cast a harsh light over the broken bedpost and glass table, shattered in pieces, on the floor. As he walked across, he saw

Kevin's legs on the bed, he was facing down into his pillow.

'You alright mate?' he said tentatively whilst knocking on the door.

Kevin looked up to see who it was and replied, 'Yeah,' before falling back into his pillow.

'Wanna talk?' Charlie asked.

Kevin sighed as he turned around. 'I just hate everything man. Why did I come to China? They treat everyone like shit.'

'I know,' Charlie said, perching himself at the bottom of the bed.

'No you don't, you know fuck all,' Kevin replied before turning himself around and propping himself up on the elbows. 'No I'm sorry, I didn't mean it like that.'

'I know.'

Charlie looked around the messy bedroom and the open wardrobe before returning his gaze towards his pitiful friend. There was a bottle of baijiu, half empty, next to his bed.

'So what's your trouble?' Kevin slurred, 'it can't be worse than mine.'

'Lesley won't release me from my contract.'

'Why do you want to leave your contract?'

Charlie explained about the job offer, and what had happened when he asked to be released.

Kevin, absorbing this information, stared blankly at the ceiling. They were silent in thought before Kevin spoke openly. 'They just don't care about what the ordinary person wants, do they? They don't care that Emma hates her husband or that you hate your job.'

'I know,' Charlie responded. 'But it happens elsewhere as well, I guess.'

'But does it?' Kevin exclaimed, sitting up. 'Does it really? … When I was at my previous jobs they always asked if there was anything they could be doing better. They wanted to know.'

'Your previous jobs in China?'

'No, no, no, back in Bristol. Even my damn job I had in the stock-rooms during the summer, they wanted to know if there was anything they could be doing better, both to the staff and to the customers.'

'I don't know, it's a different work environment I guess.'

'But it isn't. My bosses only cared about money as well but they still knew that a happy workforce was important, that … that … that, my experience mattered. I may have been replaceable but at least I had basic rights. Sick pay, weekends off, leaving my private life alone.'

'So what man? You knew what you signed up for in this country.'

'We have to show them they can't get away with this sort of shit. That, they don't control us. That … we have to have rights too.'

Charlie shrugged. 'I really don't know what you mean. I'm just waiting for my new company to think something up. Worst comes to worse, I'll just have to teach the extra eight months and hope they keep the job for me.'

'Bollocks to that man,' Kevin raised his voice, hitting his mattress, 'let's go on strike or something. Let's not work until she's forced to let you go, and Emma gets her job back.' As he spoke his eyes began to shine, as if he'd had a brilliant idea.

'For God's sake, be real,' Charlie said.

'Why not?' Kevin replied. 'What have we got to lose?'

'Just two of us? I don't feel comfortable doing that for this anyway. It won't work.'

'Then we need to get the other teachers in the school to do it too!'

'Kevin, how much have you drunk? They'll never strike. They're terrified of Lesley.'

'Yes, I know, but … but … look, all that witch cares about is that the parents want to keep sending their kids to the school so she can take their money. We just need to make her worry she might, I dunno, as they say "lose face", She'd rather rehire Emma and let you go than risk losing face or upsetting parents. You know, make the cost so high she has no other choice.'

'Mate, how are you going to persuade the other teachers to do this with you?'

'They liked Emma. Listen, if we make a WeChat group with all the teachers, we can organise it for tomorrow. If I persuade Emma to be a part of it, maybe she can persuade the other teachers to do it. If all the foreign teachers do it too, the Chinese teachers will be more likely to do it as they know the foreign teachers won't be fired for it. Look at how Emma was fired because of the affair, but I wasn't!'

'It won't work,' Charlie repeated.

'Why the fuck not?' Kevin retorted. He aggressively stood up beside the bed and towered over Charlie. 'Listen, I guarantee, all we need to do is stand outside as the parents come in with the children in the morning. The second Diana or Julia see, they'll tell Lesley who will tell them to hire

Emma again. If all the teachers work together we have nothing to worry about. I guarantee within 10 minutes, they'll curtail. She's never been stood up against. The second she is, she will keel over in fear because she would prefer to hire Emma again, than lose face!'

'For God's sake, stop with your fantasies,' Charlie sighed, standing up and moving to leave the room.

Kevin grabbed his arm and pulled him around. His eyes showed his drunkenness.

'Listen, I'll talk to Emma. I know where she lives. You talk to the other foreign teachers. We can work something out and do it tomorrow morning. I guarantee it will work!'

'Get off me,' Charlie jerked his arm away from Kevin. 'You're drunk.'

'What other choice do I have?' Kevin replied, almost whining. 'I never thought I'd say this about any girl, but I love her man. She's everything I want in a wife. I want to spend the rest of my life with her.'

'She's not, you fool, she's just another fling and you're having an early mid-life crisis.'

'Don't you fucking talk about her like that,' Kevin returned, clenching his fists.

'You think hitting me will help?'

Kevin unclenched them and sat back down on his bed before looking at his hands.

'I tell you what she is,' he sighed. 'She's the first *woman* I've met. She's the first person who's made me feel both safe and made me strive for something better. For the first time in seven years I've actually enjoyed my work,' he looked up pleadingly at his flatmate. 'She's more than just a plaything Charlie, I promise, she's a companion, I wish I could spend all my time with her, but I know I can't.'

Charlie stared at his friend. Look at this beggar now, he wondered. I never thought I would see a man turn back into a boy. Or maybe I'd been mistaken this whole time. It was a good façade. A damned good one. Through all his actions, in trying to sleep with the most women, treat others like garbage and use his friends to his advantage, he'd tricked everyone, including himself, into thinking he'd become a man a long time ago. Sitting there, with that pleading, helpless face, more like a puppy's than a lion's, Charlie saw his real flatmate for the first time; a hypocrite, unwilling to take self-responsibility, desperately in need of someone else.

'Alright … if you're sure. I'll help you.'

'Legend,' Kevin finally said, visibly relieved.

When Charlie tentatively walked back into the foreigners' office, it was only half full. Bryn, Ellie and Elijah sat at their computers with headphones on. Good, Charlie thought, these guys might be easier to persuade than the others.

'How's Kevin?' Bryn asked when he noticed Charlie, his wispy beard shuffling as he talked.

'He's OK,' Charlie replied, 'but listen, there's something he wants me to ask you.'

He motioned at the others to take off their headphones.

'There's no easy way to put this, but Emma was fired because of the affair. Kevin was kept on but naturally he thinks it's outrageous. He wants to organise a strike, and he wants all the foreign teachers to take part.'

'What?' Ellie and Bryn exclaimed at the same time.

'Hear me out,' he said. 'As long as we stand together with the Chinese teachers, we have nothing to lose. They're not going to fire us. They may want to fire the Chinese teachers, but they won't if we do it too.'

There was a moment of silence. They could tell Charlie didn't believe what he was saying.

'And you think this is a good plan?' Bryn laughed.

'Bryn please … I know exactly what you mean and I had the same doubts but I'm begging you. Kevin needs us. You know this shit works in the UK. Employee rights were fought for by stands like this. By acting together, we can hit Lesley down a notch, perhaps she'll start treating the teachers with the respect they deserve … you've spent just as much time bitching about her as I have.'

'He's right,' Elijah interjected. 'I think we should do it.'

'What's in it for you?' Ellie asked pointedly at Charlie.

'Nothing,' Charlie lied.

'But didn't you just quit this morning?'

'Yes, but what does that have to do with anything?'

'It means you can't lose your job. *You* have nothing to lose, *we* do,' Bryn said, circling his finger to include Ellie and Elijah.

'No, but that's the point,' Charlie said. 'I can't quit because she said she needs to give me a release letter.'

'So, you're striking so you can quit,' Bryn concluded bluntly.

'Yes, but also for Em ...'

'I knew it!' Bryn roared. 'No, I'm not going to join your strike just because you want to leave your job.'

'I won't either,' Ellie said.

'Guys, what about Emma?' Charlie asked.

'Kevin needs to man up. It was an affair, big deal. He'll have another if he tries again. He's been fired before. He's going to strike and risk it again, so what ... be my guest.'

'No I actually agree with him on this one,' Elijah said. 'I'm sick and tired of Chinese people with money and a little bit of power taking advantage of others.'

There was a hint of genuine disgust in Elijah's voice, but Charlie couldn't tell if it was because Lesley was a bad employer, or because Elijah was instinctively quite racist in some of the things he said, thinking less of Chinese culture compared to Western civilisation.

'I'm in,' Elijah said finally.

'I'm not,' Bryn said.

'Neither am I,' Ellie agreed.

'Alright then, 'I'll let Kevin know.'

Whilst Charlie had failed to convince the other foreigners to join Kevin, Kevin had himself proceeded to Emma's neighbourhood, and waited outside in the powerful afternoon sun. He sent her a message under the guise of saying goodbye. She replied that she would be down shortly. When he saw her at the gate, she invited him over, so they could sit in the shade of a bench in the gardens of her community. As they entered together, the security guards glared towards them.

It was a truly beautiful setting. The garden had been designed with the Chinese tradition of Feng Shui, and all seemed to be harmonised in a similar vein to Kevin's and Charlie's community. There were roses along a dirt path, which led to a small lake of pristine clear water. There must have been a filtration system built into the bottom of the lake because the bright fish could be seen swimming around within. They sat on one side of the lake underneath a large tree. The circle of apartment buildings around the edge of the community acted as a barrier to the noise of the roads nearby, which meant the garden was surprisingly peaceful. As it was around 2 p.m., they had the garden to themselves.

'Emma …' Kevin said, turning towards her, 'I love you … you're the first girl I've ever truly loved and I want it to work out.'

Emma stayed silent, continuing to stare ahead of her. Shuffling awkwardly, she gulped.

'I have an idea. I don't think this will be the end for us. It doesn't have to be … do you want to be with me?' he asked.

'Yes.'

'Then I think we can work something out.'

'What?'

He told her about the idea of the strike.

'No, we can't do that!' she exclaimed.

'Charlie is talking to the foreign teachers now. They can't get fired! I haven't been fired even though I was the one who started this. How is that fair? Listen, if you come and persuade a few Chinese teachers, I guarantee they will all follow. All it takes is for one person to do something bold and others will follow … Emma, for me,' he lifted her chin up so she was looking into his eyes, 'do it for me.'

He pressed his lips to hers.

'OK … as long as the foreign teachers do it too,' she replied, with emotion in her quivering voice. 'What do I do?'

Kevin detailed his plan. He told her about how they would all walk out after their morning meeting to stand outside in a sort of picket line. He told her what they should chant, and what they should tell the parents as they brought their children to school in the morning. He told her that she should first share the plan with the Chinese teachers she trusted, and once she'd persuaded them, she could tell the others.

Finally, he told her that once this was over, she could leave her husband and they could be married. Emma smiled when he said this.

'Just imagine,' Kevin said, 'Lesley would be so scared of you, she would treat you and the other Chinese teachers properly, isn't that what you want?'

She put her head on his shoulder as the wind rustled the leaves in the tree above them. 'I want this moment to last forever,' she whispered.

16

The next morning, the wind swirled and the sky looked menacing, its dark clouds on the verge of thunder. The rain had crashed overnight, and the pavement was hidden under puddles along the path to the school. As Kevin and Charlie sped along at almost a jog, their steps overturned some of the tiles of the pavement, causing water which had seeped underneath to spurt up and drench their feet in brown muck.

Kevin was nervous. Charlie had bluntly stated the previous night that only Elijah was willing to walk out with the other Chinese teachers. To make matters worse, Emma had said her husband wanted to leave by Friday and had already signed the lease on a new apartment in Beijing. They were now both scheduled to move within two days.

'Have you thought of what you want to say?' Charlie said breathlessly.

'No.'

'How are you going to persuade the others?'

'I don't know.'

'Slow down Kevin, I can barely keep up.'

'Walk faster.'

Kevin could feel his heart within his chest, every beat sending a shimmer of nausea to his forehead. He kept thinking about how foolish he would look if only half or, god forbid, a quarter of the staff walked out of the school with him. The weather wouldn't help.

As they approached the restaurants near the school, Kevin saw Emma inside a coffee shop with a paper cup in her hand. She looked nervous, skin paler than usual, and even from far he could see she tapped the table constantly with her finger, as if typing out a message in morse code. He walked in and kissed her.

'Remember,' he started, 'when you see me walk outside, come to me … You have to come, OK? This won't work if you're not there,' he said.

'OK,' she replied obediently, wiping a small tear from her eye.

Kevin and Charlie left the café and continued, almost bounding now, to the kindergarten. The Chinese staff meeting in the lobby was still going on. When they walked in, there was some awkward shuffling among the teachers, and a tension that was unusual for this time of morning.

Kevin walked straight for the lift, not taking any notice of the meeting, but Charlie looked around at the sullen faces of the teachers. Some of them looked lost and a few scared. They were in desperate need of a leader, he thought, as they had been since they were young. They only needed someone to tell them what to do, and they would do it.

Diana and Julia could also feel the tension, but didn't seem to give it too much consideration. They were in the middle of announcing what was on the lunch menu for the day. About a third of the teachers' eyes were on Kevin, hoping that he might say something, but he didn't look at them.

In the foreigners' office, he saw a pile of pickets on the floor in the corner. The other teachers were in and their faces seemed terse.

'Kevin …' Daphne said, speaking on behalf of everyone, 'don't do this … what are you going to gain? Emma's a nice girl but you'll find another.'

Kevin didn't pay her any attention, instead walking toward the pickets. They were light, but still large enough to be read from far way.

'Nice work on the characters,' he said to Charlie who had made them the evening before, 'did you write the messages yourself?'

'No, Emma sent me a picture of what we should write … I don't actually know what they say.'

'Anyone?' Kevin said loudly, looking aimlessly at no one in particular. He turned them around in his hands, as if inspecting a cricket bat before heading to the crease.

'Kevin, we're not going to be a part of this,' Bryn said, raising his voice, 'it's childish and ill-thought out.'

'Just stop being a nuisance for once in your life,' Ellie continued.

'I respect you Kevin, but this is over the top,' said Perry.

'You're mad,' said Amelia.

'Don't any of you care for employee rights?' Kevin demanded.

'But you're not doing it for employee rights,' Amelia replied, 'you're doing it for sex.'

'No I'm not,' Kevin roared, the aggression in his voice taking everyone by surprise. 'Do you think I would do this for any girl?' he shouted accusingly. 'I'm doing this because I am sick and tired of living in a country where the powerful take advantage of the weak. Where the employer can fire anyone because of what happens in their private life. Where the employer has all the power and the employee none. This is about more than just loving Emma. This is for the parents who want their children to have good schools with good equipment, not a school that lies and sells them a version of the school that exists only in the marketing materials. This is for the children who we all love to teach. Their education should not be the result of the profit motive, but for the sake of their growing up to be happy. This is for the teachers who slave away under a boss who doesn't care for their wellbeing. Don't you see? The disgusting culture emanates from the top. It starts with that bitch who thinks she's better than everyone else because she has money and thinks she can get whatever she wants because of it. She shouldn't be able to get away with it, and we shouldn't allow her to.'

The room fell silent. Kevin's chest heaved up and down, each breath heavy. Sweat showed beneath his t-shirt.

'So, who's with me?' he said forcefully, his voice quivering.

'I am,' Elijah said.

'So am I,' Charlie said.

They looked at the others in the room who hadn't moved during Kevin's speech, and whose heads were slightly bowed to the floor. Kevin's eyes darted from one person to the next but none of them looked up toward him.

'Cowards,' he spat. 'So, I guess it's just the three of us.'

He grabbed the pickets and bounded to the lift, his movement energetic, and with purpose. Charlie and Elijah followed close behind. On the way down, Kevin looked at the two of them. 'Thank you,' he whispered, his eyes red.

When the lift doors opened, the lobby was in chaos – they were late. The meeting had finished early and some of the teachers, as was usual, were walking towards the stairs whilst some were waiting for the lift. Another third stood bemused in the middle of the room.

'Everyone,' Kevin shouted, 'follow me!'

He darted out of the front doors and onto the pavement outside. The rain had stopped but the sky was still threatening. He chucked some pickets by the door and handed the rest to the few teachers who had exited the building with them. They were ten in all. The ones who had been queueing for the lift looked confusedly from one to the next. They hadn't been told.

Emma, having seen Kevin from afar, ran to obediently stand beside him. The noise had brought back some of the teachers who had walked to the stairs. They saw Kevin handing out pickets and a little group forming outside. Kevin, seeing them look at him, gestured for them to come and join, but they hesitated.

Emma went up and explained what was going on whilst Kevin and Charlie tried to organise those who had joined them outside into some form of line. Elijah shouted some English phrases and encouraged the others to start shouting them too in a loud, slurring chorus.

When Emma finished her little speech, the lift opened and the waverers had their choice. They looked at the empty lift, before gazing outside at the strikers. One of them asked Emma where the foreigners were, and Emma pointed at Kevin, Charlie and Elijah.

'Only three?' came the reply.

'Yes, but we don't need the others. Please join us.'

There was a decisive shake of the heads. They bundled into the lift and the door shut. The ones who had come back from the staircase too, took one look before running to their classrooms.

Outside, the commotion attracted some of the morning commuters to stop their cars and take videos of what was going on. Parents, with their children beside them, spoke to each other in fast, hushed tones. They held their children by the shoulder to prevent them walking up to the Chinese teachers, who were now chanting Chinese phrases, 'More pay', 'Hire Emma', 'Education over profit'. Diana and Julia stood in the lobby, their arms folded and their faces white as sheets. Julia had her phone out.

In her office on the top floor, Lesley was in the midst of her morning routine. When she was at the kindergarten, and not showing prospective investors around the premises, this was where she spent most of her time. It wasn't unusual that one of the first lamps turned on each morning was in her office, and that lamp was the last one to be extinguished for the night. She enjoyed the feeling of rising early and proceeding with the day from darkness to light. It was a habit she had been able to achieve in lieu of her extraordinary ability to function off only five hours' sleep a night. She believed it was her enormous capacity for hard work that brought her riches, and she believed it, too, was this enormous capability that all Chinese people shared.

From a young age, this desperation to escape poverty had been instilled in her and she had made sure, in turn, to instil it in her own children. Lesley's own experience at school was common for the time. If she was not studying for 12 hours a day, she would feel like a failure. Rigorous punishment was given to anyone perceived as lazy – it hurt her hand just thinking of the beatings that had been administered. From the age of 11 to 18, she went to the local state school, where she was housed in shared accommodation with seven other girls of her age, sleeping in narrow bunk beds with hard mattresses. At dawn, they would wake up and go downstairs for exercises on the sports yard, the entire school synchronised in their movements. They wouldn't finish their studies until 11 p.m. each day, and they were only allowed to visit home for the weekend once every fortnight.

It was a tough existence, but Lesley had excelled. Later, when she'd grown up and visited many countries, she'd realised this style of schooling was different to anywhere else in the world, and she became convinced of the superiority of the Chinese work ethic, which subsequent business dealings with gullible Americans hadn't dispelled. She believed that all Chinese people, having been brought up this way, must be like her. Only the best could reach the top, and the top meant money, but most of all, status. Anyone below in the hierarchy was there for lack of trying, and as a result should be subservient to her every whim, for it was her that gave them some form of status by having a job in the first place. It didn't matter how much she paid them, they should simply be grateful for the opportunity. This was, in particular, one of the reasons why most of her hires were teachers that had grown up, like her, in the countryside. Only those who have personally escaped poverty can know how truly awful it is. The idea of it pertaining to any nobility was farcical in her mind. But the great advantage to hiring those who had grown up with nothing, is that you can pay them next to nothing and they will still take the wage for it is an improvement.

In her mind, the girls she hired had a choice. They could slave away on a field in the middle of nowhere, waiting to marry a local boy and live in near poverty for the rest of their lives, or move to the city, with all its wonderment, in the hope they would find a rich man. As a result, the very idea of rebelling against the opportunity she had provided them was inconceivable to her. The alternative to employment under her was destitution in the countryside. With so many millions graduating each year, it was not hard to find a replacement if she wished.

It was the same with the other businesses she owned. She looked towards the map of China on the wall and sighed. She'd acquired some through mergers and absorbed the workforce, others through building something from scratch, but her employees had free choice. They didn't have to work for her, not with all the growth and jobs there were elsewhere in China. She gave opportunities for those who were otherwise destined to the poverty she had experienced when she was a child. Even if the work was monotonous, someone had to do it. Anybody who complained was undeserving.

Her phone rang loudly. She peered across above her glasses to see Julia's name flash up repeatedly.

'What does she want?' she muttered to herself. She had spoken to Julia only half an hour before, and indeed, Julia never called when Lesley was based at the school for the day.

'What is it?' she snapped.

'Lesley,' Julia gulped, 'we need to do something.'

'What do you mean?'

'Go to your window,' Julia stuttered. 'I've already called the police.'

Lesley put down the phone and walked to the window overlooking the front of the school. She peered down to see a small crowd of ten surrounded by a larger crowd of nearly 100 people, almost all of them with their phones out, filming what was taking place. She opened the window wider and pushed her head out to see that the small crowd of ten were holding raised placards and chanting loudly.

She gawped, half in disbelief, half seething at this display of revolt, whatever the cause. She felt uneasy and a slowly growing sense of fear. This was not the fear she sometimes felt in her early years when her grandparents struggled every day to put food on her table. Nor was it like the fear she'd had when she was about to go to Shanghai for the first time to start her university degree. That night she had cried because she was leaving everything she knew, she wanted her grandparents to come with her, but the train ticket for the 20-hour ride was too expensive, and they were too weak to help carry her large luggage. In the end, she only took what she could fit in a backpack. The fear she felt when looking down at those she believed to be subservient to her every wish was a new emotion. She felt pain, anger, anguish, hatred, confusion all at once. All she could think of was how this would look to her superiors within the Communist Party – this display of insubordination.

She rushed back to her desk, and put her hands on her head. She had been aware that the foreigners might do something silly like this at some point, but she'd have driven a hard bargain and appeased them somehow. For the foreigners to be joined by the Chinese teachers, and worst of all to do it on display in front of the school when the parents were dropping off their kids and locals drove past, this was the worst form of humiliation. This would entail a loss of face.

After fifteen minutes, amidst the loud murmuring of the crowd, Kevin looked sternly at Emma and whispered in her ear that she should prevent anyone from getting into the school. The crowd around them was growing and the striking teachers turned nervously toward each other as their chants became quieter and quieter. They could tell the situation was not a good one. About 50 children with their parents were pointing and laughing, wondering if this was part of a school day, or some activity they did not know about. Their concerned parents gripped tightly to their hands.

'What can we do?' Charlie quietly asked Kevin.

They were no longer shouting slogans about equal pay, and an awkward atmosphere had descended onto the street. Everyone was silent.

'I don't know,' Kevin whispered, 'I was hoping there would be more of us.'

'You know the police will come.'

'Yes.'

'What then?'

'I don't know.'

'Kevin you're leading this, what are you going to do?'

Kevin looked up. The eyes of his fellow strikers were on him, willing him to lead.

He looked towards the upstairs classrooms of the school and saw several teachers staring down at him. Daphne and Bryn turned away as his eyes came towards them.

'Kevin,' Charlie whispered, 'make a damn decision.'

He opened his mouth but couldn't speak, only a guttural gargling came out. He looked blankly at Charlie and moved his lips silently, gently swaying from side to side.

'Alright,' Charlie shouted to no one in particular, 'we're done.'

He dropped his picket and gestured for the others to walk with him toward the school, leaving Emma and Kevin alone in the middle of the road as it began to rain.

Sensing the moment was right, a small group of security guards from the business park walked across and grabbed Kevin gently by the arm, careful not to aggravate him. He was bigger than them but he resigned himself to their grip. Emma wiped tears away from her eyes as she walked back in the direction of the coffee shop she had emerged from barely 20 minutes before. In the distance she heard the growing sound of a police siren.

17

It was late July and, just as Sophia returned to Hangzhou, the torrid heat had set in. Having finished her studies in New York, she planned to start immediately working for her mother.

The first person Sophia wanted to see upon arrival was Daphne. They'd known each other since Daphne had started work at the kindergarten, and would sometimes meet up more out of loneliness than out of friendship. For Sophia, there was something familiar about Daphne – perhaps a reminder of her classmates from her childhood in the UK. For Daphne, who'd seen foreigners come and go, friendships in China were temporary, likely to evaporate upon her final return to the UK. She'd come to consider it one of those strange oddities of expat life that the people one meets in faraway lands would not be friends had they met closer to home.

Sophia, who now lived in one of her parents' many apartments in the centre of town, arrived first at the restaurant, an overly extravagant place in one of the touristy areas of Hangzhou. The buildings along the road were the pleasant mix of colonial and oriental that was common from the 1920s – huge chunks of greystone evenly cemented together in the neoclassical style.

Walking along the road, by the name of Hefang Street, Daphne inadvertently bumped into tourists coming the other way who were also staring upwards at the unique architecture, transfixed. At the end of the road to the right stood a recently made monument on one of the many green hills that litter the city. At the top stood the City God Pavilion, towering above the treeline. On clear days when the pollution wasn't bad, it gave a romantic and far-reaching view of the whole city. It was a majestic sight even from the floor. Three storeys in height but in the curving roof style of ancient China, it wouldn't have been out of place at the Forbidden City in Beijing. This particular evening, the area was beautiful, lights strung along buildings, with old-style lampposts illuminating the walk.

Sophia sat waiting at the table. Upon entering the restaurant, Daphne's nostrils tingled with the spice and heat given off by other tables' hotpots. Seeing Daphne approach, Sophia stood to kiss her cheeks.

'How is China, teacher Daphne?' Sophia exclaimed loudly.

'Ohh growing wiser and bigger by the day,' she replied happily.

It was a joke between the two women to pretend that China was one of Daphne's students, having changed considerably in the years since she'd first arrived.

'Ugh, you don't know how happy it makes me to see you,' Sophia said, sitting down, 'you know I've only been here a few days and I forgot how much I hated it. Meeting up with you, with all these Chinese faces looking at us while we speak English, I can't help but feel like some animal in a zoo ... such a perfect spot to get away from all of them,' she motioned with one heave towards the street of Chinese tourists outside. 'Foreigner this, foreigner that, internal affairs this, love the Motherland that, the greatness of the Communist Party, why I should marry someone quickly and settle down. I'm an outsider at heart and yet they treat me like I should be one of them.'

'Now come on Sophia, they all mean well,' Daphne interjected, 'Better than the bickering we have in the West.'

'Daphne, despite your Chinese skills, you don't have to listen to these people. I couldn't bear it much longer today. Father with his "weight of the world" on my shoulders' speech. Mother with her desire I marry someone! And the verbal diarrhoea they use. "10,000 deaths should not stand in the way of your victory", I know we're predicted to go into inflation soon but the only inflation I see is that of the use of language. Frankly, with my brother allowed to enjoy his lifestyle because he's a boy,

I'm the only one in the family who might do something so all the future of the company is a burden for me. It makes me sick, all of Chinese culture is so repressive. Here, I'm taught that I can't question what the government does, while in England and America, I am allowed to be who I want. I can speak up about injustice and express anger at what I want without fear of retribution.'

Daphne grew restive, as she usually did if anyone criticised the country and culture she'd married into. She sat forward in her chair, hands up, motioning as if in a debating contest.

'But Sophia you can't say that, why do you always speak so down about where you come from? I can't even begin to describe the amount of opportunities I have here in comparison to being back home! Think about what wonderful things the Communist Party has done. Think about the hundreds of millions who have been lifted out of poverty, the extraordinary growth levels that came after the 1980s. Think about how Mao unified the country once and for all. Think about how Jiang Zemin opened the country to the world. Think about how Xi Jinping rights the wrongs of China's colonial past. Do you not think things have gone in the right direction?'

'Do you want them to succeed? I don't. Besides, who were the ones who kept the Chinese of the 1950s, 60s and 70s poor in the first place?'

'Well yes but that can be explained! Without the hard times of the Great Leap Forward and the Cultural Revolution, how would modern day Chinese people be so driven to their goal?'

'What do you mean? The Great Leap Forward and the Cultural Revolution were awful.'

'Yes, but you know that old fable … well maybe it's not an old fable but it's a story my husband once told me … A man wanted to build a house and wanted three storeys, then told the builders he didn't want the second floor because he had no need for it, just build the third floor, to which the builders laughed and said, we must go through the second floor in order to reach the third floor.'

'Have you gone mad?' Sophia raised her eyebrow.

'No, it's true. Without the pain of the second floor, we could not be standing on the top of the third floor right now.'

'Ugh, you sound just like them. Using the same rubbish metaphors and all.'

Daphne continued, ignoring her remark, 'Without all the schools run by the government forcing children into boarding dorms of eight to a room, how could people be made to truly believe they are equal? Without the success of the Han people, how would the other ethnic minorities know what to follow? They are only ten per cent of the nation anyway, the Han *should* come first! Xi Jinping Thought is full of gold dust, you should read it.'

'Unfortunately I have, it was more like dung to me … there's no fellowship between Chinese people outside of families. It might be great to go for dinner with friends, drink together and talk a little, but we don't look out for each other. If one person is shamed for whatever reason, we don't want to be seen near them. Not if we want to save face. It would be awful to be associated with someone who is considered bad by the Party even if they are innocent and even if you've known them your whole life. They have no recourse to the courts.'

'Oh balls,' Daphne replied before smirking, 'besides, I find it slightly hypocritical, from you of all people, to say this when you owe all your wealth to the communist system.'

'Oh no, I'm not that critical, believe me, I don't want to lose our wealth. My family wants to make money just like all the people of the world. What I don't like is the whole awful China 2025, take Taiwan back by 2049, revenge for the century of humiliation talk that does the rounds on all the mouthpieces of Beijing in the press and these over combative foreign ministers and ambassadors who don't know when to shut their mouths. It's so nauseating. I just wish we'd give up the whole lie and actually work to improve the international system that has allowed us to make our riches in the first place.'

'But what lie are you possibly talking about?'

'The lie that we're not trying to upset the world order or expand our influence and that the Party is peaceful when all it wants to do is hold onto power. The lie that we're *investing* in Africa or other poor countries to help them rather than squeeze the life out of every country there like any other old colonial power, exploiting the world's resources until we have a monopoly big enough to satisfy the demands of 1.4 billion people. In Zambia we secured 40 per cent of their copper supply for 30 years in exchange for three football stadiums! That's almost as bad as when the British went to New Zealand and exchanged a few guns for huge swathes of land. I suppose it's a normal enough lie but it gets to our head in ways that you can't imagine. When we get to the moon, or to Mars, there's a huge yearning in Chinese people, spurred on by the national press, that we are superior to other countries. Everyone here seems to believe in cultural superiority even as they munch on their McDonald's or listen to their Western music.'

Daphne, very pleased, sat up because her favourite argument with Sophia was about to take place and she felt confident she might win it. She enjoyed it because this argument took place whenever they'd met up for dinner, and it almost always followed the same pattern. It was a very ironic conversation because the Chinese person was very anti-Chinese whilst the foreigner was loyal to the Chinese dream. Daphne had a complete admiration for the Chinese since she'd arrived for a holiday when she was young and had climbed the Great Wall, walked around the Forbidden City and eaten Peking duck, her favourite, at a nice restaurant at the top of a hotel. Her belief in the uniqueness of Chinese culture, and even its innate historical superiority as one that had developed over 5,000 years rather than only 2,000 since Christ was born was so deep, that even after her husband had told her that his family didn't approve of his marriage to a foreigner, and even after Lesley had told her she wouldn't hire a black person for the school, her faith in China hadn't faltered.

Sophia, noticing what argument was coming, sat up too, just as eager to get her side across better than it had been last time when the debate had been an inconclusive draw.

'Daphne,' she continued, 'how could you say that we are in Africa or South America or the Middle East for any other reason instead of spreading our icy fingers of authoritarian rule into other countries and enabling their faltering regimes to stay afloat. The money acts to enrich corrupt officials whilst we can rob the people of their resources. It's what the British Empire did! But I guarantee you, with modern technology we can extract more resources in 30 years from Africa than all the European colonies extracted throughout their whole centuries of existence. We're there to trade and that's it, we're not helping the local communities in any way.'

'Of course the Chinese are there to trade, but then again so are all nations! At least the Chinese are able to extract the metals that they need. Without the Chinese money that built the mines, how would the Africans have extracted the minerals in the first place. What about the railways and roads and other infrastructure that was built in the country with Chinese help? Without these regimes in place, how could African countries remain stable? Not everywhere can be a democracy. Just look at what the Americans and the British did in Iraq and Afghanistan, we went in on the basis of war to steal, and look how bad and unstable the area has become now! But in Africa, they are finally being helped by a nation that views them as equals.'

'Equals? No, no, no, no, you have it wrong, Daphne. Equals? This is just another form of exploitation, just like the tribute system that existed in ancient China where the "barbarians" of Korea, Indochina, Mongolia, Burma and Thailand would send taxes to the emperor so he didn't invade them and take it himself. There's nothing equal about the relationship. If the Africans didn't kowtow and actually fought back against the Chinese we'd get out just as quickly as we went in … You see,' Sophia continued, 'the only countries that have developed with few problems are the ones that have been flush with Western cash. Singapore, Hong Kong, Australia, Europe after the war. This money came with the disclaimer of being transparent about what it was being spent on. The Chinese don't care, the less transparency the better!'

Daphne always interrupted when it arrived at this part of the conversation. Waving her hand eagerly, her face lit up. 'But have you not seen within China how wonderful things are now! China is now respected on the world stage. Yes, there's less transparency but that doesn't matter if things are successful. There are schools for the poorest students and a meritocratic system of government that means only the best reach the top having proved themselves. Donald Trump would never have made it past a district official were he Chinese!'

'Of course, I don't mean to say the Party since the 1980s hasn't improved the country somewhat, but at what cost? What level of pollution is OK to continue spewing? What incentives are there to ensure the people at the top aren't doing the wrong things? In the West they *must* listen to the people, otherwise they are voted out of office. In China, there's no such reliable feedback system. People are too scared to criticise because they'll end up in jail. Just look at what happens if you criticise Chinese medicine as a qualified doctor … you lose your licence to practise!'

'But you have to realise that your system at its worst happens in the UK anyway, we're just not told about it. You don't think the government in the UK reads my messages? You don't think my government lies to me too? At least you don't go invading other countries like we do.'

'Hmm, and yet we end up extracting the same concessions you would after a war. Money is power, and if you have money you can use it as leverage to pursue your agenda. With our money we can silence critics in these countries in the same way a colonial power would after a war. There are almost 100,000 Chinese students in the UK, each paying enormous fees to cash strapped universities. One word from the Communist Party that they should leave and study elsewhere, and all those 100,000 will leave, so universities go out of their way not to upset the Communist authorities. They silence their own academics' free speech. Think about it, if you're an academic in a foreign country trying to research China's forms of influence in your own country, you won't be allowed the visa into China in case you uncover something the Party doesn't like. China is using its sway to block any research into its influence. It even stretches up to the stinking UK Government. When the Premier of China went to the UK in 2014, he threw a tantrum and threatened not to come unless the British broke all protocol and allowed him to have tea with the Queen despite him only being head of the government and not head of the state. Those money-obsessed wet-wipes Cameron and Osborne were desperate for Chinese investment so caved in and allowed it. The line between respect and arse licking seems to be getting thinner and thinner by the day.'

'But ... but ... but you are being too tough on your own country, think about all the infrastructure built in China which didn't exist even 10 years ago. The growth is astonishing! A bridge that takes five years to build in the UK takes two days to build in China.'

'Not that the local people have any say over what gets built and where,' Sophia mumbled in return, 'besides, any country like China that was poor has huge potential for growth as we have seen. The Asian tigers grew so quickly because they started from such a low base. It is the same in China, only here, because the country and population is so much bigger, the numbers seem almost miraculous. It will come to a crashing halt soon enough, you'll see. Anyway, it seems you like all that's happened in China whilst I've been around the world, and I don't like what's happened. I would chuck this Communist system quick enough if only it didn't pay.'

'Surely you don't mean that, otherwise you'd tell your mother so.'

'Unfortunately I'm afraid she'd never understand,' Sophia sighed, 'she's just so engaged in her spreadsheets and her money … it's better I just shut up and put out.'

At that point the waiter came across with a large wok-like bowl split down the middle and placed it in a dent in the table that had a heating system underneath it. The liquid in the bowl began to bubble up almost immediately as the waiter placed plates of meat and vegetables around the table. Within the bowl, spices and herbs dotted around rose to the surface and moved like twigs on a lake. The girls used their chopsticks to lift the food into the bowl letting each bit of meat and vegetable cook for a few moments before being flicked into their mouths.

'You know Sophia … we may not agree on things but I'd almost forgotten that there are still some Chinese people out there who don't just gobble up everything their government tells them as if it's scientific truth.'

The girls sat in silence for a few minutes, nibbling the food they picked up with their chopsticks.

'It's funny,' Daphne continued, 'all of what you just said, that's the sort of thing Kevin was talking about when he did that strike thing last month. Did your mum tell you about that?'

'Yes she did,' Sophia said quickly, looking up gloomily, 'I wish I'd been there, I'd have been able to talk him out of it.'

'But I thought you didn't like him?'

'I don't mind him. I'm sceptical about everything, as you've seen … but I didn't dislike him. I just thought he was weak, we'd never have worked out. That doesn't mean I wanted him to go to jail like he did.'

'Hmmm, yes I guess.'

Daphne scratched her hair with painted fingernails and sat back, trying to subside the spicy pain in her mouth with a large swig of beer. Sophia continued to prod at the remaining food in the wok.

'I just wish I'd been there,' she repeated, 'I could have done some-thing.'

'I dunno … you didn't see him … he tried to persuade all of us to go.'

'And why didn't you?' Sophia asked, almost accusingly. 'I mean you know perfectly well the other teachers aren't treated the same way you are.'

'Yes I know … but … I didn't … I mean it doesn't affect me so why should I care?' Daphne replied.

Sophia laughed loudly. 'And there it is! You're Chinese at last.'

After they'd finished eating, they paid the bill and went out into the night, walking towards the metro station. Erhu music, like a sort of whiney violin, came from the shops they passed.

'What happened to the other foreign teachers on the strike?' Sophia asked.

'Oh, I mean now it's summer holiday so they're all travelling around but I know Charlie left for Shanghai.'

'Charlie? Which one is that?'

'Tall one, a little lanky.'

'Oh yes, I know him. What's he doing now?'

'I'm not too sure actually. Not teaching anymore I think, he's got some job as a researcher. Somehow, they were able to find a loophole allowing him to quit. I think he just wanted to get away from here. I'm surprised he wasn't put in too.'

'They only need one scapegoat,' Sophia mumbled ominously, 'but he'll have to be careful, if he pisses off my mum again she might really find a way for him to join Kevin in jail. She was furious about what happened.'

18

The early August weather in Shanghai goes through spells of both extreme heat and monsoon-like rains crashing fiercely to the ground. This particular day in early August, the morning was a blistering heat, the air shimmering as if a desert mirage.

Charlie woke cold and naked – his apartment's A/C had been on overnight. Eyes half open, he touched around for the blanket before noticing Areum curled up with it next to him like some caterpillar in a cocoon, her round cat-like face poking through a hole at the top. Charlie shivered as he tried to snatch some of the quilt back but she moaned and held on tighter before turning over and offering him a small corner that covered half his chest. He grabbed the remote from beside the bed and turned the A/C off. Almost immediately the cold wind, like the breath of a fridge, stopped and the room became warmer.

It was a dark, musty room, which had been converted from a storage facility in an old building into what constituted a flat. There was a small window at one end next to the bed, which just about squeezed into a 'bedroom', cut off from the living room by a thin white wall that looked like it would collapse should any weight be placed on it. The living room had a dull purple sofa opposite a TV which Charlie hadn't figured out how to use, whilst in the centre of the room sat a small coffee table. By the entrance was a small room with a toilet and a showerhead above it.

The place didn't have a kitchen but this made no difference to Charlie who bought his breakfasts and dinners from an old gentleman who had a restaurant on the avenue outside – a small hovel converted into an indoor kitchen with a few wooden chairs placed on the street outside underneath a large pine tree. There were many restaurants like it in these small pockets of the French Concession, but this particular man, with his seeping yellow eyes, crooked back and toothless smile cheered Charlie every morning and evening when he returned from work, exhausted.

Charlie specifically chose this flat because of its location in the heart of the French Concession, surrounded by the greenery and cafés he fell in love with when he first came with Gabriel in May. It was an odd building. An old home which had been hastily converted into flats as most buildings were once the Communists came to power, but this one had a few migrant workers sleeping underneath the staircase. They slept in what looked like a bed that had been moved from a dumpster into the building, broken and slanted, covered in a large red blanket – red being the colour of fortune – with a few belongings spread around them. To give them some privacy in this windowless hole, they placed a piece of cardboard over the view from the staircase, though this failed to cover much. During the days their little dwelling was empty, but when Charlie returned from a night out or a late evening of work, he would sometimes look in and see the tanned, ageing, exhausted faces of manual labourers.

The other occupants of the flats weren't much wealthier, mostly living in smoke-filled rooms which hadn't been redecorated since the 1970s. Behind brittle wooden doors Charlie could hear each of the arguments, but perhaps worst of all, each spit too. At one point a neighbour had spat on the floor just in front of him as he'd walked past, almost staining his trouser leg with a goblet of snot. Charlie, aware of the sort of jealousy that had existed with his former co-workers at the kindergarten, didn't even bother to raise a protest.

Despite all this, he enjoyed the flat, it was his home which he didn't have to share, and it was paid for by the money he earned from his job. Living here gave him a greater sense of independence than even moving from London to China for the first time. The flat, as such, was all that he could afford but he didn't mind, most of the time he tried to be social anyway, spending less than ten hours during the week stuck indoors when he wasn't sleeping. On weekends he would sit in the cafés of the streets outside or at the many bars in town which he hadn't been able to do in Hangzhou. The salsa scene was much better in Shanghai and, apart from his neighbours, the locals more friendly to foreigners.

Charlie stood up and pulled on a pair of underpants before opening the curtains to the blistering heat of the sun outside. He wiped the condensation that had formed as mist on the glass with one swipe and looked onto the street. The sun was high in the sky as cyclists on the busy street below pedalled slowly in the heat of the day – he could faintly smell the old man's fried food seeping through his window.

'What time is it?' came a moan from behind him.

'Eleven,' he replied curtly, still peering outside.

'Wake me at 12,' came the reply, 'my train's at two and I don't want to miss it.'

'Alright, I'm gonna go grab some breakfast … what do you want?'

'Bagel.'

'I was just going to go to the old man.'

'Ooooh, not again, his food's lubbish,' she said, not being able to form her r's properly.

'Ugh alright, what kind of bagel?'

'Ummm … bacon and cheese.'

He pulled on a pair of shorts and a t-shirt before slipping into some flip flops and charging out the door. The humidity slowed his stride, and by the time he'd reached the staircase, he could feel his t-shirt clinging gently to his back. The homeless person's hovel was empty but the stench of cigarette emanating from his neighbour's rooms was strong as ever.

He dived out of the entrance to his building, then turned left and darted away from the old man, trying to avoid his glance which he imagined would be one of disappointment. The glare of the sun in the sky was sharp, causing Charlie to raise his forearm to cover his eyes. He looked out of place on the streets in his mismatching t-shirt, shorts and flip flops. Most of the people in the coffee shops he passed were dressed fashionably and they ignored him as if he were some beggar.

After buying two bacon & cheese bagels and a coffee for both him and Areum, he paced back to the apartment, avoiding the gaze of any foreigners he might recognise. He'd only lived there a month, but already he felt he knew too many. He recognised in each and every one of them the degenerates, and the naïve – like two categories no less distinguishable than the male and female sex.

Back in the apartment, Areum slept peacefully in bed, whilst the temperature of the room had reached that of the outdoors. He placed the food and coffee on the coffee table and jumped in the bathroom for a pee. After a quick splash of water on his hands, he returned to the bed before kneeling on it to stroke Areum softly with his fingers. She moaned and curled into the duvet once more, so he pulled the duvet up and began tickling until she let go.

'Ahh, no, no,' she cried.

'Come on I have breakfast.'

'Oooh yummy.'

She jumped up naked and grabbed Charlie's dressing gown which was strewn across the end of the bed.

'Which one's mine?' she asked.

'They're both the same,' Charlie replied as he made the bed before going into the living room to sit beside her on the low couch.

'Hmmm,' she said, holding the bagel with both hands and taking a large bite.

They sat for a few minutes quietly eating their food. Charlie scrolled through his phone whilst Areum peered around the room.

'When did you move here again? I can't remember when the first time I came was. I know this is my third.'

'Errrr, it was in July, just after the kids broke up for summer.'

'Oh yeah. That's right.'

For someone who spoke English as a third language, Areum spoke it remarkably well. She was a few years older than Charlie but had the mind and appearance of someone much younger. She had a roundish face with prominent cheekbones, ears that stuck close to the side of her head. Her shoulder-length jet black hair was thick and looked graceful, even when messy.

'You know, I think I stayed in a hotel down the road when I first came here a few years ago,' Areum said.

'Oh really? What for?'

'When my company first was thinking about transferring me to Hangzhou.'

'Why'd you meet here and not Hangzhou?'

'Pff, I don't know, you ask them.'

She flicked a crumb off Charlie's chin.

'Do you miss Seoul?' he asked.

'A little bit, but I didn't want to live with my parents anymore.'

'You still lived with your mum and dad?'

'Yeah … Seoul is expensive and I don't have a husband yet.'

'Are you going to go back soon?'

'I don't know, I haven't decided. After three years this place feels more like home, and I have Miki now.'

'Miki?'

'My cat.'

'Oh,' he laughed. 'I thought you meant you had a kid or something.'

'Oh no, I don't want a kid yet. I need to get married first.'

'Why haven't you?'

'I haven't found the right person. Mom and Dad tried their best but I didn't like any of them.'

'Does your mum mind you dating foreigners?'

'Um … No, well, a little. But she did say as long as they're white.'

'Seriously?'

'What do you mean?'

'Kevin told me that teacher he had an affair with said the same thing.'

'Some Asian parents view things that way. It's changing though.'

Charlie finished off his bagel and scrunched the wrapper into a small ball before throwing it towards the bin. He opened his coffee lid and drained the last contents before throwing it after the wrapper.

'You know, I'm surprised how fast we've become so close,' Charlie said suddenly turning around. 'To think I only asked you out because I was leaving for Shanghai.'

'Me too. Maybe we shouldn't have slept together that first night.'

'Are you kidding? That was the best bit.'

'No, that's not what I mean,' she replied. 'What I mean is that you just moved to Shanghai, and it's a big city, maybe you shouldn't start a relationship with someone in Hangzhou while you're making new friends in this one. Besides, you just said you would have to do some work today and it's a Saturday.'

'OK ... we don't have to be boyfriend girlfriend anyway.'

'No we don't ... don't worry about it.'

She gave him a kiss which tasted of bacon.

'What do you need to do this afternoon anyway?' she asked, taking another bite of her bagel.

'I just need to look over my notes from work. It's not too much, my boss and me are going to a conference on Monday evening where there'll be a lot of British and American clients. This time it's my job just to work out if they're interested in getting some due diligence done.'

'Due diligence? What's that?'

'It's like ... err ... let's say you want to do business as a foreign company in China, but you don't know if you can trust the people you're going into business with for whatever reason. You know, difference of culture, lack of transparency, are these businesses even legit? That sort of thing. Well my company does the background research for you. We work out if you can trust Chinese people. There's a lot of corruption in China so there's a lot of business to be made. It's not even just that. For example, when I first arrived my boss just told me a story of a company in Thailand where another one of our offices is based, that wanted to hire this man who said he was Chinese. They wanted to make sure he wasn't lying on his CV etc ... My boss looked into it and basically the guy said he'd done economics at a university in China in the 80s. Apparently that wasn't a very done thing in that day and age, so my boss did more digging. It turned out the guy wasn't Chinese, but was in fact North Korean and therefore likely a spy who wanted to work in this Thai company.'

'Interesting.'

'As you can imagine my boss was chuffed at finding that out. I guess another example I ... oh yeah, I don't know if you saw this because it was a British newspaper, but over Christmas there was a story in *The Sunday Times* about a Christmas card which had been bought in a big chain supermarket which contained a scrawled message along the lines of "send help … find this man John Humphreys … we're forced to make these here" or something like that. Anyway, after that we had some supermarket chains from across the Western world get in contact with us and ask if we could research the people they already had contracts with in China to make products, because if any of the production lines were sublet to prisons, or slave labour, they wanted out. Apparently my boss didn't find any but it's that kind of thing.'

'But you don't speak Chinese very well. How can you be any help?'

'I can do some research and write some reports in English, plus go through all the English contracts they have then look for any discrepancies with what we find after we've completed our research. I'll get to a stage where I'll end up writing the reports in English once I'm qualified enough to understand all the data we get. At the moment my boss does it but English is his second language so he doesn't always write very well.'

'You sound important,' she chuckled.

Oh well, if this is what she likes to hear, Charlie thought.

'There's more, I feel I might be onto something.'

'What do you mean?'

'Well, remember my old employer, Lesley, and how I told you she had some businesses that had gone public on the New York Stock Exchange?'

'Yes, what about it?'

'Well, I've been looking up as much as I can about her steel business. Online reports, statements and yearly profits. They've been going up and up and up.'

'That's expected, isn't it?'

'Sure … but the numbers are too good. Like I'm talking 100 per cent increases in value annually. Her business volumes are tripling in size year on year, at weirdly rounded numbers, but in one of the statements, she said she didn't expect the need for further investment in space for at least five years. Something's fishy about this.'

'So what are you going to do about it?'

Charlie hesitated in thought. 'That's the problem … I don't really know. I'm going to raise it with my boss but unless a client comes and asks us to do research … well there's no point using resources to explore the company more.'

'I guess you'd have to be around for a few years to figure that out ...' Areum said quietly, 'is this a career you want to be doing for the long term?'

'No, not really, I imagine I'll do it for a few years but I don't know what I want to do afterwards ... just see where life takes me.'

'Hmmmm ... you know ... that's why I don't think we should see each other again.'

Charlie turned his head towards her. 'What?'

'You're 12 years younger than me. I can't keep my life on hold just for something where you don't know what you want.'

'But I want you.'

'No, you don't.'

'But ... but I really like you,' he stuttered.

'I know, but you know what it's like with expats, we all live temporarily in one world with no intention of really staying there for too long. Maybe for a few years but especially not in China. I don't mean to be brutal about it but I've been doing this a lot longer than you.'

She grabbed his cheeks between her thumb and forefinger of her right hand. 'Listen ... maybe we can meet up again and have a fun night like last night again, but I'm not going to make a habit of coming here.'

Charlie sighed, his head felt heavy and he swayed a little.

'Oh come on,' Areum smiled, 'don't be silly, you're still young. I didn't have my first boyfriend until I left Korea to go to Australia when I was 26, you have plenty of time ...'

She looked at her phone and pushed herself off the bed before drifting slowly towards the bathroom. 'Like I say,' she continued, 'if I'm not in a relationship and you're not either in a few months' time, maybe we could have another night like this ... but pull your pants up for now.'

She took off the dressing gown before entering the bathroom, leaving Charlie to stare wistfully after her.

'Oh well. What would Kevin do?' he mumbled to himself.

19

It was approaching Christmas, the temperature was cold and the sky was turning greyer day by day. Charlie bounded down the street in chinos and a shirt, about to meet his colleagues for Christmas Lunch at a sports bar in Shanghai. About ten minutes' walk from his house in the French Concession, this was his regular hide out for world sport and a spot many Westerners enjoyed frequenting, for the food and alcohol was good. It was only 8th December, but the interior already brimmed with Christmas decorations. Today was the biggest lunch of the year which all its usual guests would sign up for, followed in close succession by Thanksgiving and every Sunday Roast they had done since they'd been founded ten years before.

The bar was situated on the 4th floor of an old office building, whereas its interior had been redesigned to match that of a Hooters. Once you were out of the lift, one was met with a surreal atmosphere of jeering and loud music alongside sports commentary. The inside was enormous, stretching back at least 60 metres. The first thing you saw when you entered, the *piece de resistance,* was a large screen, the largest Charlie had ever seen on top of the bar and behind it the kitchen, windows allowing the customer to see their food being prepared. To the right was a baseball net where players could bat away the afternoon, frequented mostly by Americans but also some Japanese and South Koreans. Behind the entrance to the right were basketball nets and a big screen suspended above them. At the back to the left of the bar was situated an array of snooker and hockey tables, constantly in use by groups of boys tossing darts nearby.

It was about 2 p.m. when Charlie finally arrived, and the room was uproarious – people were drunk and the music blared, with the latest songs from America and some Chinese music thrown in for good measure. The room was at various stages of lunch, with some early birds already having a go at the sports opportunities situated around the room, whilst some like Charlie had just arrived and were trying to find their party. It was hard to see through the ecstatic room of people, some of whom were dressed as Santa Claus, others as reindeer. It felt like a Stag do and Hen Party wrapped into Christmas.

For people like Charlie, far from home and slightly lonely, the celebrations took on a special significance. Indeed in China, where the tackiness of seeing some Christmas decorations up year round, those who celebrated it properly did so with new friends and old alike. The spirit of being an expat drew together people who, in their native countries, might not usually have been friends.

As Charlie searched through the crowd for his colleagues, he bumped into a few drunken people, who turned around and screamed 'Merry Christmas!' before darting off again. He dodged and ducked as more people aimlessly jumped in his way or fell off chairs into his path. The atmosphere of the room was exhilarating, and he looked forward to seeing a side of his Chinese colleagues he hadn't seen before, for they had been reserved and hidden since he'd arrived five months earlier.

To the left, he saw his boss waving towards him, himself from Thailand, dark skinned, with a smile which showed off his fake teeth. As Charlie walked across, he could see his Chinese colleagues a little be-mused by what was going on around them. They were pointing and laughing, and lifting their cups in frequent '*ganbei*!'; the Chinese version of Cheers! Christmas was just a Western version of the Lunar New Year celebrations to them.

'Ronnie! Happy Christmas!' Charlie shouted when he was within hearing distance.

'Happy Christmas!' he returned.

Ronnie was the founder of this company and spoke fluent Thai, English, Spanish and Chinese. He'd interviewed and ultimately given the job to Charlie who had established himself as the right hand man. The job Charlie had turned out to be a mix of Research Assistant, Salesman, and Secretary to Ronnie. As the only white man in the firm, he was a jack of all trades, attracting people from the West who wanted due diligence checks on Chinese companies, and being shown off to current Chinese clients. Charlie didn't mind at all, he enjoyed the conferences and sales meetings it entailed, and he still got to use his legal mind when his job entailed research.

After a round of '*ganbei*' with his other colleagues, he grabbed a seat next to Ronnie and the jovialities began. Despite being the only group at the bar with a predominantly Chinese make up, these were Shanghai Chinese and more confident in participating in whatever their boss asked of them. When another table jeered, they jeered back. When some foreigners came up to start talking to them, they talked back in friendly terms. Most of them only spoke limited English, but alcohol bridged the gap of understanding.

'Charlie,' a colleague called Yu started, 'we all came together and bought a present for you.'

Charlie looked towards Ronnie and smiled.

'Don't look at me,' Ronnie replied putting his hands up, 'this was them.'

'Yes, in China we like to welcome friends from abroad and we're so happy you came to join our firm. We've all really enjoyed having you around and we hope you can stay for a long time.'

Charlie took the gift Yu held out in front of him. Its wrapping paper glinted as he moved it about in his hands.

'That's so kind of you,' he said tugging to open it.

'Oh no, don't open it. Also be careful, it's delicate,' Yu laughed.

'Why not?'

'This is China, that's rude!'

'Oh, sorry.'

'Don't worry about it. Ganbei!'

After the main course of turkey, cranberry sauce, trimmings and roast potatoes arrived, Ronnie took Charlie by the arm and led him to the bar. As they weaved through the crowd, Ronnie whispered in his ear, 'You'll be happy with the lead I've got.'

'I will?'

'Yes,' Ronnie found it hard to contain his smile.

'Well go on … explain.' Charlie gestured.

'OK, I haven't told anyone this yet but I want you to work on this with me as this will be personal to you. I'll be the lead so we get it absolutely right. Honestly I think we can make a killing from this.'

'Go on,' Charlie repeated.

'So, remember when you told me about your old boss and how she owned a very diversified portfolio of investments, indeed that she'd listed on the New York Stock Exchange with some of them, and you thought there was something fishy about it. Well, I've done as much research as I can and put out some feelers and I've found a hedge fund in the US which owns some of the shares in one of her companies who became really confused when I told him what you told me. They've gone over the numbers since and got back to me last week. They've realised they can't trust the company's accountants. The numbers just don't add up but because the shares keep going up and up in value, they hadn't thought to check them out before.'

'Uh huh,' Charlie nodded.

'I did some digging myself and realised it was PwC China which did the checks on the firm and gave it the seal of approval to list on the NYSE. Now I know a couple of people at PwC from my days as part of Deloitte's due diligence team, so I asked them if they were aware of this company. I went for a drink with one of them in particular and he told me that they hadn't even bothered to go to the factory.'

Ronnie paused to let this sink in. Slowly, as if still trying to work it out, Charlie replied. 'So you're saying they just gave the seal of approval without any actual checks on whether the company was telling the truth about its output?'

'Yes.'

'So, all Lesley did was get a mate of hers to sign a document saying the company was ready to list on the NYSE and the investment bank that did her IPO took her at face value?'

'Yep.'

'This is huge!' Charlie said, almost shouting, 'so she defrauded American investors out of over $100 million!'

'Keep your voice down,' Ronnie replied, grabbing his arm again.

'But if she listed three years ago, that means she must have sunk her earnings into the school and used ill gotten money for it.'

'Yes exactly.'

'So what can we do about it?' Charlie asked. 'How can we prove she is lying?'

'Well, we need to write a report and get it in the press in the US. Our hedge fund clients just want to make money out of it, so if we tell them to short it after getting legitimate proof and then planting the story in the news, they will make a killing.'

Charlie stopped for a moment. 'But hang on, how many of the shares of her company does this hedge fund own?'

'Only about a $1 million worth at present, but they'll short the position and who knows how much they could make,' Ronnie replied, taking a sip of his recently arrived beer as they stood at the bar.

'So they might make a killing, but what about the other people who own the other $99+ million of shares?'

'Well they won't, but not everyone can win from this.'

'But if it's mostly funds which are investing in this, that could be

American people's savings and retirement?'

'Well, yes, you're right …' Ronnie said, hearing the tetchiness in Charlie's voice, 'but it's worthless stock to begin with. Look, if we can prove the link, her name in America will be ruined, her two other businesses listed on the stock exchange will go down and she'll never be able to defraud American investors again. We'll have cleansed the markets. Hell, if we do it right, we could get the Securities & Exchange Commission in on it, and the next time she's in the States, she could get arrested! Isn't that what you want to do after she ensured your friend was tossed in jail for two years?'

Charlie took a long sip of his pint, he was torn despite the attractiveness of the deal. Was it right that he would take part in something that would lose pensioners in the US a lot of money whilst making one hedge fund much richer?

Ronnie, noticing Charlie's reluctance soothed him with the language of a man who had a profound understanding of the blurred line between right and wrong. 'Look, I understand you're conflicted on this, but if we don't do it, someone else will. There are lots of due diligence companies in China, I was just lucky enough to know a guy who knew a guy at a hedge fund in the US who wanted to know the actual value of their shares. If we don't help them, they'll go to another one of the firms in Shanghai who will, and they'll make the commission from this deal. Pensioners will still lose money, and if not done correctly, which is why I want you to help out, your old boss will get away scot-free.'

Charlie took another long, cool sip of his pint. 'OK, let's do it,' he said, biting his lip. 'Where do we start?'

'Lovely … alright, first thing Monday, come and see me in my office and we can discuss our strategy.'

After they'd clinked glasses, they returned to their table with the round of drinks to a rapturous round of applause from their red faced, tipsy colleagues.

On Monday, Charlie, dressed in his usual suit, almost leapt as he walked to the company's HQ in a discreet part of Pudong, the south-east part of the city. Despite living in the French Concession, he was only a 30-minute commute away by metro, which was convenient and allowed him time to perk up before work. All he could think about on Sunday had been the thought of Lesley in jail and how he could send news of it to Kevin.

He knew, however, that this would have to be secretive and he would have to be careful who he told. He definitely couldn't tell the other foreign teachers from the school. After the incident, the school had been temporarily closed down as the Chinese teachers who had taken part were duly purged and their teaching licences revoked. Elijah and him had gotten away with it because they were deemed more 'valuable' to Lesley, but Kevin, as the ringleader, was charged with civil disobedience and contributing to a breakdown in social order. Thankfully, the company in Shanghai came back with a way for him to exploit a loophole in the visa system, and he was able to quit soon after.

He entered the tower block that housed the company and caught the lift to their 12th floor office. The view of the city from the windows was marvellous – in the distance stood the financial district, rising as it did towards the sky. The office was small and only had enough desks for the ten employees, but it felt homely. At the back was a heavy steel door behind which ongoing cases were filed. It was 07:30 and the office was still empty bar Ronnie whose office door was ajar. Charlie knocked on it and Ronnie shouted for him to come in.

'So what did they get you?'

'Who? … Oh Yu. It was a tea set.'

'A tea set?'

'Yes, a very nice one. I don't know what it's made of but it looks good.'

'Clay probably. An odd gift.'

'I mentioned it a few weeks ago actually in passing to Yu. He must've told the others.'

After taking a seat on the other side of Ronnie's desk, the boss started.

'OK, so the crux of the issue is, that this particular factory is saying it did over $50 million dollars of business last year in China alone. It shouldn't be too hard to prove as this is a steel manufacturing company, it's not a software company, so the product should be easy to see coming and going. The factory should be in pristine condition too.' Ronnie took out one of the reports, 'Look here, the company has said in all these press releases that they have contracts with large road building contractors and companies that build housing projects. In order to fulfil these contracts given the size of their clients, the company should be shipping about three dozen truckloads of steel per day. They should be loading and unloading goods all the time with hundreds of employees and plenty of truck drivers. Let's set up a camera outside the front gate, and check out the factory as potential investors.'

'Is that legal?' Charlie asked.

'Is what legal?' Ronnie replied.

'To observe what a private company is doing.'

'Of course not, but we have to get them somehow. As long as we're not caught, it should be OK.'

'But this is just one company. How can we take down Lesley?'

'Well look, this is just one of the three companies she listed on the NYSE, and the one that the hedge fund hiring us has shares in. Believe me, if we prove this, the other companies will lose value straight away because her name is attached.'

Charlie clapped his hands. 'OK, when can we get started?' he asked excitedly.

'We'll organise a trip down there for next week, I'll buy the camera equipment in the meantime. The factory is in Jiangsu, near Changzhou, about an hour and a half train away. If we all act like prospective investors, we can have a tour of the plant.'

20

The radio in the rental car blared Chinese music as they went deeper into the industrial area of Changzhou. It was an awful assortment of softly spoken Chinese words attempting romance and longing. The use of a saxophone was out of place, and the singer would suddenly shout into the microphone like some teenager unable to control their emotions. The melodies were slow and all the songs repetitive, but this didn't stop the driver from humming to each tune as they sped along the highway, barely able to see ahead in the pelting rain.

Communist style utilitarian blocks rose on either side of the motor-way, much like they did in Hangzhou, but without the greenery and pleasantness of the ancient city. They looked empty, and stretched out into the distance, each without the character that could've made looking at them a little more pleasant. The sky was a dark grey and the rain ferocious.

'How do you like Changzhou Charlie?' Ronnie asked, turning around from his seat in the front of the seven-seater.

'I wonder why I ever wanted to live in Shanghai when I could've lived here,' Charlie replied.

'I grew up in a place like this.'

'You did?'

'Well, when I say a place like this, I mean a place like this would've been 30 years ago before these factories came here, when it was mostly not very arable farmland.'

'Is that what this was?'

'It would've been flat, yes. A bit like the very edge of Bangkok on the way towards Burma. You ever heard of the Bridge over the River Kuai?'

'Yes.'

'Well, it was near there.'

Ronnie looked at the surroundings once more, and sighed. 'It was idyllic growing up there. You see these lonely old men just wandering around? They would've grown up here, they would've remembered what it was like before. Sure the Bund looks far more beautiful and futuristic now but the ordinary peasant, who had so little to begin with, has lost the one thing he clung to that gave him purpose.'

'What's that?'

'His family, his way of life, his home. For generations his bloodline would've toiled in these fields, now look at them, they're wastelands. This old man would've been there when the Communists took over. His family would've been so full of hope that his life prospects would improve, that the corruption of the Kuomintang had been stamped out, that the imperialists would be gone forever. What do you think they'd say if they saw him now?'

'They don't seem too angry about it.'

'Development has its ups and downs. Perhaps the worst down is the familiar becomes the unrecognisable. It's great for people like you and me who can live it up in Shanghai, but what about these people?'

The lonely old men looked in the car's direction as it drove by. They had sullen bronzed looks on their faces, and crooked backs.

'You see those sheep over there?' Ronnie pointed out to the other side of the road where a couple of sheep lazily grazed on a small grassy land. 'I have a story about sheep, want to hear it?'

'Sure, why not.'

'Well it was lambing season on the farms nearby where I grew up once, and I was asked by the local villagers to help out – nimble hands you see.'

'How nice.'

'Sometimes the sheep need a little bit of help.'

'Is that so?'

'Anyway, one of the sheep had a bit of a problem. The farmer was sure that after two lambs had come out, there was still one left. He gave me this large condom-like glove to go in with my skinny arms and drag it out. Firstly I had to catch it, which is harder than it looks, I ended up tackling it with a two footed football-like tackle. I think it was more stunned by what I was doing than anything so it stopped in its tracks. I grabbed it and put it in place. Reaching round the back, I whispered gently to calm it down and eased my hand inside. My first thought was "wow this is tight", my second was "ooh this is warm" and my third was "where the hell's the lamb?" I thought, alright maybe I need to go deeper, which I did, by now I must've been up to my elbow and there was still nothing closely resembling a sheep. I was so into the process that I'd forgotten to keep the sheep calm and I realised I had to whisper in its ear some more, but, looking up, I could tell by her cross-eyed expression looking directly at me that something was amiss.

'So I looked back at my hand and realised I was in the wrong hole … I've been banned from midwifery ever since … that sheep still looks at me to this day in a funny way.'

'Sounds like a good … er … bonding experience,' Charlie replied, a little stunned. Ronnie had these odd, eccentric ways of bringing up stories when he was reminded of them. It's what made him great with new clients, but a very different boss.

His colleague, next to him in the middle of the car, held out a small jar offering Charlie some pickled radish, which he politely declined.

'Do a lot of people eat that?' Charlie asked, his face grimacing in horror.

His colleague looked at the jar, then back to Charlie before saying in a heavy Chinese accent, labouring each word as it came out, as if trying to recite a poem.

'Those who like it, eat it. Those who don't like it, don't eat it.'

Charlie looked at the jar of pickles.

'What wisdom,' he muttered.

The smell of the pickled radish wafted around the car, and he shuffled around uncomfortably in his oven-like suit. It didn't help that the driver had turned the heating to its highest setting; Ronnie's story also hadn't helped and he started to feel sick. This was not how he'd planned to spend his Wednesday – they hadn't even needed him apparently, he'd only joined out of an interest to see how Lesley made her money. He started to regret it as soon as they arrived outside the station at Changzhou, where the surroundings gave the impression that a bomb had just gone off. Among the shattered grey walls of the old buildings, people had been scavenging in the rain for bricks and bits of scrap, as if in a third world country, not the second wealthiest nation on earth.

The monotonous view out of the window continued for at least 30 minutes until they turned off the motorway onto a single road leading into what felt like the apocalypse. Driving along with wasteland all around them – decrepit old factories with holes in the roof – the car trundled along a heavily potholed road, swerving between crater-like holes.

Charlie's stomach ached, and he opened the window slightly to let in some fresh air. As they bumped along, he felt some vomit at the back of his throat, but was able to put his hand over his mouth just in time. The sickly taste rose in little bursts as he tried to prevent more of his breakfast coming up by taking long swigs of water.

While Charlie struggled to compose himself, Ronnie was thinking aloud. 'What the hell kind of truck carrying steel can get down this road …'

Charlie undid his seatbelt to release the pressure on his stomach just as they hit a pothole which made him jump out of his seat and his head bang the roof of the car with one hollow thud.

'Charlie shut up back there, I'm trying to think.'

'Sorry,' he said meekly, having landed on the floor.

The driver, little caring for the state of the car, nor the safety of his passenger, continued humming along to the music, and staring at the road. Despite the heavy rain, the ever-present smog still hadn't lifted and it was hard to see further than 50 metres ahead. Some time later, the road turned into a dirt track, and Charlie, already feeling queasy, sighed with an air of self-pity as he crashed to the floor of the car again. His Chinese colleagues giggled at the sight of this tall white man fumbling about.

When they finally arrived at the factory, the rain had stopped but the sky was still a threatening grey. Charlie, having only just survived the journey without vomiting, opened the door as soon as the car stopped at the entrance and ungracefully fell out, white as a sheet. Ronnie, with his sunglasses on, despite the lack of need for them, slinked like a panther the ten metres to the security guard and explained they'd made an appointment as prospective investors to see the site. The man picked up the phone and spoke quickly with someone before telling the arrivals to wait for a few minutes.

The outside of the factory was a lot smaller than they'd imagined. There was steam rising from one of the two chimneys in the complex, but the building seemed worn down by many years of harsh weather. It was a metal tomb, rusting corrugated metal lining the roof of a concrete structure that looked like it might crumble when the rain started again. There were food wrappers swirling in the wind around the perimeter of the site, which was only a wire fence, barely tall enough to prevent trespassers, should there have been any in this wasteland. There were only a few cars in the parking lot, which itself had potholes and broken walls which had once been adorned with flowers, but since been neglected leaving only dead, heavily brown strands of plant. The smog covered everything other than the factory, it being suspended as if in some hazy dream. Charlie half expected zombies to suddenly limp slowly towards them out of the wilderness.

'What do you think?' Charlie asked.

'You know this one factory apparently made 400,000 tonnes of steel last year,' Ronnie replied. 'That's just over 1,000 tonnes a day. It's just gone midday … do you think they've made 500 tonnes so far today?'

Charlie looked at the decrepit factory, then back to Ronnie. 'Hard to believe it makes anything.'

As he stood in disbelief, looking at this building that seemed more like it should be a Berlin nightclub than a cutting edge factory making high value metals, a rat ran across the path ahead.

A small group of heavily tanned people in obviously hastily put on high vis jackets and hard hats that were two sizes too big shuffled towards them at the entrance – one even had his hard hat on backwards.

Briefly speaking to Ronnie, they ushered the group in giving them little umbrellas as they did. The security guard invited the driver, who looked identical to him, fat and thumb-like, into his cabin for a cup of tea.

As they approached the main building, Charlie was hit by a smell like the back of a garbage truck, sewage like and unpleasantly filling his nostrils; it tingled his sinus and made him screw up his face. The others didn't seem to recognise it, continuing to walk up ahead. The barren tarmac outside the unloved factory seemed ghostly; puddles of water strewn around the uneven floor.

The guide opened a big metallic, gate-like door, more suitable at an allotment than a profitable steel factory. Charlie had hoped the inside would be warmer, steel on the whole needing a high temperature in the production process. They were instead met by a barren sight of rusty structures. It was obvious the arrival of random investors had set the workers into a frantic state, trying to look like they were doing something of importance. Old men, barely able to pick up a chair, let alone operate clunky machines, stood around, as if awoken from a nap, rubbing their eyes and limping aimlessly. In its day, the factory with its vast expanse and size, must've been able to produce a fair amount of steel, but this part of the factory looked like it hadn't been used in at least a decade.

'Are they going to show us the bit where they actually make steel?' Charlie asked.

'I've already asked … you owe me a drink if you can guess what they said.'

'Err …yes they'd love to?'

'It's apparently only open to employees because of safety concerns,' Ronnie raised his eyebrow.

'Uh huh,' Charlie replied.

'Notice this,' Ronnie said, raising his index finger and swirling it in a small circle, 'the number of cars in the parking lot would suggest these are *all* the employees in this room here.'

The guides meandered awkwardly from side to side, looking at each other as if begging one of them to take authority of the tour and competently answer all questions that might come their way. They were particularly disconcerted by the appearance of a foreigner in their mix.

'How many tours of investors do you usually take here?' Ronnie asked.

'Er … you're the first one in three years. At least the first with a foreigner,' came the reply from the youngest looking man – though that could have meant anything between 30 and 50 years old.

There was an awkwardness in the air. The workers looked at the investors, the investors looked at the guides, the guides tried to avoid eye contact.

'How many employees do you have?' Ronnie asked finally.

'200,' came the quick reply.

There must've been 50 people in the room at most.

'Where is the toilet?' Charlie asked.

He was shown by one of the old men to a room which made him feel queasy once more. The smell of mouldy faeces wafted in the air. The floor around the urinals was covered in liquid, and on the other side of the room, was a row of barely covered alcoves. The dividing walls between the stalls was about a metre high, and the occupant was invited to put two feet either side of a gutter like hole in the ground which joined all the cubicles together. Charlie, who'd come to expect these sort of facilities in China, carefully avoided squatting above a giant mound of faeces in the cubicle which looked cleanest. Flies buzzed around his bum as he grimaced at the smell. The man who had accompanied him had also decided to relieve himself, and sat effortlessly on his hind legs whilst typing something into his phone. Charlie tried not to look up in case their eyes met – the wall dividing the cubicles being just below head height – not that they would be able to speak, the man was shouting into his phone in the Jiangsu dialect.

After he'd carefully extracted himself from the squat position and wiped what he could, he walked to the basin and searched for soap only to see a small, chewed up bar in the corner of the bathroom. He washed his hands with the jet stream of freezing cold water the tap offered, and rapidly turned around to join the others; his sense of smell completely distorted.

The others had moved from their position back outside to the front of the factory where they were receiving a lecture on the history of Changzhou and how steel factories had first been built there during the Great Leap Forward.

'Have fun?' Ronnie asked.

Charlie, whose face had turned deathly white, shook his head.

'You know what ...' he finally replied, 'perhaps I'll leave this to the professionals next time … What's the plan now?'

Ronnie tapped his nose, 'I'll tell you when we're back in the car.'

'Where's Ming?' Charlie asked.

'Aren't you observant!'

After some pleasantries where the guides betrayed an obvious look of relief to have bluffed their way through the tour unscathed, Charlie and his colleagues turned around to head towards the main entrance, where they saw Ming laughing with the security guard and driver. After a quick goodbye, they got back into the car and started on the long journey back to Changzhou station.

'So … Ming … where were you?' Charlie asked in his limited Chinese.

'I did what you asked me to, boss,' he said to Ronnie.

Charlie paused before turning to Ronnie. 'What did he say?'

'He said he did what I asked him.'

'Oh, anything more?'

'Nope.'

'Well can someone tell me what's going on?' he said, exasperatedly.

'He set up some cameras outside the entrance, Charlie,' Ronnie replied.

'What? How? Surely the security guard saw him?'

'No, I asked the driver to make sure he was occupied throughout the whole time we were having the tour. Ming went outside to take a call before disappearing, and sneaking out the entrance to install them.'

'Oh, I see. Did we get the pictures we needed?'

'Yeah, don't worry, the camera in my tie was working before we went in, that's got more than enough evidence alone of what the inside of the factory looks like. Now we just need to link that up with what we find in the next few months from the camera outside.'

'Do you think we can trust anything they say?'

'Look, I think they made *some* steel here. That chimney wouldn't be smoking for no reason and they would've needed samples to show investors three years ago. Though I suspect they also hired a few hundred people to look like they worked here the last time investors came. Besides, most steel making equipment needs to be kept on 24/7. *But,* I reckon they make at most five tonnes a day, which suggests they should be getting a truck every other day … I can't imagine the quality is very good either. This stuff probably goes to some of the minor cities in Anhui.'

'How do you know so much about steel?'

'Did you not read the pack I sent you on this stuff?'

'No,' Charlie replied sheepishly.

'The information is all out there. Just need to look in the right places, and know the right people. No one can hide,' he said, winking at Charlie. The car continued along the road at a leisurely pace. Charlie had recovered from his queasy feeling, and presently felt in a good mood. Perhaps it was the upset stomach of earlier, or the worry about the unknown when they had been on the way to the factory, but hope had now turned to certainty that they were on their way to finding something big. So far, his work for the firm had mostly been limited in scope, uncovering dodgy individuals and writing research reports. This was the first time he felt he was changing the face of something – he felt he could bring down a big fish and send a message to the world. It was an exhilarating feeling of power which he allowed himself to indulge in.

21

Christmas Day was particularly cold. As the only Westerner in the office, Ronnie gave Charlie the day off. He decided it was best to go back to Hangzhou and spend it with the few people he knew well in China.

On the train across, Charlie looked outside the window at the passing countryside covered as it always seemed to be in a haze of pollution. Sitting near the back of the train, he kept shaking his left leg, visibly annoying the person next to him. Charlie was anxious to tell the other teachers what he knew, but had to keep reminding himself it wasn't the right time yet. Besides, if this happened, they could lose their jobs, and however much they disliked Lesley, they had shown by their reluctance to take part in the strike that their jobs were more sacred to them than their principles. He carried with him a secret-santa gift he had prepared to give Ellie, some chocolates and a scented candle – she liked yoga and things that were sweet, and these were the first things that came to mind.

When he arrived at Hangzhou East station, he took a taxi that went past West Lake, reminding him of the good and bad times he had experienced in the beautiful city. He imagined himself walking by the lake, and drinking on the roof terrace of the salsa bar, attempting to flirt with girls, yet always failing though not through lack of trying. He hadn't been back to Hangzhou since moving to Shanghai in late June, but he had fond memories even though he'd been there so briefly.

The taxi passed a group of school children on a field trip. They were in a line, two by two, and between each child was a ring attached to a rope, designed to keep them in some semblance of order. Meanwhile, their teachers struggled to keep them together as they jostled and walked into one another, pointed and fell in the way only children can fall, splaying their limbs out in all directions. Charlie smiled, remembering how much fun it had been to play with the kids at the kindergarten, their bluntness at once innocent and hilarious.

As the car pulled up at Daphne's neighbourhood, Charlie leapt out and waited at the gate for Daphne to come down and let him in. He was a little shocked when one of the kids he used to teach waddled up to him, obviously a child who lived in the same community as Daphne.

'Charlie teacher! Charlie teacher!'

'Hello Jason, how … are … you?' he said, reverting to his old teaching style of slowed clear speech and wide eyes open with a large smile.

'I … am … happyyyyy,' Jason responded with a grin, accentuated by his two little forefingers pulling his mouth even wider to make him look like a small clown.

'Wow!' Charlie clapped, 'Well done!'

Just then, Daphne came to the gate and opened it for him.

'I do not miss that one bit,' Charlie said quickly under his breath after he'd waved goodbye to Jason and his grandfather, who had filmed the whole exchange with his phone's camera.

'Oh, have you already started?' he said, entering Daphne's apartment.

Everyone else was in festive jumpers and had opened their presents. Gift wrapper littered the floor, whilst Daphne's cat licked empty sweet wrappers. Her apartment was cosy, homely, and without any trace of mess other than the gift wrapper. In the corner, like in his old flat, was a balcony more attuned to the hanging of washing than sitting outside on a summer's day. As in all Chinese homes, Daphne had adopted the custom of asking her guests to put on slippers when at the door of the house, and keeping them on whilst inside. As Charlie was the final arrival, he had a choice of a fraying pair which the cat enjoyed peeing on, or a pair of small frilly pink slippers which Daphne's husband had bought her years ago which she'd only worn once – her favourite colour he had since realised, being purple. Charlie elected to wear the latter and stumbled a few times whilst he got used to their feel.

'Sorry we didn't hang about for you!' Daphne apologised. 'We just couldn't wait.'

After festive cheer was passed around and he'd given a hug to everyone, he raised a glass of sparkling wine and finished it in one glug before joining the rest on the sofa who had already started watching *Love Actually*.

After an hour, Daphne called everyone to the table and brought out a vegetable nut roast as Charlie took a seat next to Elijah and his fianceé Vivian. They talked about what they'd been doing since the incident. Elijah had tried to get a job at the same international school that Vivian was at, but failed without the right number of qualifications. As they talked, they avoided the topic they knew was still on everyone's mind, and Charlie tried to hide his sadness at the thought of his friend all alone in an unheated cell, eating rice.

'You know, I regret not striking with you guys now,' Daphne said suddenly. She stared wistfully at the vegetable roast as she said it, 'I really do.'

Silence engulfed the room. Each person seemed to stop eating all at once.

'Since you left Charlie, the school's really gone to shit. Some of the parents took their kids out because of the "teachers' bad influence", but not enough to shut the school. They've really clamped down on our freedoms now. We have to stay in our office for the whole of our three hour lunch, and we're not allowed to speak to the Chinese teachers outside of school. I'm sure they're monitoring our WeChat messages somehow. When I tried to message my afternoon teacher the other day, she said she hadn't received it when I asked for her response the next afternoon.'

'As much as he did it for what I think were the wrong reasons,' Bryn said. 'I have to agree. Together we would have been more powerful and the school would've listened. I don't think they could've fired all the teachers if we'd stood together in solidarity.'

Charlie listened to this with a dour look on his face. So now they repent, he thought to himself. In the aftermath they had been intolerable, gloating with stupid expressions on their faces about how bad an idea it was, and they didn't even realise they'd been the missing key. They were the few individuals who could have made the difference between success and failure. There was no sin worse than wasted opportunity.

'Have you kept in contact with anyone who got fired?' Charlie asked, looking at Daphne.

'Yes. My old morning teacher is now a delivery driver, and your old afternoon teacher,' she said pointing at Charlie, 'has become a retail assistant in a clothes' store.'

'Do they still blame Kevin and me for what happened?'

'No, they actually seem pretty OK about it. They smile whenever I bring it up in a sort of "can't be helped" shrug of the shoulders.'

'If someone made me lose my job, I'd be angry,' Charlie laughed.

'Yes, but you're not like them. Maybe it's the Daoist philosophy of being unable to change things and not complain about it or something, but they don't blame you, only themselves. Even then they don't seem to be dwelling on it much. Besides, they earn as much as they did at the kindergarten. I honestly wonder all the time why they decided to work in the kindergarten when they were treated so badly.'

'They're like it everywhere,' Elijah interjected. 'The management at every business are a bunch of wankers – fucking Chinese … No offence Felix!' he said looking at Daphne's husband.

'Good holidays at schools I guess,' Ellie pointed out, 'better than only five days of annual leave per year I hear some people get at other jobs.'

'How much do you get?' Daphne asked Charlie.

'Five days,' he said, nodding.

The room went silent again. They'd finished the pudding by now and lay back on their mismatching chairs, loosening their belts a little and belching from the feast. The booze of the morning was already beginning to wear off, so they opened another bottle of wine and continued their drunken haze. Daphne's cat silkily moved through the legs of each diner below, marking her territory as she rubbed her neck onto legs. When Amelia tried to pick her up, she hissed in return.

'And what happened to Emma in the end?' Charlie probed.

'Oh, from what the other Chinese teachers were telling me, she and her husband moved to Beijing together. His company allowed him to transfer and she's started at a Chinese school that not only has no foreign teachers, but teaches Japanese as a second language instead of English.'

'Blimey,' Charlie replied.

Charlie tried to eat the last chunk of custard and cake, the warm cream overflowing from his mouth onto his chin. The cat, seeing an opportunity, jumped up from the floor and licked his face. Amelia and Perry laughed, but Daphne continued to stare into her pudding bowl, moving the spoon around wistfully.

'I just really want to leave the school to be honest,' she finally said.

'Me too,' Elijah agreed.

'Me three,' Bryn said whilst the others around the table nodded their heads.

'When do all your contracts finish?' Charlie asked.

'Almost all of us signed two-year contracts last Christmas, so we have about a year left on them,' she said glumly.

'You know ...' he hesitated ... was it right? They all seemed to have the same opinion as him, he thought, surely they wouldn't tell anyone. 'What if I told you I had a secret which I knew would mean Lesley going out of business.'

'We'd call bullshit,' Elijah replied.

'Hear me out ...'

Charlie explained what he'd discussed with Ronnie that early December morning. How Lesley had defrauded people in America and the likelihood the school was being run by dirty money as a result.

'So if I can prove this ... not only will she be arrested in America ... but depending on how the US plays this, they could seize the assets such as the school. That last part would be a long shot though as the Chinese authorities probably won't play ball – I don't even think there's actually a law against Chinese companies screwing over foreign investors. However, if we time it perfectly, we could get her the next time she's in New York,' Charlie said.

'That seems a bit far-fetched,' Vivian intervened.

'But what did you find when you went to the plant?' Daphne inquired.

'Nothing as valuable as was being said in the marketing material for the place. There was rubbish all over the factory floor. The road leading to it wasn't even suitable for our car, let alone trucks. We set up the cameras when we went about two weeks ago.'

The room went silent. People looked at their drinks in thought.

'So, you said there should have been about 30 trucks a day … how many have there been so far?'

'Six,' Charlie replied.

'Six per day?' Daphne gasped.

'Nope. Six in two weeks.'

The room murmured in shock.

'How long is it going to be until you have enough proof?' Amelia asked.

'My boss says it's best to have about half a year's worth of footage to prove it's a fraud. At least wait until the Q1 figures for 2019 come out into the open and we can compare them. In the meantime, we have to do background research into all sorts of things. We need proof of the number of people at the plant, we need to know the destination of the trucks. We need to know how Lesley operates them. I think we genuinely have a case here.' He took a long gulp of his wine, 'so cheers to that!'

The others raised their glasses and drained them too.

'So how will you be able to finish it? What's the stage after the proof?' Elijah asked.

'Well … first we need to compose the report, comparing the figures to our findings with the evidence of videos, pictures etc … then we need to wait for the perfect moment for it to be sent. If we want to arrest Lesley, we need to release it to the press when she is in New York, but by then the SEC will be up her arse with all the proof.'

'But her daughter doesn't go there anymore,' Daphne replied. 'I don't think she goes often. Besides, like Vivian said, this all seems so far fetched, how would you get the timing right? Do you even know anyone there?'

'No, no, no, luckily because she got greedy, she has two other businesses that went public on the NYSE. She'll have to go to a share-holder briefing there at least three times a year, one for each of her businesses. The next one is in February, which is too early. But if we work hard once the evidence is in, I reckon we can nab her in early May when she's there over the holiday of the first week.'

'Don't hold your breath,' Vivian said, 'is this what your boss has told you will happen?'

'I figured it out myself mostly but I'm confident it will.'

On the train back to Shanghai that night, Charlie, drunk and swaying in his seat, let himself smile at the thought of Lesley behind bars. He didn't think it was wrong for him to have told his friends, they all seemed to hate her as much as he did. Kevin had been a popular character in the office. He thought it good that the others were regretful of what had happened, the only problem being it was too late to change it. 'A wasted opportunity,' he sighed.

A kid next to him looked up at his swaying and whispered to his mother that the foreigner looked funny. She told him to shush but Charlie had already seen the kid in the corner of his eye.

In terrible Chinese he said, 'Big monster!' and tickled the child.

The parent laughed and took out her phone.

For the rest of the journey, she tried to get Charlie to pose with the child. She spoke the small amount of English she could, and the child screeched with delight every few minutes. By the end of the journey, he was asleep in Charlie's lap.

In the light of the prospect of getting what he wanted, he remembered there were some things like this that he loved about Lesley's kindergarten. There was a tinge of sadness as he realised that the children, whom he'd loved like his own for the five months he taught, might be forced to move schools and be taken away from what they had come to know. In addition, the teachers he'd been friendly with would be unemployed as a result of his actions, likely to find it harder to seek employment again in education because their names were tarnished by association with their previous employer.

'Omelettes and eggs,' he murmured to himself as he exited the train in Shanghai, barging his way through a throng of people.

22

Sat at the desk of her office in the main HQ building, Lesley viciously hit her keyboard, the continual crash of keys echoing about her room. She looked out of the window towards the river.

'Mrs Li, this is very serious you must pay attention,' the men in suits had said in the aftermath of the incident when she'd been called to explain herself.

'We're disappointed in what happened, Mrs Li.'

The chairman of the local committee had sat behind a desk with his vice-chairmen on either side. They wore dark navy suits with bright red ties and CCP pins on their lapels.

'Sir, I can explain.'

'There's no explanation to be made, you allowed your workers to get out of control. Why and how did this happen? Were there rumblings in the build up to this? Why weren't they quashed?'

Lesley had taken a sip of water before clearing her throat.

'It was the influence of the foreigners.'

'Ha, the foreigners … When we gave you a licence to employ foreigners, you assured us they would have no negative influence on the community. I've looked over the file, you specifically said, and I quote, "they will be paid handsomely and provided with sufficient accommodation".'

'And they were.'

'Then why did this happen?'

'I can't control the emotions of my staff. I conducted a quick investigation after the incident and it transpired that one of the foreign teachers had been conducting an extramarital affair with one of my Chinese employees.'

'Yes, this Kevin individual, why did you hire him? I've looked into his past and it's tainted with debauchery and insolence. And yet you hired him.'

'They're all like that, Sir … and …'

'That may be,' the chairman interrupted, 'but it is under your watch that he exploded and caused a scene. This is an open country and we the Party do our best to only allow legitimate individuals to live and work in this country, but as you know a society is not happy unless everyone does the groundwork. You shouldn't have hired him, and you should have fired him before this issue came to light. Why didn't you seek the opinions of your other employees? In order to maintain harmony you must know everything that goes on. Do I make myself clear?'

'Yes, Sir.'

'You have a stellar record, Mrs Li. This has tainted it somewhat but I expect you to cleanse your businesses of bad elements and thoroughly reaffirm your commitment to the Party and the country.'

She shook her head and returned to typing. Her email inbox had piled up since she'd implemented a new system of watching over all her businesses. She'd set up cameras in every room, not just in the school, but in her factories as well. She'd hired a team of workers to pore over the footage and report any funny goings on and received a daily report on the overall status of her businesses.

At the school in particular, she'd stamped down as best she could, but the numbers signing up to start at the school after the Lunar New Year holidays were vastly smaller than previous years. She could barely fill one new class in the nursery, let alone the three she had initially hoped she would. As she looked at her figures again with an air of angst, they didn't add up. She tried to establish if there was any way out of this hole.

'We're going to have to close down the school at this rate,' she told her daughter, who was sat next to her.

'Blast it,' Sophia said, 'how bad is it looking?'

'Very bad,' she replied, 'half the parents have given notice they're taking their children out at the end of June. We're lucky we told them to pay a year up front in May last year, otherwise they would've taken them out earlier.'

They sat staring at the sheets of paper on the desk.

'At least the *other* businesses are doing fine, perhaps I should announce record levels of sales at the next board meeting after the New Year.'

Lesley laughed whilst Sophia looked at her quizzically. 'Hmmm, silly Americans,' she continued. 'I could sell their own daughter back to them if I wanted to. They're gullible as pigs.'

There was a knock at the door. Fu Gui stood at it and announced there were two of her foreign staff there to see her, though they hadn't made an appointment. Lesley gestured without looking for them to come in. Fu Gui opened it and ushered in the couple that were waiting to see her.

'Hello Amelia and Perry. How can I help you?' she asked, pointing for them to sit at the sofa. Lesley and her daughter sat at the chairs around the sofa. Sophia poured some tea for all of them.

'Thank you for seeing us, Lesley,' Perry said.

They sat in silence for a few moments.

'Well, what is it?' Sophia asked, gesturing with her hand for a response.

Perry and Amelia looked at each other uneasily, then Amelia, as always the spokesperson for the couple, spoke up. 'We have some information you might want to know about,' she started.

'What information?' Lesley enquired as she raised her eyebrow, shuffling in her seat.

'Well, it refers to something Charlie told us about the other day.'

'Charlie? What does he want?' she spat.

'He doesn't want anything, but if I told you he had something to make you lose a lot of money on your steel plants?'

'I would laugh at something so preposterous,' Lesley said.

'Well, what do we get in return if we can prove it to you?'

'Prove? There's nothing to prove, you don't know what you're talking about.'

She was in an especially feisty mood after looking at the financial figures on her desk. Amelia ignored what she'd said and continued to negotiate, she leaned in, circling her forefinger around the rim of her teacup.

'If you can promise both of us 500,000RMB each and a release from our contracts, we'll tell you.'

'What!' Sophia roared in laughter. 'Mum they're taking the mick,' she said in Chinese.

'Now hang on,' Lesley said, waving her hand, 'what do you know?'

'First you need to promise us what we just asked for.'

'What if I don't like what you tell me?'

'You won't, that's why we want to tell you, but first we need your acceptance of our terms.'

'That's almost £120,000, my mother's not dumb,' Sophia said.

Lesley sat back in her chair, placing her hands together as if in prayer. She knew she might be discovered some day for her inaccurate business dealings, but she hadn't expected it to come so soon. She hadn't finished milking the American cash cow.

'Sophia, would you go outside for a moment,' she said.

Sophia obediently rose up, but not without a little protest in her facial expression, and walked to the door. After she'd exited, Lesley leaned forward again. 'What do you know?' she asked, eyebrow raised.

'Oh fuck!' Charlie shouted from his desk in the office, 'Fuck! Fuck! Fuck!'

He stood up and ran into Ronnie's room. Ronnie was in the middle of a call, walking aimlessly around his table, but he'd heard the profanities from the other side of the building. He cleared some magazines off a sofa in his office and gestured towards it. Charlie sat down, grabbing some whiskey Ronnie kept on the coffee table, and poured himself a large glass despite the fact the sun was still high in the sky.

After Ronnie put the phone down, he turned to Charlie. 'What's the problem?' he said, 'go easy on my whiskey.'

'The bitch just sold all her shares in the steel company, she's made $50 million.'

'What?' Ronnie replied, 'How? Why?'

'Ronnie, we have to get our report out now, we have to at least stop her selling the other two businesses! Fuck, why is she doing this?'

'But it's only the start of January Charlie, we don't have enough proof to bring her down and the Q1 results aren't out yet.'

'Fuck em! They're there for the whole world to see! We have to do it. Everyone will agree with us that there's something fishy and then investigate the other two companies.'

'But the client …'

'Fuck the client!' Charlie shouted, he'd worked himself into a rage and his eyes burned with a passion he had not usually shown in his calm exterior.

'Charlie, the client wants the stock to tank so he can make the money, if this report goes largely unseen or written off as shoddy reporting, that won't happen, and she'll get away with it.'

'But if we don't do it now, she'll get away with it! And with more money!' Charlie said.

'We're doing this for the client Charlie! There's 100,000RMB sitting on this and I don't want to lose the money we've already invested in time and camera equipment … It's not time yet. Besides, it's done. She has made money on this particular business. With or without the report she's made $50 million … Look, I'm sorry for what happened to your friend, I truly am. But we have to do this right. If we release the report too early, it'll be written off … nobody will win. The clients won't get to make their money, we won't get paid, and her reputation in the US won't be ruined. Hell, she might even be able to register a few more of her companies onto the Stock Exchange. But if we wait until the Q1 results come out in mid-April, we can ensure our clients make money, we get paid, and

Lesley's other businesses will come into question. We might even get a shot at investigating them too' Charlie was silent. 'Now that we are where we are, this is the best outcome that can happen … I'm sorry, but we have to think rationally. I know you're charged up about this and I would be too, but this is the best outcome we can hope for.'

Charlie's eyes welled up.

'I can't believe she's going to get away with it' he said, putting his head in his hands 'What if she sells the other businesses in the meantime?'

'It's a risk we have to take in order to get paid,' he said, sitting next to Charlie and rubbing his back. 'Now why don't you head home for the day, I don't think you'll be good for much work. Actually you know what, take tomorrow off too. That'll extend into the weekend. I think you need a little break.'

Charlie rose, finished off his whiskey glass and placed the glass on the table, before walking out without saying a word. Ronnie sighed and sat in his chair behind his desk.

As he exited the building, filled with disgust, he almost bumped into a passing jogger. Crossing the road for the metro, he paused, before deciding to walk the distance home. As he strolled, hands in pockets, braced against the cold, he sighed heavily before wondering aloud.

'How did this happen? Why did this happen? Can it really be? Did I say too much at Christmas? I thought I could trust them. They all share the same values as me, surely? They all agreed with me. They'd all regretted not taking part in the incident. Maybe it was Felix? God I can't trust any of them. Married a Brit, seen how we live and he still pledges allegiance to other fucking Chinese … Calm down, Charlie, there's no reason to think it was him … Well who else could it fucking be? Everyone else in there was Western. We all think the same way, don't we? No, it has to be Felix, that snivelling yellow …' he stopped in the middle of a pavement and shook his head.

'Stop it,' he continued. 'Leave Felix out of this, he's a nice man, one of the nicest you've met, it can't have been him. Besides, it's done.'

He sighed heavily again.

When he was almost home, he saw an empty table outside one of the French Concession's cafés and grabbed it.

He waved at a street vendor passing by with a large box of cigarette packets and bought one. Before he realised he didn't have a lighter, the vendor had disappeared. He looked around and noticed a Chinese girl with a cigarette in one hand and a book in the other on one of the other tables.

'Excuse me,' he said in poor Chinese.

'Yes,' she replied in English.

'Oh, of course …' he laughed, wiping his brow, 'may I borrow your lighter please?'

She handed it over and he lit one of the cigarettes with shaky hands.

'Thank you,' he said, before coughing after his first inhale.

The girl laughed. 'You don't smoke, do you?'

'No, no I don't.'

'Ah, one of those boys,' she said dismissively before returning to her book.

'One of what boys?'

She put the book down.

'I'm meant to fall in love with you now, aren't I?'

'What? No.'

'Oh, all you foreign boys use the same trick.'

'What's that?'

'Ask for a cigarette lighter then start asking me deep questions as if I'll fall in love with your intellect.'

He looked at the cigarette and then back at the girl.

'My, your English is very good.'

The girl smirked. 'What's your name?'

'Charlie.'

He took a long draw from his cigarette.

'Phoebe,' she said.

'Well, now I know your name I'm going to have to sit with you.'

She laughed.

Charlie took a seat opposite her.

'Don't you have work or something? You're dressed quite smart.'

'I needed a break,' he replied. 'What about you?'

'I'm on holiday.'

'Oh, where are you from?'

'Beijing.'

'How come your English is so good?'

'Everyone learns English here.'

'Yes, I suppose that's true.'

Charlie dropped the cigarette butt in the ashtray and reached into the packet for another.

'Two in a row? Has talking to me made you a chain smoker?'

'No,' Charlie smirked, 'it's been a stressful morning.'

He used her lighter once again.

'Want to talk about it?'

'I'm afraid I can't. Confidential.'

'Oooh, confidential,' she leaned over, 'so Mr Bond, you work for the British government?'

'Nothing like that. It's just sensitive. I'd rather not talk about it.'

'Suit yourself.'

They each looked at the slowly busying pavement. A man with a wheelbarrow of vegetables trundled by.

'Have you eaten yet?' Charlie asked.

'No.'

'Do you want to have lunch together?'

'I'm afraid I have a boyfriend.'

'Oh … well I di …'

'But we can have a coffee and talk,' she interrupted. 'It's good for my English you see.'

'Yes, of course.'

Charlie waved to a waitress who'd just taken the order of a man in a baseball cap and round spectacles some tables across. After ordering two lattes and a cake for himself, he took another cigarette out of the packet and lit it.

'So where's your boyfriend?'

'He's at work, back home.'

'You went on holiday by yourself?'

'Is there a problem with that?'

'No, no, of course not … It's just something I haven't come across in China before.'

'We're not all the same, you know.'

'Naturally, but … are you not afraid or something?'

'Afraid of what?'

'I don't know. Being robbed or kidnapped?'

'Does it look like that stuff happens here?'

'I guess not.'

'Look, I'm not a fool. Of course we have bad things that go on, but I don't need someone protecting me, besides, I'm old enough to look after myself. I know you sometimes get these scare stories in the foreign press about child abductions but it's very rare.'

'Well anyone can be abducted, not just a child.'

'What a nice topic of conversation for a morning.'

'Sorry.'

The waitress returned with their coffees and cake, along with two forks. Charlie picked up the fork and greedily separated a large chunk. The girl looked at him and narrowed her eyes. 'I guess it's crossed my mind before though,' she started.

'What has? Oh, do you want some of the cake, my bad,' he replied, shoving the plate in her direction.

'No, not that,' she continued, 'I mean the kidnappings. When I was younger my mother would always hold my hand when we walked in crowded areas. Even when I was ten.'

'Mine did too, though not when I was ten. I'd have forbidden it.'

Charlie slurped some of his coffee.

'Just some of the stories you hear,' she continued, 'kids getting trafficked off. Everyone knows it happens.'

Her face had taken a serious tone to it, and she stared blankly at a lamppost nearby.

'What happens to them?' Charlie asked.

'I don't even want to know,' she shivered, 'sex, slavery, factories, farms. Who knows where they end up?'

'Factories? But there are laws against that.'

'Laws aren't always upheld.'

Charlie ate another piece of cake and returned the fork slowly to the plate.

'What kind of factories would take a child anyway? They're hardly good enough for labour.'

'I don't know.'

Charlie thought about this conversation as he walked the short distance back to his apartment. The cigarettes made him edgy and his heart pace had quickened.

What kind of factories? He thought. What kind indeed. Just like

Victorian Britain I suppose, at least they were paid. I guess these ones might be paid too. Maybe they work in steel factories? No, work would be too heavy. Clothing?

Charlie stopped walking.

'Clothing,' he muttered to himself, 'clothing …'

23

'Where are you going mate?'

Charlie looked up from his phone across the aisle. The foreigner was dressed in shorts and a t-shirt, chewing gum relentlessly and, with each smack of his jaw, the sound irritated Charlie.

'Excuse me?'

'Where are you going?'

'Guangzhou,' he replied before returning to his phone.

'Why didn't you get the plane?'

'I prefer the train.'

'Lol, all eight hours of it?'

Charlie looked up towards him. 'Yes, all eight hours of it.'

'You know we're not getting in until 10 p.m. or something.'

'That's fine by me.'

The foreigner looked at him quizzically.

'You're not very talkative. Want to go for a drink when we get to Guangzhou?'

'No, I have some work to do.'

'Do it now, who works at 10 p.m. Lol.'

Charlie stood up and walked towards the dining car.

'Loser,' came a mutter behind him.

He moved out of the way for an elderly man coming in the opposite direction, then strode towards the doors of the car. The restaurant was small but there was an unoccupied table and he sat at it.

He took out his phone once again. Is there really a way I can go in alone? He wondered. Even at the steel factory they were suspicious of me. I don't even speak Chinese. Perhaps I can get a translator before going. No, don't be silly, they've got no loyalty to me, I can't explain what's going on.

He looked at a map of Guangzhou again.

I guess I can get a taxi out, he thought, it's only 20 kilometres from the city centre. But then what?

He looked at the passing countryside from the window and tapped his fingers agitatedly against the tabletop. Each mile, the scenery outside became more tropical, and although the carriage was air conditioned, he could feel the humidity changing.

'I guess I need to book a hotel,' he finally said aloud to himself.

After finding a place which still had rooms just off the central square in the city, he put his phone out on the table in front of him and closed his eyes.

Come on, think … think … think. If you can't go around the plant, what can you do? Hire somebody to do it? But they won't understand. They won't get it right. There must be a way of doing this. But what exactly are you trying to find?

The decision he'd taken had been so spur of the moment, he wasn't quite sure what he was hoping for.

Maybe this is a mistake, he thought. If there was any way to truly get Lesley, Ronnie would've thought about it. Or would he? He's more interested in money. Boy, I need a drink.

He waved to the waitress at the bar and said the Chinese word for beer. She nodded and brought across a frosted can of Tsingtao. The fizz felt good against his parched throat.

The taxi driver looked at him through the rear view mirror curiously, angling back to the road whenever his passenger raised his eyes to meet his. Charlie sighed heavily. Even he wonders why I'm doing this, he thought.

The road emptied as they approached the factory. Charlie looked at his watch just as it approached 9 a.m. He sighed again. In all his time in China when he felt out of place, and there were many, he'd never felt this hopeless.

His mind drifted to the first time he'd met Kevin, and the debauchery they'd had on that first night, and every night out they'd had since. The days seemed so long ago, like a previous life that he'd died in. His hatred of Lesley had grown ever since to a point where he wasn't quite sure if he was angry at Lesley, Kevin, or himself for getting involved in this situation in the first place.

It felt like he'd had his life and it was over. He could always go back to being a teacher if he chose. This wasn't the first time he'd thought as such. He could start afresh, as Kevin had done, and head to another city, then reinvent himself. If he kept from thinking about the broader world and his place in it, it would be marvellous. He was fit and healthy in a way other expats often weren't. His pleasures were different from theirs. He could make an attitude that he didn't care for the university degree he'd done nor the actual work he was qualified to do, and over time if not already, he would lose his ability to do it. The comfort of the past year had all but dulled him and softened his will to get ahead that used to see him at his best, and often happiest.

And what of Kevin? Even though many of the foreigners he met in China reminded him of his friend, there were others who had truly made something of themselves instead. Created business, found love. Not everyone needed to destroy their talents by not using them. Not everyone betrayed themselves through drink and sloth.

And yet, he felt like he'd made money this whole past year through no talent of his own, rather his appearance and his language. Two rights of birth he'd never had to earn, and without earning it, he felt a deep sense of guilt.

The driver pulled up outside the factory and Charlie got out slowly. As the car drove off, he looked around. The factory entrance was fenced off and there was a stern looking guard staring at him from behind a desk under an umbrella. He approached the guard cautiously and smiled. Taking out his phone, he typed a message: *I want to have a tour. I am an investor.*

He handed the phone to the guard who held it and looked at him bemusedly. Charlie turned the translation feature to its speaking setting and the man spoke quickly. He looked back at Charlie, who looked at the phone.

No.

Charlie raised his head and looked angry.

Why not he typed.

The guard shrugged before returning to his desk and taking out a walkie talkie.

A man walked out of the building dressed in orange overalls. 'Need you help?' he asked.

'Excuse me?'

'Sorry, English bad,' he pointed at Charlie before pointing back to himself, 'you need me help?'

'Yes, I want to go in.'

'Ohh, no, not possible.'

'Why not?'

The man looked around at the empty streets. 'You only?'

'Yes.'

'No, not possible,' he repeated.

'But I travelled a long way.'

'Not possible, goodbye,' he turned to leave.

Lesley and Sophia walked towards the beach. They'd travelled to Xiamen the previous day for the weekend and after settling into their hotel on the island of Gulangyu, had dined on lobster and champagne in the colonial style dining hall of a nearby restaurant.

Since it was winter, the island was less busy than usual, although no less beautiful.

'I still would've preferred we go to Sanya,' Sophia sighed.

'That's why we didn't. I know what you get up to when we're down there,' her mother replied. 'Besides, we've been over this, your father and I married here, it's important you see it.'

'But we've been here before.'

'Not for many years … and stop that attitude young lady, I grew up in far different conditions from you and …'

Before she could finish, the phone she carried in her hand rang loudly.

'Yes, you've said this all before mother.'

'We're not finished … Yes, hello,' she said into the phone.

Sophia could hear a man's voice on the other end though it didn't sound like her father's or her brother's, who'd failed to turn up as usual.

'Uh huh,' Lesley said into the phone, 'OK, bye.'

'Who was that?' Sophia asked as Lesley slid the phone into her handbag.

'I was hoping that would be the end of it,' she replied aloud, though looked towards the beach.

'End of what?'

'That boy Charlie is making trouble for us again.'

'Oh Mum, I told you not to pay those two …'

'It's not them … at least I don't think they're involved anymore. From what I was told, they boarded a flight as soon as the money went into their bank accounts.'

'Then what?'

'He's gone to one of our factories in Guangzhou.'

'So? Also how do you know this?'

'I've had him followed.'

'OK, well he's gone to a factory and I guess they didn't let him in?'

'Correct.'

'So what's the problem?'

'Dammit, Sophia, don't you see? He's going after us.'

'We knew that before, hence why we sold all our US holdings.'

'Not all of them, only the steel ones. I didn't think he knew about our clothing plants.'

'Well, of course he knew about them.'

'No you misunderstand me, if he knew about the problems in the steel plant, he must know about the problems in the clothing plant.'

'What problems? Do we overstate our production there too?'

They walked from the tarmac onto the sand and towards a restaurant some way along the beachfront. Lesley removed her shoes and her long flowing dress skimmed the top of the sand as she walked. 'We don't,' she gulped.

'Then what do we do?'

Lesley sighed. 'I had been waiting to tell you this at the right time … I've told you before why we're so successful, haven't I?'

'Because we make the cheapest product.'

'That's right. But how do you think that's possible?'

'Material? I don't know.'

'Labour costs dear.'

'Do you underpay them or what?'

'No, we hire children.'

Sophia took this information calmly. 'That's what all our competitors do,' she finally replied.

'But not all our competitors run kindergartens.'

'So what?'

'It's the PR, that's the problem. No one in America cares if their goods are made by slave labour or children. As long as they're cheap and last long, who cares where it comes from. Just look at Nike and Apple. But they do love the image and branding of a firm. And with me as the figurehead of the firm, this could blow up on us. I can see the headline now, "user of child labour runs kindergarten that hires foreigners".'

'Mum, you're not thinking rationally here.'

'I don't care, I want him gone.'

'Gone?'

'Table at the beachside,' Lesley told a waiter as they approached the restaurant.

'Mum, what do you mean gone?'

'You know what I mean. Now, we're on holiday, what are you drinking?'

It was nearly two o'clock in the afternoon and the weather was cool. Charlie sat with a beer outside an internet café about 200 metres along the road from the entrance to the factory. The café wasn't particularly busy and the owner stood awkwardly near his table. He wished the man would stop looking at him, but they all did it, he thought to himself. So little to live for in some parts of the world that all they'd do is stare at those they believed to have everything. Well, he didn't have everything. Far from it. He was a failure in China. A spectacle to look at but not remotely useful. It didn't matter if he taught English well, or researched on behalf of Ronnie. All that mattered was he looked good whilst doing it, and acted servile to his boss' needs.

He thought about that time in Rome when, alone and just finished school, he'd tried to find a new personality for himself. Trying a different hostel within the city every other night, he was determined to find persons of interest, whose stories he could make his own and take with him as he started university.

But he found no such persons. There were the student eurorailers from America and the UK, and northern Europeans who enjoyed drugs, even southern Europeans who came for the whores, but there were no interesting types. They all shared the common characteristics of failure. A failure of determination, and they were in this part of the world drowning their sorrows in a sea of each other's failures, making up stories of what they could have been and violently pushing back on the idea that they had to share any responsibilities.

He'd tried to fit in with these people, and one night having tried to fit in, he followed a Scot with a long beard who had been cycling since he'd left his home in Glasgow, and had been cycling for two years since. They'd visited a local bar and the owner made them pay upfront for their beer, tip included. They'd tried to talk to the girls on a table nearby but they were ignored. Finally, the Scot, upset on behalf of the two of them, walked over and hit his hand on the table at which the two girls sat. They screamed and he was dragged away by the owner who pushed him into the street and spat at him before turning and striding towards Charlie. Charlie had stood up and put his hands out defensively, hearing mocking laughter from the other tables.

He took a sip of his bottle and realised it was empty. Before he could turn to order again, the waiter came with another, his fourth so far, the bottle cold and with fingerprints around the logo.

That was why he'd come to China, he thought. He'd had such different expectations. If Europe had its faults, and it had many, and if Europeans had faults, he didn't expect the same faults to have made it to a place like China.

And yet he was wrong.

If Europeans were too sloth-like and out to take advantage of you, the opposite was the case in China. The Chinese were too intense, too keen in a way that was dangerous.

He thought back to the first time he'd seen the Monday morning flag raising ceremony at the kindergarten. The whole school lined up, staring fiercely at the fluttering five-starred flag. A few of the children furthest away in the corner were distracted by a passing car and their teacher hit them before pointing back to the flag. Charlie had swept his eyes down from the flag toward the three, four and five year olds screaming the national anthem like some banshees, the older ones raising a hand in a salute too. It was only later he figured out the words of the anthem included "Braving the enemy's fire, march on, braving the enemy's fire, march on" as if the country were on the verge of war.

Or the time he'd seen a child hit by his parents as he sat waiting in a hospital. The child's sin seemed to be that he'd fallen asleep instead of reading his textbook whilst they waited to be seen by the doctor. It had struck Charlie that had he grown up in China too, perhaps this would have happened to him. But it hadn't. He was a European.

Nor could he forget when Gabriel had told him he'd convinced his first boyfriend to confess to his parents that he was gay. Gabriel hadn't heard from him for months and when he saw him in the street and ran over, the boy had burst into tears and explained he'd been married to a girl he'd known for two days before the wedding.

The bottle of Tsingtao was empty and the man by the bar, occupied by another customer, hadn't brought another. Charlie turned drunkenly, slightly swaying in his plastic white chair and raised the bottle until he'd been seen. The man then brought another across.

But it was something deeper, more sinister within China that Charlie disliked. These individual circumstances were plain to see and unique in a certain way. In another, they felt all too familiar. The arranged marriages, the corporal punishment, the nationalism, the social pressure to conform all reminded Charlie of lessons he'd learnt about Victorian Britain. And in the same way as China was now, unequal, tense and rigid, Britain of the 1800s was the same. The one common strand that both shared was a face saving culture. The inability to admit when one had made a mistake. The pressure put on oneself to abide by the norms of the age. The only difference was at least the literature and arts of Victorian Britain shone a light on what was worst in society. Charles Dickens had free reign from censorship in a way that no one in China did.

Those of the Victorian era claimed a superior society, and in their inability to comprehend another opinion, hurtled head long into two wars that would destroy much of the world.

Charlie thought back to the children screaming about 'braving the enemy's fire' and shuddered.

He looked at his watch. 17:48. The sky was darkening fast and he stood up as he downed the final, now flat beer in the bottle. Putting his hand up to the man he knew would be getting him another beer, he meandered slowly towards the café desk and paid for what he had drunk.

He turned around and nearly fell over a chair as he ambled towards the street. He stumbled along the road, narrowly missing people coming the other way.

What was in that beer, he thought. I only had a few. He meandered further before needing a seat on the curb. He could see the factory entrance and that was all he needed. Maybe he could still see if children came out after their shift.

He took a cigarette out of his pocket and felt in his jacket for a lighter which wasn't there. He turned around and stood up again. A man in a baseball cap and round spectacles with his head low tried to walk past him but Charlie grabbed his arm.

'Scuseee me,' he slurred, 'duyu av a ighter?'

The man shook his arm away without protest and walked on.

What the hell's wrong with me, he thought.

He took his phone out and tried to open it with his fingerprint but couldn't. He tried again, and again, and again. His forehead felt sweaty and his heart pounded.

He saw a yellow car approaching and waved his hand at it, almost falling in front as it stopped. He opened the door and slumped himself across the back seat. 'Sent-er,' he slurred.

The driver said nothing as he drove away, and Charlie closed his eyes.

24

'Did you do this for me?'

'Huh?' Charlie sleepily stirred.

'I said, did you do this for me?'

'Do what?'

'Go after her.'

'Where am I? What's going on?'

He could hear Kevin's voice but he couldn't see him. 'You're safe here,' Kevin said in a hushed tone.

'What happened to you?'

'I've been in prison this whole time.'

'Have they treated you well?'

'No.

'Kevin I've tried my best. I went after her.'

'I know.'

'Are you proud of me?'

'Am I what?'

'Are you proud of me?'

'Of course I am.'

'I'm sorry I let you down.'

'You didn't.'

'What's going to happen now?'

'I need you to wake up.'

Charlie started and, panting, opened his eyes. He could feel the familiar outline of his bed in Shanghai and the smell of his bedroom. Even though the curtains were drawn, he could just about make out the pattern of the room. He tried to sit up but his head pounded. He lay back down and looked around him for his phone. As he was fully clothed, he reached into his pocket but it wasn't there. He attempted to sit up again and with great effort, heaved his feet off the bed and onto the floor.

He felt his heart beating in his chest and groaned as he stood up, trying to feel his way towards the window. He opened the curtains and saw it was dark outside.

'Charlie.'

'Ah,' he cried, turning around fast.

It was a man who looked mildly familiar.

'Who the fuck are you?' he screamed, raising his arms up as if for a fight.

'Calm down,' he said. 'I'm David, I'm Lesley's son. I'm sorry but it had to be this way, we don't have a lot of time. Sit down.'

'No, I …'

'Sit down,' he said sternly.

Something in his voice made Charlie obey.

'Can I get some water? My head is killing me.'

David walked to the kitchen counter and took a dirty glass from the sink before filling it with water from the tap.

'Er … I don't think I should drink that.'

'It's fine,' he said.

He greedily took the glass and drank it in one.

'Can I have some more?'

He took the glass and filled it again. After downing it a second time, Charlie put the glass on the bedside table. 'So …' he finally said, gesturing at him. 'What the hell's going on?'

'You need to leave.'

'What do you mean?'

'Leave China.'

'No, I …' before he remembered who he was speaking to. 'I have a good job and I'm onto something.'

'Charlie, this isn't a joke. Who do you think just tried to have you arrested?'

'What do you mean? I wasn't arrested.'

'No you weren't. But had you stayed in Guangzhou you would've been.'

'For what?'

'Drug trafficking.'

Charlie's mouth opened before closing again as he looked bemusedly towards David.

'OK, I don't know what your sister or mother have told you but now I'm just confused.'

He sighed.

'My mum knows all about what you were up to down there in Guangzhou, at one of our factories.'

'What do you mean?'

'Don't play dumb Charlie, she knows we employ child labour down there and you're trying to pull something on us like you did with the steel plant.'

'Too right, you shouldn't be …'

David gave him a fierce look that made him stop talking. 'Whatever you think of my mother, that is not me or my sister.'

The room fell eerily quiet before David continued. 'That's why we drugged you.'

'You did what!?' he exclaimed.

'You're lucky I used to get her guards to sneak me alcohol when I was younger, in my summers. One of them has been following you for a while now. I don't know how long, but I was able to get in touch with him.'

'But why?'

'Had you gone back to your hotel room that evening once you'd finished up whatever you were doing, there would've been a "random visit",' he gestured, 'to your room from the police, and they would've found two large packs of cocaine stashed in your bags.'

'What?'

'So, I persuaded him to find a way to drug you. If you hadn't made it so easy by drinking in a café all day, he would've bundled you into that car that brought you here and injected you with something.'

'I don't understand, I got in a taxi and told it to go to the city centre.'

'God Charlie, can you stop being so naïve? I hired that taxi as soon as Sophia told me what was going on and told him to wait in advance, then bring you back here when the time was right. He was waiting all afternoon apparently. In fact, it turns out both the guard and the driver were surprised you lasted so long before the drugs kicked in.'

'Err … experience?'

David laughed. 'Whatever it was, that doesn't change the fact you have to get out of here. Now.'

'But I don't understand, I've done nothing wrong.'

'It's only a matter of time. My mother wants you gone.'

Charlie looked solemnly towards him. 'Why are you doing this for me? You don't even know me.'

'I don't. But my sister told me everything and even though we don't talk all the time, neither of us like the way our mum operates. I might have to love her but that doesn't mean I have to approve of how she does business.'

'What's going to happen to you?'

'Nothing, why?'

'Won't she know you've done this?'

'Pff, my mum gave up on me a long time ago. Sophia said she would've tried to do this herself but she's with my parents down in Xiamen right now. Besides, she won't know I was involved. All she'll hear is that you went straight from the factory to the train station and took a train back to Shanghai where you packed your bags, waited a day, then got out on a flight.'

'I still don't get it. Why do I have to leave?'

'Because my mum is ruthless. According to Sophia, she says she wants you gone. And when she says gone, that's not out of her life in a "delete your number from her phone" way, but a way where you're arrested or worse.'

'I don't buy it. This is all a little fishy to me.'

'That doesn't matter. As long as you're gone, you can no longer bother her. If you're arrested, you're gone, if you're out of the country, you're also gone. It's down to what form of gone you want to be.'

Charlie looked around his apartment. 'But what about my stuff?'

'Take the most valuable with you now and I'll take the rest and send it to you.'

'But what about my bank account?'

'Charlie, for god's sake, they have banks in the UK, just take the money out with your card there. Do I have to think everything up for you?'

He sat on his bed and stared out the window. He didn't want to go.

'The car's waiting downstairs Charlie, jump in it and get the first flight out of here.'

The lights of the city flashed into a blur as the car sped along the highway. He had a small bag with him containing his documents and laptop whilst the boot contained half his clothes in a suitcase.

He thought about how the neighbour that first night, cold and alone in his apartment in Hangzhou, had brought him dumplings. The smile of the old lady and her husband standing in the doorway with a bowl and pair of chopsticks. Neither said a word as they handed over the bowl and Charlie, who hadn't even learnt the Chinese word for 'thank you' yet, embarrassedly reached into his pocket and took out some money. The elderly couple laughed as they turned around and shuffled back into their apartment.

Gabriel recently told him that since then, the wife had died and the husband had moved in with his children in another part of the city. Charlie had never had the chance to say thank you for the dumplings.

He remembered the best of his time in China. The children, laughing in the playground. The smiles he received from strangers on the street, and the warmth with which he'd been invited into his colleagues' lives both at the kindergarten and within his new firm. Well, old firm now, he guessed. What would Ronnie think? Perhaps this was an overreaction on his part? The company had a branch in Thailand, maybe he could go there. He had never asked about it because he had for some reason always pictured himself as staying in China for a number of years.

The skyscrapers of Shanghai faded into the rear view mirror as the car continued onwards towards his final destination. He turned around and sighed. All that futurism. The lights on each building, the forward vision that it all entailed. How long would it be before the UK caught up to China in making life as easy as it was here? The payments systems, the metros they'd built in almost all big cities, the undeniable confidence that came with such an angling towards the future. I don't want to miss out on that.

Perhaps it was better to have a society that blocked out the bad, he thought. At least then you could feel you were safer, part of something better. He was already worried about what might happen in the UK when he returned. It was hard to think of anything other than the safety of his bubble in China.

What opportunities would there be for him when he went back? Here, he could walk anywhere and be respected as someone who went to a good university and dressed well. He could apply for a role in any educational institution and it didn't matter if he could do that job well.

He thought back to how his old salsa instructor Ray had described China as the future America. 'The government is more powerful than corporations here,' he had said over a drink in the salsa bar as the night wound down, 'That's a good thing,'

'What do you mean?' Charlie had said, 'Why should a bureaucrat do a job that the private sector can do better?'

'That's beside the point. Everyone here is lifted up when the government is so powerful. When the private sector is powerful, only the most privileged do well.'

'That happens in China. Just look at the emphasis put on *guanxi* all the time. It's all anyone ever talks about. Relationships are everything. That's why Xi Jinping is the leader, no? He was a son of one of Mao's friends. That's entrenched privilege if I've ever seen it.'

'But just look at me,' Ray had said. 'I'm from a poor background and worked damn hard and I couldn't make it in America. I come here, try half as hard and I have a much better life. It's like everything we're taught to believe about the American Dream, it's actually the Chinese Dream. Don't you see that?'

For us foreigners maybe, Charlie thought to himself in the back of the car as it approached the airport. Only for some was China really a place of reinvention and unlimited opportunity. Then again, those of us who have it, shouldn't waste it.

The car stopped behind a policeman who gently tapped the bonnet outside the departure gate. Charlie hesitated, and looked at the policeman. The driver sat in silence, as if he could sit there for as long as it took.

Charlie opened the door laboriously and stumbled out, clutching his bag to his chest. He walked around the back and removed his suitcase. The evening air was cold against his face as he slammed the boot. The driver looked at him in his rear view mirror and slowly started off.

Charlie stood still as it swerved into another lane and approached the end of the causeway. The car disappeared, and he looked longingly after it, then toward the international departure gate, then to his bags.

A taxi pulled up next to him and a Chinese person in a suit stepped out.

'Excuse me,' Charlie asked, 'Do you know how to find domestic departures?'

'It's down the escalator,' the lady replied.

'Thanks.'

Charlie picked up his bags and walked toward the escalator, each step echoed with a loud thud.

As he descended, he looked behind him to the Chinese person as she went into the international departure gate, the automatic doors shutting behind her.

No, he thought, those of us who have it, shouldn't waste it.